MEN OF MAPLE MOUNTAIN

BOOKS 1-7

SADIE KING

LET'S BE BESTIES!

A few times a month I send out an email with new releases, special deals and sneak peeks of what I'm working on. If you want to get on the list I'd love to meet you!

You'll even get a free short and steamy romance when you join.

Sign up here:
www.authorsadieking.com/free

This is a work of fiction. Any resemblance to actual events, companies, locales or persons living or dead, are entirely coincidental.

www.authorsadieking.com

CONTENTS

MOUNTAIN MAN'S OBSESSION

MEN OF MAPLE MOUNTAIN BOOK ONE

MOUNTAIN MAN'S OBSESSION

MEN OF MAPLE MOUNTAIN BOOK ONE

His one obsession is her...

From the moment Colette sweeps into my bar, I can't stop watching her. Even when she doesn't know I'm looking. *Especially* then.

My cameras record her every smile, every frown, every moment. I study her until I know my girl inside out, my obsession growing, overwhelming me, demanding I act.

She'll never find out my secret, will she?

Mountain Man's Obsession features an OTT obsessed mountain man and the curvy innocent woman he claims as his own. It's high heat, oh so sweet, and always with a happily ever after.

The Men of Maple Mountain series is set in the world of the Maple Springs. Each book is a standalone but best enjoyed together.

1
BEAR

Her fingers pause in their flight across the keyboard. She sits back, nibbling the tip of her thumb, a self-conscious gesture, unaware of me watching her.

She sits upright in the booth her chestnut hair hanging in loose waves under her headphones.

"I guess she doesn't like your choice of music," Kit, my best buddy, quips as he follows my gaze.

Dragging my eyes away from the beauty in the corner, I pull him a pint of strong ale and set it on the bar in front of him. "She's concentrating."

He takes a sip, his gaze resting on her a little longer than I'm comfortable with.

"I wonder what she's writing."

My body stiffens. I'm not happy that he's showing interest in my girl. Well, not technically my girl yet, but she will be.

I cut a look at my best buddy but his gaze has already left her. He sips his beer and scans the room. Either he knows she's mine, or he's not interested. Hopefully the latter. I'd hate to have to fight my best friend.

"Historical romance."

He gives me a pointed look. "You've spoken to her, then?"

That's not how I know what she's writing but I'm not going to tell him my secret. "We've met. Her name's Colette."

The name swirls around my tongue and sends a shiver of longing through my body, my blood thumping in my ears.

My Colette.

To hide my reaction, I grab a tray of glasses from the dishwasher and start drying them. Kit gets the hint and drops the subject.

While I put the glasses away, Kit leans against the bar. Suddenly he sets his beer down and his eyes narrow. "Who's that with your sister?"

I follow his gaze, and my chest tightens.

Ursula's seated at her usual table with her best friend, Heather. I served them low alcohol vodka in their cocktails, but they don't know that.

There are two guys at the table with them. One is leaning over Ursula with a leery look on his preppy boy face.

I know everyone of drinking age in Maple Falls, population 1,300-ish, and I don't recognize these kids. They're either up from Maple Springs for the night or tourists, here for the hiking trails.

Since my parents passed in a climbing accident eight years ago, I not only inherited the bar, but responsibility for my little sister as well. It was easier when she was still at school. But now she's twenty-two and just home from college, and every randy boy on the mountain is trying to get in her pants.

Not on my watch.

Slinging my dishcloth over my shoulder, I approach her table and cross my arms, so my muscles are on display alongside my tattoos.

I fix my eyes on the skinny boy staring at my sister's tits. "Evening, gentlemen."

My voice comes out as a low growl. I'm a big guy, six-foot-five and almost as wide as the mountain.

The kid jumps when he sees me and the leery look slides off his face.

Ursula looks like she wants to stab me in the eye. "Bear. What are you doing?"

"You know this guy?" the spotty kid stammers.

"He's my brother." Ursula rolls her eyes. "Here to protect my virtue."

I keep my eyes on the kid. "Can I see your ID?"

Kit comes up behind me, as if I need back up, but he's almost as protective of my sister as I am.

The boy fumbles in his pocket and shares a look with his friend."We, um left it in the car. I'll just go get it."

They scamper through the door and Kit follows, trailing them all the way to the car park.

"Do you think they're coming back?" Heather asks wistfully.

"No," says Ursula. "Would you come back if this guy threatened you?" She gestures at me.

"You'll thank me for it one day, sis."

"When I die a lonely old maid?" She gives me a sarcastic smile, but her eyes are dancing, and I know I'm already forgiven. My sister's too smart to go for a gangly kid like that anyway.

Kit returns and I motion him over, putting my hand on his shoulder. "Keep these ladies company would you, Kit? Make sure those young bucks don't come sniffing around again."

"Sure." He doesn't hesitate, which is why he's my best friend. Always willing to help out, even if it means babysitting my sister.

On my way back to the bar, I do the rounds clearing tables and talking to my regulars.

The Amery brothers are in town, Chase as chatty and good natured as his brother Rowan is surly and silent. Rowan's ex-military, and I give him a drink on the house whenever he's in town. Which isn't often. Doesn't like people much, that one.

They're at a table with Colton, another surely mountain man whose beard is even wilder than my own. He only stops in if he's in town for supplies. We talk a bit about his solar panel hook up and how he's entirely off the grid now.

The only person I don't chat with is Ewan, the recluse who never talks. He likes to sit on his own, staring at the mountain and sipping his whiskey. I can't imagine what demons he's wrestling with inside. But it's not my place to judge, only to serve.

His glass is empty, and I bring him another whiskey. Scotch, to go with his Scottish accent. He nods at me and silently raises his glass in thanks.

By the time I get around to Colette's booth, she's gone. There's an empty coffee mug and a napkin. On the napkin is a faint imprint of her lips, shiny and coffee stained, like she's pressed them to her lip-balm covered mouth.

Glancing around the bar to check no one's watching, I press the napkin to my own lips, right on the imprint. It smells like cherry lip balm and coffee, exactly how I imagine she'll taste when I finally kiss her.

Slipping the napkin in my pocket, I take the empty mug to the bar.

Later that night, the last punters finally go home, so I lock up and go upstairs to my apartment above the bar.

With eager fingers, I open my laptop and pull up the CCTV feed from the bar. The live feed shows it's all quiet downstairs, but that's not what I'm here to look at. I scroll back until I find the recordings from earlier tonight. Until I find Colette.

There's one CCTV camera trained on the bar, another one pointing outwards toward the door, and a third pointing to the left-hand side of the bar. Then there's the one I installed last week, after the first time she walked into Bear's Brewery.

She blew in with a flurry of autumn leaves, all five-foot-nothing and wrapped up in a red coat and matching knitted hat, her hair splayed out behind her. Her cheeks were rosy red, her eyes bright, and her beauty so surprising that the glass I was holding dropped right out of my hand. It shattered on the floor along with my heart.

She smiled at me and ordered a coffee then selected the booth in the corner, the one overlooking the mountain.

While I burnt the coffee and over-frothed the milk, she pulled out her laptop and put on a set of headphones.

For the first hour, she just stared at the mountain, letting her coffee go cold. It made me agitated, watching her. I wanted to know what she was doing, where she'd come from, but she was in such a reverie I didn't want to disturb her.

Then she began to type.

The next day, she came back and repeated the ritual in the same booth.

That night, I installed my fourth CCTV camera, above the booth. That's the feed I pull up now.

I've watched her every night since. Replaying the feed, pausing and zooming in to see what she's writing, to catch her smile, to examine the lines of concentration on her face when she's thinking.

I know every expression, every turn of her mouth. I know the thumbnail on her right hand is worn down from nibbling it when she's thinking. I know she sometimes hums along to whatever music is in her headphones. I know she smiles along with her characters and mouths the words when she's writing dialogue.

There's no explanation for this obsession. I should talk to her, ask her out. But then I'd have no reason to watch her. And I like watching her.

She's so petite, but there's nothing petite about her curves. She must think I'm a brute with my height and bulk and rugged beard. Plus, she writes romance. I know this from reading her screen. What does a guy like me, raised on the mountain from a long line of mountain families, know about romance?

So, I watch, and I wait, looking for the right opportunity to show her we're meant to be together.

I scroll back to when she arrived today, pausing on her face as she stares out the window. There's a serenity to her, a peacefulness that's endearing.

Under her coat she wears a tight sweater. Her breasts pushing against the fabric. That's what catches my eye now – her tits straining to be let out.

I imagine them in my hand, caressing her nipples as I ravage her body.

Undoing my fly, I catch my dick in my hand. Thinking about her curvy body writhing under me, I thrust into my palm.

Remembering the napkin, I grab it from my pocket and press it against my nostrils, inhaling her scent. It's all I need to send me over the edge, shooting hot liquid into my palm.

Breathing hard, I set the napkin down alongside the other memorabilia I've collected.

One day, I'll talk to her, make her mine. But for now, I'm content to watch.

2
COLETTE

"This ain't no place for a lady, Elizabeth." His amber eyes sparked like fire. "I'll see you safely down the mountain."

Elizabeth picked up the hunting spear, still dripping crimson from the morning's catch.

"You may as well spear me through the heart if you send me away."

My nose crinkles at the screen and I delete what I've just written. After a moment's thought, I try again.

"A trapper's life ain't the life for a lady." His amber eyes shimmered like the embers in the grate.

"I'll judge what life is best for me."

My fingers delete that too. I pull my headphones off and rest my head on my hands in frustration.

I came to Maple Falls to find inspiration but today I'm

nothing but distracted – and by one big burly distraction in particular.

"Another coffee?"

The sound of Bear's voice makes me jump.

He grins sheepishly. "Sorry, I don't like to disturb you when you're working but, it looks like you might need this."

He holds out the cup like an offering and I gratefully accept.

"Thank you."

Our fingers brush, sending a tremor of heat coursing through my veins. My hand wobbles and a dribble of coffee slips over the rim of the cup, pooling on the saucer.

Bear may not want to disturb me, but he sure is. The man exudes a pure animal magnetism.

Every time I lay eyes on him, my heart wobbles and my panties dampen. I tried staying away from the bar and writing in my rented cabin, but being away from him was even worse. I spent the whole day wondering what he was doing and who he was talking to.

He may think I'm sitting here working all day, but the truth is, I spend a lot of my time people watching, and when I say people, I mean Bear.

Even when he's not in my line of vision, I can hear the reassuring rumble of his deep voice through my headphones. The hairs on the back of my neck stand on end when he's clearing a table behind me. More than once, I've turned around and found him staring straight at me.

There's an attraction between us, for sure. I've written and read enough romance books to know that a pull like that can't be ignored. Sooner or later, the pull will get too strong and our bodies will collide. I'm waiting for him to make the move, and in the meantime, enjoying this delicious cat and mouse attraction.

My favorite author Ava Grayson came to a mountain and found her mountain man, I read about it in Writer's Weekly.

Her own real life romance story. I had to see for myself if the hills were teeming with rugged men waiting to fall in love. I don't know about love but I'd like to fall into something with Bear.

It's been three weeks since I arrived in Maple Falls, the tiny town halfway up Maple Mountain. My new series is set in a small town in the 18th century with rugged mountain men who are trappers and hunters. Problem is, I grew up in California, on the beach with no idea what it's really like to live up a mountain. So, I decided to find out.

I found a cabin to rent and came for a week. That was three weeks ago. Once I saw the mountain, I knew I had to stay longer. Then I met Bear, the growly bar manager, as rugged as one of my characters.

In fact, as I've gotten into the story, when I write William, the hero, it's Bear that I think of. William has suddenly become very tall and wide and protective.

"How's the writing going?"

Bear seems genuinely interested, and I'm flattered that he's asking. But then, he's a bar manager, it's his business to talk to the clientele.

"Some days are better than others," I confess.

He nods sagely as if he knows what I mean. "Maybe you need a break."

He's probably right. I tend to go all-in when I'm working on a book. There are many long, frantic writing days, and I don't come up for air until the book is finished.

There's an old trapper cabin I've heard about that's a short hike up the mountain. Maybe tomorrow is a good day to take off from writing and go take a look.

"Do you know the abandoned trapper cabin in the mountain?" I ask.

Bear pulls on his beard, a long, luscious beard that I'm longing to run my hands through. "Which one?"

"There's more than one?"

"Oh yeah, the mountain's full of them. My great, great, great, great grandaddies on both sides used them."

My breath hitches. This guy really is the quintessential mountain man. It's in his blood. And there's something so attractive about that.

He opens his mouth like he's about to say something else when there's a shout from the bar.

"Can't a man get a beer around here?"

Bear spins around, his face like thunder. When he sees the large smiling man at the bar, his expression slackens. "Be with you in a minute, Colton."

He shrugs apologetically as he turns back to me. "That's my buddy Colton, he doesn't come down the mountain much. You'll have to excuse his manners."

He holds my gaze and I could get lost in his deep grey eyes, the same color as mountain stone.

"Hey!" Colton shouts again.

"Duty calls," Bear says, tearing his gaze away from mine.

He saunters over to the bar and claps his equally big friend on the shoulder. Their deep voices boom through the bar. But it's the rumble of Bear's voice that rolls through my body, causing a rush of heat between my legs.

Yeah, I definitely need a day off to cool off.

Pulling out my local guidebook, I find the page with trappers' cabins in the area. There's one about an hour's hike from town on a main walking trail. I circle it in the book before slipping it back in my bag.

3
BEAR

Sweat beads at the back of my neck and I undo a button of my shirt, letting cool air circulate. It's a warm day for autumn and Colette has set a steady pace. She's surprisingly nimble for someone of her stature. She's definitely petite in height only, there's nothing petite about her wide hips and heavy breasts.

My throat goes dry just thinking about her curvy body. Stopping behind a bush I quietly pull my water bottle out of my backpack and take a long cool drink.

She's a few feet ahead of me on the track and has no idea I'm here. When I saw her circle the cabin on this trail in her guidebook on the camera last night, there was no way I was going to let her walk all over the mountain on her own.

I could have invited myself along, and I almost did. But I get the sense it's a writer's thing, something she wants to do on her own. Maybe visit the place where her characters might have lived and let her imagination run wild.

She's probably got all sorts of visions going on in her head right now that I don't want to disturb.

Better to leave her alone with her own thoughts and not disrupt the creative process.

Besides, I enjoy watching her when she doesn't think anyone is around.

Humming reaches my ears from further up the trail, the sweetest sound that pierces right to my heart and causes me to grin like a maniac.

Colette continues to hum as she walks and sometimes breaks into song. Old country music mostly, sad and sweet.

Carefully stuffing my water bottle away, I shoulder my backpack and follow the humming.

A half-hour later we're at the old, abandoned trapper's cabin. It's a single room log cabin, tucked between ancient trees. The wood is dark from rot and the roof is caved in and coated in moss.

Not far away is a rock ledge and this is where I approach the clearing from, having cut into the trees a while back. I quietly slip behind the boulder stack as I watch Colette explore.

Her wide-eyed excitement is endearing; she's like a kid in a toy shop, running her hand over the ancient wood and taking pictures.

A wood pigeon startles and flies out of a nest on the roof, squawking angrily. Colette squeals and pulls her hand to her chest. When she realizes it's a bird, she laughs at herself, a silvery peel that echoes through the forest and straight to my heart.

Carefully, so as not to make a sound, I climb the boulders and lie on my stomach at the top. From here, I have a good view of the area and can watch her as she takes photos and scribbles notes in her notebook.

She walks over to the boulders and I dip my head down, but

she doesn't look upward. When I dare to peer over the edge again she's sitting below me, her back resting against the boulder.

She pulls her sweater off and I get a bird's eye view of her substantial cleavage.

As she gets a snack out of her backpack, I can see right down her top to the lacey edge of her bra.

Heat jolts through my veins and my blood thumps in my ears. My cock hardens instantly and my throat goes dry.

She sits back and her tits press together forming a perfect V. How I'd love to slide my cock between them, feel her soft tits around my hardness.

My breathing is so heavy I'm sure she must hear me. The pressure in my dick is unbearable as it presses into the rock. I have to move or I'm going to injure myself.

Sliding my legs around the boulder, I knock a pile of loose pebbles and they go cascading over the side.

Shit.

My body freezes, waiting to see what will happen.

The stones tumble to the ground landing right next to Colette. Any second now she's going to look up and see me lying here, watching her with a hard on like weird pervert.

I'm sprung.

Before she looks up, I slither quietly backward and then jump to my feet. Shouldering my backpack and untucking my shirt so it hides the bulge in my pants, I walk to the edge of the rock, as if I've just gotten here.

"Hey," I say, as calmly as I can muster. "I wondered if I might find you here."

4
COLETTE

My neck swivels upward to the boulder above me, wondering what caused the mini rock fall. I shield my eyes from the sun and in the next instant, it's blocked out by an impressive figure. My breath catches in my chest when I realize it's Bear.

He's standing on the top of the boulder with his hiking gear and rugged beard, looking like he's just stepped out of the 18th century.

"Hi," I manage to squeak.

He scrambles down from the boulder and, standing beside me, is no less impressive. "Good day for a hike."

He trains his pale eyes on me. My heart flutters in my chest and there's a pull in my belly that sets my core aching.

"You're not working today?"

"My sister's looking after the bar."

He sets his backpack next to mine and leans one shoulder casually against the boulder. It's the closest I've been to him and my knees feel giddy. I lean on the rocks for support.

"You here to see the cabin?"

"I want to see how the trappers lived." I remember that I

mentioned it to him at the bar yesterday. Did he know I would be here, at this one? Then again, I guess it's the closest and the one most popular with tourists.

"What brought you up this way?"

"This is one of my favorite trails." He looks away when he says it and I get the odd feeling there's something he's not telling me. But what do I know about this man? He could be up here for any number of reasons.

"You must have been just behind me on the trail."

He pulls on his beard. "Yeah. Must have been."

He turns his gaze to me and takes me by the elbow. It's like a bolt of heat shooting through my arm and all the way down my body. I look up sharply, wondering if he felt it too.

His slate gray eyes give nothing away.

"I'll show you the cabin." He leads me over to the shack in the trees.

"My great, great, great, great, great, great grandaddy Bear used to come up here and stay weeks at a time gathering and preparing skins to trade."

"Your ancestor was called Bear too?" I'm fascinated by this man, a piece of living history right in front of me. My skin tingles and I don't know if it's my writer's curiosity or something more.

"Oh yeah, family tradition. So was my dad and his dad before him. First son is always called Bear."

A vision pops into my head, a baby boy in my arms, a boy called Bear. Wow, I barely know this guy and I'm fantasizing about having his babies. My cheeks flush.

Stooping to get through the door frame, Bear enters the cabin. The floorboards are uneven and he holds his hand out, helping me inside.

He keeps my hand firmly tucked into his as my eyes adjust to the dark. When they do, a rusted metal cot frame is the only sign of human habitation. The floorboards are rotten and debris from the forest litters the place.

"There's not much here."

He squeezes my hand, sensing my disappointment. "It's been abandoned a long time, and tourists have come through looking for souvenirs."

I look around the tiny cabin trying to imagine what life was like here. "There's not much space for a man to live."

He pulls at his beard, nodding. "Aye, it was a hard life for hard men. Ain't no place for a lady."

The line is from my book. I look up sharply.

Bear's studying the wall, running his hand over the wood. "Always lots of hooks in old cabins like these."

He seems completely oblivious to the fact he's just quoted a line from my book. And why wouldn't he be? I just wrote it yesterday, there's no way he could have known. It must be a coincidence. I put the thought out of my mind.

"It must have been lonely for the men up here."

My arms go around myself and I shiver. I think of the men staying out here alone, no women for company.

"Most of them managed to find a woman eventually, or at least my ancestors did, or I wouldn't be here today."

He turns around suddenly and in the cramped space his body is so close we're almost touching. I feel the pure magnetism of him. This strong pull that emanates from my core.

"Let's get back out into the light. I can't see you properly in here."

He takes my hand again and we walk back to the boulder. My mind is in a whirl and my body is on high alert. This was supposed to be a break, a time for me to recharge. But with Bear around, I'm agitated, my body hot and flushed.

Pulling my water bottle from my backpack, I wrap my lips

around the bottle and take a long, slow drink. When I lower the bottle, Bear is watching me.

His dusky grey eyes are fixed on my lips and he's breathing heavily. My pulse quickens.

I realize that I love his gaze on me, his intensity. I want him to keep watching me like that. My tongue flicks over my lips and I bite the lower one.

A low growl comes from Bear's throat that echoes through my body and rattles my bones. He closes the distance between us and his lips smash into mine.

White hot heat shoots through my body, and I feel his kiss all the way down to my toes. Bear's hands go around my waist and he lifts me up and sits me on a boulder so I'm level with him.

"Colette." My name rumbles off his lips sending a delicious shiver all the way through me.

"I've been wanting to kiss you ever since you walked into my bar."

He says it as his mouth crawls over my neck, his hot breath making every hair stand on end. "I've wanted this too," I admit.

His mouth reaches mine and our tongues tangle, putting all the pent-up passion from the last few weeks into the kiss.

My legs straddle his waist and his presses in between them. There's a hard lump poking into my belly and I moan when I realize what it is.

Bear makes a deep grumbling sound. "You make that noise again, and I'll take you right here, right now, against this boulder."

His eyes are stormy and hooded, full of desire, and I believe what's he's saying.

I moan again.

"You're in trouble now."

He claws at my top, grabbing my left breast in his giant hand, rough and needy. I moan again and again and again as his hand slides to my shorts and he tugs at the fly. My pussy is on fire and I want this man with every nerve ending in my body.

Suddenly, there's the sound of a branch snapping and human voices. Bear pulls away from me, turning quickly and shielding my body.

I almost cry out at the loss of him. I'm aching for his touch and my hard nipples chafe against my top.

Then I see why he pulled away. Strolling into the clearing are a couple, hiking packs on and chatting amiably.

Trying to get my breathing under control, I scramble to do my shorts up and straighten my top.

"Hello!" the couple calls cheerily when they see us.

"Morning," says Bear in a low grumble that sounds like he wants to kill them.

I giggle, and he turns to me.

"You're lucky they turned up, or you were about to get ravaged right here."

I suck my lower lip, my body aching for what it just missed out on. "I don't feel lucky."

My eyes travel down his body and I giggle again.

"What's so funny?"

My head jerks pointedly at the stiff bulge protruding from Bear's khakis. "You might want to hide that or you'll scare the tourists."

He gives a sheepish grin and pulls his shirt over his waist.

"Come on," he says, helping me down from the rock. "Let's get back to town."

We hold hands on the hike down the mountain. It feels so right, so natural to have his big hand over mine.

He asks me to his place for dinner, but we both know what he means. We've got unfinished business. My body tingles in anticipation the whole way back.

5
BEAR

A few hours later, I'm stirring bolognaise sauce as I wait for Colette to arrive.

The trek down the mountain was a master class in self-restraint. Now that I've had a taste of Colette, my blood's running hot in my veins. I'm agitated and restless knowing I was so close to having her, to claiming her as mine.

I could have taken her into the bush and rutted like wild animals on the side of the mountain, but I restrained myself. The first time should be special. It should be on my bed with a soft pillow under her, not a hard rock.

There's a knock at the door and I turn the element off, giving the sauce a final stir. If I can make it through dinner without ravaging her, it will be a miracle.

My place has two entrances – the staircase at the back of the bar that leads straight to the living room and the outside entrance. She's used the latter, likely so no one at the bar sees her and gives her a hard time.

I open the door and my jaw hits the floor.

She's wearing a figure-hugging black dress that clings to

every curve of her perfect body. My heartbeat thumps in my ears and my dick stands to attention.

All my resolve melts with one look at her body.

"Come in." My voice is low and growly.

I've been aching for her ever since I laid eyes on her, and since kissing her at the boulder today, I've been in a state of arousal that's blissful torture. Her body brushes past me as I shut the door behind her. It's too much.

"I like your place..." Her words turn to a squeak as I pull her toward me. My arm wraps around her waist and her hot, plump body is pressed against mine, sending sparks of desire coursing through my veins.

My mouth finds hers and she kisses me passionately, as hungry for this as I am.

"Colette." My mouth moves down her throat. "You're driving me crazy."

Her hips wiggle against me and I groan, my hard on straining painfully against my fly. Fuck waiting for a soft bed, I must have this woman – now.

My hands run over her soft rump, down her thighs, and to the hem of her skirt. Sliding up her thigh, my pulse races as I near her hot center. My hands slide over her soft inner thighs and straight to her soft, sticky mound. My fingers stop and I pull back to look at her. She bites her bottom lip, looking sheepish.

"You're not wearing underwear."

She giggles like a naughty schoolgirl. "I was going to tell you at dinner and watch you squirm."

"Oh honey, I can't wait till dinner."

Her breath grazes my throat, barely a whisper. "Neither can I,"

Her hands fumble at my fly and my pants drop to the floor. She gasps when she sees my thick cock sticking straight out and already dripping.

Her eyes are wide and she looks slightly terrified.

"Don't worry, honey. I'll get you good and warmed up first."

"Bear, there's something you need to know."

I freeze. This is where she tells me about the boyfriend back home or her husband or something. She bites her lower lip and looks away.

"What is it, honey?" I tilt her chin so her eyes meet mine.

"I'm a virgin."

Holy fuck. This just got ten times better. "You mean no one's been here before?" As I say it, I run my fingers over her soft pussy folds.

She shakes her head. "No one."

Not breaking eye contact, I slide a finger into her dripping entrance. "No one's ever been inside this sweet little cunt?"

My finger slides in and out slowly. Her eyes go wide and she pants. When she speaks, it's a whimper. "No. I was saving myself."

I give her two fingers and she groans. "You were saving yourself for me, weren't you?"

She nods.

"Say it, honey."

Dark eyes, full of need, fix on me. "I was saving myself for you, Bear. Just for you."

My name is like honey on her lips. It speaks to something primal deep inside me. I growl as I capture her mouth, nipping at her lips while I finger fuck her, feeling her pussy suck me in. My palm rubs against her hard nub, making her squirm.

"It feels so good, Bear. Don't stop."

"I'm not gonna stop, honey, not until you come all over my fingers."

She moans, a high-pitched noise that makes my body tremble and my dick drip with longing. I slide another finger in.

"Oh god, Bear, something's happening."

"Don't fight it, honey, come for me."

She screams out my name as she shatters around me. Her pussy grips my fingers and releases a hot stickiness. I hold my hand inside her until she stops trembling, then slowly withdraw.

"That was amazing." She's breathing hard, her tits heaving up and down in her tight little dress.

"I'm not done yet, Colette."

I pull the dress over her head and drop it to the floor. She's in nothing but her black lacey bra, the most gorgeous sight I've ever seen.

My cock throbs for her, and my whole body will explode if I don't get inside this woman. I grab her hips and lift her against the wall, spreading her legs open.

I imagined our first time in a bed, but I don't have time for that. I need her now.

"Hold on, honey."

She clings to me with her legs while I push her up against the wall, my dick finding her entrance.

My tip grazes her folds and even that contact is like an electric shock through my body.

Thoughts of taking it slow flee my mind. The animal inside me takes over and in one quick thrust, I impale her on my cock. She cries out, her nails biting into my back. I pull back, only to slam into her again.

"Bear!" She cries out and I pause, balancing her on the end of my dick.

"What is it honey, am I hurting you?"

"No, don't stop, it feels so good."

She's right. It feels fucking amazing. Her pussy tugs at my cock, sucking me in and wringing me out until I feel completely undone. Unable to control myself. I slam into her sweet cunt again and again, pulling her hips down so she rides my cock.

She's screaming my name, and the way she's loving it spurs me on till I'm in a fucking frenzy. She is mine, all mine.

Her screams get more high-pitched and her pussy tugs at my cock as she orgasms again. It's too much, and I explode as well, shooting myself deep inside her and coating her walls with my seed until I've got nothing left to give.

She's taken all of me, all that I am.

Holding her close, I carry her into the bedroom. As I lay her down on my bed, I'm already getting hard again. The first time might not have been in a bed, but the second time will be.

Fuck dinner. I'm dining out on Colette tonight.

6
COLETTE

Two weeks later...

My fingers fly over the keys as I type the last scene of my book. I'm sitting on Bear's couch with my laptop balanced on my knees.

Since we hooked up two weeks ago, I've spent most of my time here. It's nice to write in the bar sometimes, but Bear is too much of a distraction. Whenever he's in the same room as me, my thoughts are scattered and my body longs for him.

At least up here I can focus on writing for a few hours a day.

My characters have found each other and, in the epilogue, they have a brood of mountain children. I try to come up with a name for a young girl character.

Looking for inspiration, I open an internet browser and type in *girls names western America 18th century.*

The round icon on the corner of the browser spins, but nothing comes up. That's odd. I try again and this time a message tells me I've got no internet connection.

It's a part of mountain life I'll have to get used to – dodgy internet connections. I smile at the thought. It's not being said yet, but I'm sure Bear and I feel the same. When my book's finished, there's no way I'm going back to California. My life is here now, with the big bear of a man I love.

Smiling to myself, I put my laptop aside and go over to Bear's desk in the corner to check if he has internet connection.

Opening his laptop, I bring up an internet browser. It does the same twirly button thing and I sigh in frustration. I'm closing the browser when something on the desktop catches my eye.

There's a folder titled "Colette".

My heart is in my throat as I click the icon, wondering what I'll find. The folder contains video files; I click one to start it playing.

It takes me a moment to realize what I'm looking at. It's the bar, but not just any part of the bar. This camera is trained on my favorite booth. And it's zoomed in on *me*.

My skin prickles and my belly clenches.

I open another video. It's me, writing at the bar on a different day. I try another one and another and another. They're all videos of me.

Sitting back with my heart racing, I put my trembling hands between my knees.

That's how he knew I was going to the cabin that day, that's how he knew the line from my book. Bear had been watching me, all this time. He engineered our whole relationship.

My mind is in a whirl, my skin prickly with heat and my chest constricted. Our whole relationship is based on a lie.

There are other folders on the desktop and with trembling fingers, I click through them to see the other CCTV feeds of the bar.

In one folder I find the live feed. It shows what's going on downstairs right now. Bear is at the bar drying a rack of glasses and talking to some customers.

I force myself to look at him hard. He looks happy, carefree, like the man I love, not some weird voyeur.

One of the men says something and Bear tilts his head back and laughs. I can imagine the sound, the deep rumble of his voice.

Just thinking about it makes my core melt and my panties dampen. I clamp my thighs together. I've just found out he's been watching me without my knowledge! I shouldn't be having this kind of reaction.

But the more I watch him, the wetter I get.

He dominates the bar with his big frame, confident and sturdy. One hand rests on the bar and I know that hand, I know what it's capable of doing. My nipples pebble and the heat between my legs becomes unbearable.

I slide a hand into my pants and palm my nerve center, needing some relief. One hand rubs myself while the other slides down my bra, teasing my nipple. All the time, I keep my eyes on Bear. He doesn't know I'm watching him and that makes it all the more thrilling.

He pours a beer for someone, his muscles flexing as he does it.

That's my man, I want to scream, my man.

My core explodes, and my pussy contracts, coming over my fingers. I squeeze my eyes shut tight as the orgasm races through me, feeling all its intensity. The way it shatters my body is delicious release.

When I open my eyes, I look to the screen. Bear's not there.

Leaning in, I scan the other feeds, trying to get a glimpse of him somewhere in the bar. Then I hear the door open.

7
BEAR

It's been two hours since I kissed Colette goodbye and headed downstairs to the bar. And that's two hours too long.

Ursula's just arrived, so I leave the bar in her hands and bound up the stairs to see my girl. I push open the door that leads straight into the living room and freeze.

She's sitting at my desk, my laptop open to the CCTV of the bar.

Shit.

I'm an idiot for not getting rid of the videos of her. I knew I should've deleted them, but every time I try, I can't bring myself too.

"I found the files." Her voice is husky and her cheeks are flushed.

"I can explain." I stride across the room and kneel in front of her. "I love you, baby. From the moment I saw you, I couldn't take my eyes of you."

She's breathing hard and I don't know if that means she's going to cry or scream or what.

"You're so fucking beautiful; I just want to watch you all day."

Fuck, this isn't coming out properly. I need to make her understand. "You're my world, baby, you're my everything."

She's looking at me, her eyes dark and hooded, her chest heaving up and down. I wait for her to say something, knowing my whole future depends on her reaction.

Then she does something completely unexpected. She takes my hand, opens her thighs and presses my palm between her legs.

Her panties are dripping wet and I catch a strong musky scent, like she's juiced up and ready to go.

"Colette?" I'm totally confused. Is my girl telling me it's all right?

"I found the files, and I found the live CCTV feed." As she speaks, she moves my hand over her wet pussy, rubbing herself against my palm.

I'm mesmerized by her intense look; my heart is in my throat and my dick's as hard as stone. If this is her way of telling me to fuck off, then it's pretty confusing.

She leans in and brushes my ear with her mouth, her warm breath making me shake.

"I watched you."

Holy fuck. "Do you mean…"

She moves her hips and slides them forward, rutting against my hand. "It means I'm really fucking horny, Bear."

Holy crap.

She's pulling at my belt and my cock's out in an instant.

My girl knows I watch her, and she likes it. Holy fuck, I've hit the jack pot.

Pulling her out of the chair, I hitch up her skirt and tear her panties off. I lift her into the air and line my dick up with her hole.

"I fucking love you, Colette," I say as I slam into her. She bucks her hips, wriggling against me as I carry her to the couch.

Still inside her, I sit on the couch, keeping her impaled on my cock. She straddles me as I slide her up and down my length.

"I fucking love you," I chant with every thrust.

"I love you too, Bear."

It's the sweetest thing to hear with my cock buried in her. I take her over the edge then explode inside her. The intensity of the orgasm makes me see stars.

Afterward, I pull her tight and kiss the top of her head.

"I like watching you, Colette. But if you want me to stop, I will."

She leans back and looks at me. "You don't have to stop, Bear. I think I like watching you too."

My heart soars. She gets me, she understands.

"You're perfect for me, honey. How about you stay here and be my mountain girl? We'll get married."

Her eyes go wide. "Are you serious?"

"Of course," I growl. "You're mine and I want to make it official. What do you say?"

"Yes!" She throws her arms around my neck. "I say yes!"

EPILOGUE

COLETTE

Six years later…

The keyboard blurs as my fingers race over it. I'm working on my latest book, writing it in my favorite booth at Bear's Brewery.

The scene comes to an end and I sit back, sighing triumphantly.

Through the window the mountain looms, solid and dependable, and I catch my pale reflection in the glass.

I'm wearing a low-cut t-shirt and without looking at the CCTV camera on the beam overhead, I lean forward, letting my top fall open.

My breathing becomes shallow, knowing that later tonight, Bear will be watching this.

The bar's pretty empty for a Wednesday afternoon and I give a quick glance around. Bear's behind the bar talking to Kit, his rumbling voice like a beacon to my soul.

Slowly, so no one notices, I slide my hand down my top. Now I do look at the camera, giving it a long, sideways glance. I bite my lower lip and tilt my neck back as my hand runs around my nipple.

Before anyone sees, I pull my hand out of my top and slide it between my legs under the table.

That'll give Bear something to watch later.

Feeling pleased with myself – and horny as hell – I try to concentrate on the words in front of me.

It's been six years since I came to Maple Falls and I've never left. Mountain life suits me and as long as I'm with my mountain man, I'm happy.

The door of the bar opens and the sounds of children laughing make me spin around.

Bear jr runs in, the twins, Wolf and Coyote, toddling behind.

"They've been no trouble," Ursula calls to me.

Bear comes from behind the bar and scoops Coyote up in his arms. She squeals with delight, grabbing his big beard. A real daddy's girl, that one.

"Pizza, pizza," Chants Wolf.

"All right," Bear booms. "I'll get the pizzas going."

I close my laptop as my booth is invaded by little people.

Wolf puts his little hand in mine and crawls onto my lap and Coyote snuggles in next to me.

Bear comes to join us and the little ones all scoot over to make room.

"Did you have fun with Aunty Ursula?"

"We had ice cream," says Bear jr, grinning. One leg moves restlessly, kicking the booth. At almost six-years-old he's tall for his age and looks like he'll be as big as his daddy one day.

Smiling as my family surrounds me, I realize we're growing the next generation of the mountain. And I couldn't be happier.

* * *

Mentioned in this book...

Curious about Colette's favourite author Ava Grayson who finds love with a mountain man?

Read Ava's story in His Big Book Stack.

MOUNTAIN MAN'S CAPTIVE

MEN OF MAPLE MOUNTAIN BOOK TWO

MOUNTAIN MAN'S CAPTIVE

MEN OF MAPLE MOUNTAIN BOOK TWO

Trapped in the woods and tied up by a mountain man...

First, he captures me in a hunting net, then he binds my wrists and feet to a chair.

I can't decide if this rugged mountain recluse is an axe murderer or a kind human trying to save me from myself.

What I do know, is one look and my body is on fire. I yearn to break free from my bindings and run my fingers through his thick beard.

Am I supposed to enjoy being held captive this much?

Mountain Man's Captive features an OTT obsessed mountain man and the curvy innocent woman he claims as his own. It's high heat, oh so sweet, and always with a happily ever after.

1
ANNIE

Branches scrape my arms as I stomp through the forest. My sweater catches on a bush, and I tug free, feeling the fabric tear.

Great, ruining my favorite sweater is another crime to add to Mark Granger's list of wrongs. Although alongside bullying and sexual assault, it's one of the lesser ones.

Tears sting my eyes and I wipe at them furiously; I will not let that asshole make me cry.

I can't believe I was stupid enough to let Mark Granger drive me up here.

Come see the stars with me, he said.

I know a great spot to watch the meteor shower, he said.

Now I'm halfway up the side of a mountain in the middle of the night with no way to get home to Maple Springs.

I glance at the sky, hoping to see the stars. If I can find Polaris, I can figure out which way I need to be heading to get back to the road.

All I see above me is blackness. I'm not sure if it's the canopy of trees or the thick storm clouds that have been gathering all day.

Mark told me it would clear up, that the storm would pass, and he had the perfect spot for star gazing.

Stupid, naive me believed him. I was too flattered that a boy had asked me out, because boys never ask me out. Least of all good-looking boys like Mark Granger.

Just because we're in astronomy club together, I trusted him.

I shouldn't have.

Once we got to this apparent star-gazing spot, he had his hands all over me. I told him no, but he wouldn't listen to my protests. He said I should be grateful. That a big girl like me wasn't going to get laid any other way.

But he didn't count on one thing, a big girl like me has strength. I kneed him in the balls, scrambled out from under him and gave him a punch on the nose for good measure.

That's when he swore at me, pushed me out of the car and drove off.

He left me here, halfway up the mountain in the dark. What kind of asshole does that?

A bird calls in the darkness and there's a snuffing noise to my left. I give a yelp and head to the right. I don't want to be some wild animal's dinner.

I waited for Mark to come back, not believing that he'd really leave me here. My phone must have dropped when he pushed me out and I couldn't find it in the dark. After a while, I realized he wasn't coming back.

In the dark it was hard to see the gravel road and after a while I lost it. So here I am, lost in the wood, in the middle of the night halfway up a mountain.

A sob escapes my lips and I grit my teeth and swallow down my hurt. I will not cry over this.

Through the trees I catch a glimpse of a warm orange glow.

My heart leaps. It's the first sign of human's I've seen since I've been wandering these woods.

It might be a house, or a cabin. Or it might be some crazy ass axe murderer.

I pause, the sounds of the woods mingle with my heavy breathing and the blood pounding in my ears. A cool breeze rattles through the trees and I wrap my arms around myself to fight off the cold.

An animal howls in the distance.

That does it. Deciding I'd rather take my chances with an axe murderer than spend the night out here alone, I head toward the light.

As I get closer, I can make out a log cabin sitting on its own in a clearing. Who the hell lives out here alone in the woods?

Treading carefully, I sneak toward the clearing, scanning the property for clues as to who lives here, friend or foe.

Running the side of the cabin are raised vegetable beds and a line of fruit trees. The light from the window falls on the trees illuminating plump red apples.

I relax a little. An axe murderer wouldn't have an apple orchard. Would he?

Moving forward, I'm almost at the clearing when I stumble over what at first seems like a tree root.

There's a clicking noise, and then the sound of rope rubbing along bark. Something closes around my foot and I let out a scream as I'm thrown upside down.

My head never hits the ground because as I fall, I'm pulled sideways and into the air. The rope closes around me and I'm swinging, upside down, trapped in a thick rope net.

Oh god, I'm caught by an axe murderer.

2
COLTON

A scream pierces the night and penetrates the walls of my cabin.

Grabbing my gun from its rack, I pause to check the security cameras. The infrared picks up something hovering off the ground on the edge of my perimeter.

One of the traps has been sprung and there's something inside, dangling from a tree.

I'm not sure what I've caught that makes that kind of high-pitched scream. It looks too big for a raccoon. Could be a bear, but they seldom come down this far.

I catch a flash of a leg and an arm protruding through the rope. Hitting zoom on the camera I go closer to see what I've caught.

"I'll be damned."

Wriggling in the net like a caught fish, is a woman.

Her hair is splayed out around wide eyes and the plumpest bee stung lips. Her body is pressed against the rope and I get a flash of heavy breasts and a curvy ass.

"Holy shit." She's gorgeous. The breath goes out of me and a strange sensation runs through my body making me hot all over.

I'm transfixed by her image on my screen. What is this beauty doing on my mountain in the dark and how the hell did she wander onto my property?

Grabbing my head torch and strapping it round my forehead, I venture out to see what I've caught.

My light pierces the darkness of the forest illuminating my path to the trap. The beam sweeps over the net picking up her upside-down body, caught awkwardly in the trap.

"My boyfriend's hiding in the woods with a shotgun trained on you."

Her words make me pause. Boyfriend. I don't like the sound of that. Even though she's lying through her teeth.

"I'm not gonna hurt you."

She snorts. "I'm upside down and caught in your trap. Already hurting."

"If you stop wriggling, I'll let you down."

"You take one more step toward me and he'll shoot."

I move toward her and crouch so I'm eye level. She's got the deepest brown eyes and they're blazing with anger. There's no gunshot.

"Let me down, you monster."

She flails her arms and one of them slips through the rope, causing her to roll forwards.

The more she thrashes, the tighter the rope pulls around her, until she's bundled up like a cute bale of hay.

But I can't release the rope until she's still, otherwise she'll go crashing to the ground.

I sit back on my haunches and wait for her to stop wriggling.

Finally, she gives up. Her arm trails almost on the ground and she looks at me with a wary eye.

"If you're going to kill me, just get it over with."

She looks resigned to her fate, which almost makes me laugh.

"I'm not gonna kill you."

She eyes me warily. "That's exactly what an axe murderer would say."

"Do I look like an axe murderer?"

Her eyes travel over me and I feel heat under her gaze.

"Yes. You're a big, bearded man with a gun slung over his shoulder who lives alone, I assume, on the side of a mountain. It's the MO of an axe murderer."

I chuckle, and the sound surprises myself. I spend so much of my time alone I barely get an opportunity to laugh.

"I'm glad you think it's funny. Or are you stupid too?"

Wow, this woman's got a mouth on her. She's bold for someone who's swinging upside down from a tree.

"Now that wasn't nice."

I stand up getting ready to cut her down when the beam from my light sweeps over her body.

Her leggings are torn giving me a glimpse of a silky pale calf. In the beam of the torch, I trace the line of her body. Plump ass, curvy as hell. Even all pushed up and awkward looking in my net I can tell she's beautiful.

My cock stirs, a sensation I've not felt in a long time. Of all the times to get a hard on. That'll scare her even more. At least she won't be able to see in the dark.

I pull my hunting knife out of its sheath on my belt and she screams.

Goddamn, what does she think I'm going to do, hurt her or something? I already know I'd never hurt this beauty.

With a quick movement, I slice through the rope that's holding the net up. It crashes down, unfurling the net and disgorging its precious catch. I'm standing underneath, and she falls right into my arms. She's so surprised it knocks the scream right out of her.

Her huge brown eyes look startled. There are scratches on her face and her clothes are torn. That didn't happen from hanging out in my rope trap.

"Where did you come from little fish?"

Her mouth flops open and closed but she doesn't speak. Her body presses against me and it feels so good, so natural, like she belongs there.

"Let's go inside and get you cleaned up."

Reluctantly I lower her to the ground so I can retrieve my knife. I'm slinging it into my belt when there's a shooting pain in my shin.

She kicked me. I spin around in time to see her disappearing through the trees. God knows where she thinks she's going but there's a sharp cliff face another hundred feet or so that way and there's a storm about to hit. I can't let her run around my mountain in the dark, it's too dangerous.

Catching up easily I put a hand on her shoulder. "Hey..."

The kick comes out of nowhere and she's got me in the shin again.

The girls got some spirit in her. But she's heading to danger and I can't have her running blindly through the forest.

"I'm not going to hurt you."

"Let me go." She tries to shake my hand off her but I'm too strong.

"Can't do that. Too dangerous."

She's struggling to be free and though I hate what I'm about to do, it's the only way to stop her running into danger.

"You're gonna hate me for this."

In one quick movement I catch her around the waist. She gives a surprised yelp as I sling her over my shoulder.

"Put me down." Her fists pummel my back.

"Nope." My arm wraps around her legs, pinning them against me so she can't kick. Her mound is pressed against my shoulder and I catch a musky scent, the scent of her.

My nostrils quiver and it's like an electric shot straight to my dick. It stands to attention and now I do feel like the bad man of the mountain, but Christ, this woman's got my body going all sorts of crazy.

"I'm not going to hurt you, sweetheart. But the mountain side is no place to be in the dark."

There's been a storm brewing all day and as I stride to the cabin, the first thick raindrops hit my face.

I push open the door to my cabin and she stops wiggling. I'm hoping she sees that it's a safe place.

There's a fire burning in the grate and the smell of roast chicken from the dinner I just ate permeates the cabin.

I carry her to the fire.

"If I let you down, do you promise not to run?"

"Fine."

As she slides off my shoulder her breasts press against my body and a wave of desire washes over me. Christ, if she knew what I was thinking…

"Sorry about…" My words are cut short as she makes a break for the door. I move quicker than she does and block the entrance.

"It's not safe out there."

I try to explain but she's got a determined look about her and she's eyeing up my shins. I'm pretty sure her kicks could be lethal to a smaller man. But I'm not a small man, I'm six foot six and as thick as the mountain I live on.

"Let me out of here." Her eyes flash anger and I really hate doing this but there's no way I'm letting her wander about out there in the dark. Even if she hates me for it.

"Nope. Not in the dark."

Capturing her up in my arms there's only one thing to do.

Slinging her over my shoulder again I carry her to my supply cupboard.

"Let me go, you brute." Her fists pummel my back

"I don't like to do this to you. But it's for your own safety."

There's a shelf full of rope and I grab a thin one, perfect for binding. With my leg, I swing one of the wooden chairs toward the fire and plonk her on it.

Her head twists wildly and when she sees the rope her eyes widen.

"You're not seriously going to tie me up?" She sounds incredulous.

"Yup. Until you learn to listen to me and let me keep you safe."

I stand astride her, keeping her legs pinned together while I bind her arms. I must concentrate on what I'm doing and not the curvy woman below me or I'll get hard and then she really will have something to scream about.

She's peering at me now and I feel the scrutiny of her gaze. "Is this how you treat all the women who visit your cabin?"

"Only the ones who are hellbent on killing themselves in a storm."

With her hands bound behind her, I bend down and work on her legs, binding the ankles together.

Satisfied she won't be able to break free I stand up. The fire's warm on the back of my legs. But that's not the only thing making me hot. With her hands behind her, her tits are pushed out showing off two voluptuous mounds.

Too bad she's looking at me like she wants to kill me. I'm really trying not to be the bad guy here, but I know this doesn't look good.

"I hate doing this, but if you go out in that storm tonight, you won't survive."

I'm not sure if she hears me. She's breathing hard and her anger is palpable. I don't blame her.

I've just met the woman of my dreams and I've got her tied up in my cabin. I'm pretty sure this is the shittiest seduction ever.

3
ANNIE

Rope rubs at my wrists as I wriggle my hands trying to get free.

Of all the shitty luck. the one cabin I stumble across is a freakin axe murderer. Except he's wearing a knitted sweater with a moose on it and he's got a kindly smile. Not how I imagined a murderer would look.

The man is speaking but I can't hear what he's saying over the sound of the blood thumping in my ears.

Something about a storm.

He watches me with a frown on his face. His cool blue eyes peek out of his rugged beard. When he had me over his shoulder, I could feel his beard scratching against my thighs where my leggings had ripped.

It caused a ripple through my tummy and a damp sensation between my legs that was so confusing it made me thrash even more.

Now he's watching me intently and I feel it again. A tug, deep in my core. My body shivers and something weird happens to my nipples. They're hardening and I hope to God, he can't see them through my shirt.

Are you supposed to get turned on by the man holding you captive? But he was so gentle when he tied me up and apologetic. Is that some weird thing murderers do?

He's got his arms folded and seems to be waiting for me to do something. I'm not sure what. He looks exasperated. Maybe I'm not behaving like most of his victims.

But then I've never been in a situation where I'm about to get murdered so I'm not sure how to behave.

The rope isn't done up too tight, but I can tell there's no way I'm getting it loose. Suddenly feeling exhausted, I stop struggling.

"There's a storm coming. You can't go out there."

He's speaking slowly, like I'm a child. But finally, I get what he's saying.

There's a storm. I shouldn't go out in it; I need to stay here in his remote cabin alone with him. He'll keep me safe. Sounds plausible, but it also sounds exactly like what an axe murderer would say.

As if to back him up, a smattering of rain hits the window. I glance over to it and back at him.

"See, a storm." He points.

My body slackens. Maybe he is telling the truth? Maybe I'm safer here with him than out there in the rain.

"I'm not going to hurt you. You got caught in my net."

Or maybe not. He did set a trap to catch me.

"What's the net for?"

He pulls one of the other chairs around and sits opposite me.

"Racoons mostly. They kill my chickens. Sometimes I catch a wood hen. I've never caught a woman before."

There's a smile playing on his lips and his eyes are dancing in a way that makes me want to touch him. If only my hands were free.

"My name's Colton. You're in my cabin. You'll be safe in

here."

I snort. "Safe? I'm tied up."

"Yeah." He rubs his beard. "I know that looks bad. But I'm keeping you safe."

The rope presses against my skin and with the way he's looking at me and my breasts pressed forward like this, it is causing a strange sensation to creep over my skin. A hot itch, a longing. Surely not for this brute?

His gaze travels over my legs and I feel a tug of desire. I press my thighs together, trying to banish it.

"You're bleeding. I'll get the first aid kit."

While he's out of the room I scan my surroundings. On the ledge above the fire are pictures. Him with an arm around an older woman who I guess is his mother.

Another one with a bunch of guys in a fishing boat. Holding up decent size fish. I squint at the pictures. One of the guys looks familiar, I've seen him working in the bar down the mountain.

Relief floods over me. Colton may just be a regular guy who likes solitude. Then I notice the gun rack above the door. And next to it a set of three knives.

There's no axe, but at least one of the knives looks big enough to chop up a body.

Oh shit. I've got to get out of here.

Colton comes back into the room and I quickly look away from the wall of death.

He crouches next to me and sets the first aid kit and a tub of water on the floor.

"This might sting."

My pulse is racing and I'm not sure if it's because I'm scared or turned on. Is he or isn't he going to kill me?

Gently, he presses the cloth against my bleeding leg. His touch is so tender and the look of concern on his face so genuine.

"You live here alone?"

"Yup, just me and the chickens."

Oh great, so no one will hear me scream.

"I'm completely self-sufficient."

For a moment I forget he's maybe an axe murderer. I have a vision of him tending the orchard I saw and clearing land with his bare hands.

"That sounds nice."

He smiles and I look away. Damn, I'm not here to have a conversation, the man's tied me up for Christ's sake, I'm angry at him. Only he is exceptionally hot, kind, and tending gently to my wounds.

"You got a name?"

I'm not willing to tell him that yet so I remain silent. After a few moments he tries again.

"What were you doing out in the woods on your own?"

The last thing I want to do is tell this man about my stupidity. How naive I was to be lured out here so a teenage boy from astronomy club could try to take advantage of me.

I close my lips.

"You don't want to tell me, that's fine."

He finishes dabbing at the blood and rubs a salve into the wounds.

"How do your wrists feel?"

I narrow my eyes at him. "My wrists hurt."

It's only partly true. They ache a little and there's something nice about being tied up with this man looking at me that I'm enjoying. But the knives have me creeped out and this could be my chance to get away.

"If I untie these. Are you going to promise not to run off into the dark?"

Keeping my face straight, I nod.

"Because there's a cliff face not too far from here and record rainfall expected tonight. I need to keep you safe."

"I promise." I cross my fingers behind my back.

Even though this man has a gentle touch and is doing things to my body I don't understand, there's no way I'm sticking around to find out if he's a murderer or not. He must be near an access road and if I can find that I can find the main road and get home.

He unsheathes the huge knife that he keeps round his belt and slashes through the bindings on my legs. As they fall away, he comes round the back and frees my hands.

I stand up slowly, stretching the tension out of my wrists.

"I'll go dump this water."

He goes through the door to what I guess is the bathroom. As soon as he's through the door, I make a break for it.

Sprinting across the room, I pull open the front door. Rain lashes my face and a bolt of thunder booms overhead making me jump.

I hesitate, this storm looks mean, I could get lost in it, never find my way out. Maybe Colton is just a good guy trying to keep me safe.

A flash of lighting follows the thunder illuminating my surroundings and I glimpse the access road that would lead me home.

If I'm going to go, I need to go now. Wondering if I'm being incredibly stupid, I bolt down the steps and into the night.

4
COLTON

The sound of the door banging brings me back to the living room. It's wide open, the rain falling in sheets against the dark sky. The woman is nowhere to be seen.

"Damn." She won't last ten minutes in this weather. Striding to the door I fix my head lamp back on my forehead.

"Hey!" The rain drowns out my voice. Not that she'll come to me anyway. Am I really that frightening that she'd prefer to be out here alone then safe in the cabin with me?

My feet carry me down the steps and I cross the yard, moving my head from left to right to illuminate the area. The driving rain makes it hard to see anything.

A tightness constricts my chest thinking about her out here alone.

My feet trip over something and I stumble. In the beam of my torch, I find her, crouched on the ground and shivering with mud streaks down her face. She must have fallen.

She looks up at me with doleful eyes, the look tugging at my heart.

My arms go around her and this time she doesn't resist as I lift her up.

"You're okay, sweetheart."

Her hair hangs in wet clumps around her mud-streaked face and she burrows it into my shoulder.

I carry her inside and sit her on the chair, this time not using restraints. Her wet clothes cling to her body showing off every curve. I have to look away before I lose it.

Water drips off her forming puddles on the floor and she hangs her head.

"If you're going to murder me, can you just get it over and done with."

Christ, does she still really think I'm dangerous?

"I'm not going to murder you." I hold out my phone. "Go ahead and call whoever you need to call. The road into town is closed so you'll have to stay here with me for the night. My name's Colton Bray. And I live at Wildwood Cabin. Tell them to call the ranger, Kit, if they want to check I'm legit."

She looks at the phone suspiciously. "You have signal up here?"

"Living off the grid doesn't mean shunning technology. I've got my own satellite dish."

She looks at me wearily like there's something else she wants to say.

"Why are you wearing a moose sweater?"

A smile plays on my lips. "My mother knitted it for me. I wasn't expecting company."

The answer seems to satisfy her and she relaxes and takes the phone.

While she makes a call, I head to the bedroom to change into dry clothes. I can hear her talking to someone and when I come back to the room, she's looking sheepish.

"They've closed the road into town for fear of washouts."

Just like I told her.

"Do you believe me now? That you're better off in my cabin than wandering round out there on your own?"

She looks away and bites her bottom lip. It's fucking adorable and I feel a rush of protectiveness over her. She's walked onto my property and that makes me responsible for her.

"I spoke to my mom," she says, "apparently she knows you."

I wonder who her mom is. There's not a lot of people I have much to do with these days.

"Or she knows of you. She's seen you at Bear's."

Bear's Brewery, it's the bar in the little mountain town halfway between here and Maple Springs. My buddy Bear owns it and I go there occasionally for a drink.

"You live with your mom?"

She nods.

Christ, I'm lusting over this woman and I don't even know if she's legal.

"How old are you?"

"I'm eighteen."

Holy shit, I've got twelve years on her. The protective feeling grows stronger. She's mine to look after, mine to protect.

"Your mom doesn't need to worry; I'll deliver you home safe as soon as this storm clears."

She looks up at me, her eyes wide and for the first time there's no fear in them. I guess she finally trusts me.

"Thank you."

She's dripping muddy water on the floor and starting to shiver."You need to get cleaned up and warm.

I hand her a towel and point her in the direction of the bathroom. "Shower's through that door."

She pulls open the bathroom door and then stops and turns around.

"Annie, my name's Annie."

I try out the sound on my lips, but already the door's shutting behind her.

"Annie."

She'll be peeling off her wet clothes, pulling her shirt over heavy tits.

I dig my nails into my palms and try not to think about the naked goddess in my bathroom.

To distract myself I head to the kitchen. She must be hungry and I get to work cooking an omelet.

She's still not told me what the hell she was doing on her own crashing through the forest at night. If someone's hurt her, they'll have me to answer to.

The shower turns off and a few minutes later the bathroom door opens. She's wearing one of my shirts, which is like an oversize dress on her, trailing all the way to her knees. As she towels her wet hair the hem creeps up giving me a view of her thick thighs.

I turn away quickly adjusting my dick. Does she have any idea what effect she's having on me?

With a monumental effort, I still my racing blood. She's only just starting to trust me; I can't scare her now with a giant hard on.

When I've got my dick under control, I set the omelet on the table in front of her.

"Did you make this for me?"

Her delight is palpable. She gives me a smile and peeps up at me through lowered lashes turning my heart to liquid and my cock to steel.

She's mine.

The thought comes into my head and it's too right and so natural. As I watch her eat, my fist clenches impatiently.

This little fish got caught in my net for a reason. I may not be an axe murderer, but that doesn't mean I won't ravage her.

5
ANNIE

Colton's staring at me intently over the table. It's a look that makes me feel giddy and flushed all over. I don't understand what this feeling is but I like it.

"So, um what do you do out here?" I chatter nervously trying to calm the heat between my legs.

"Raise chickens, hunt, live off the land."

It seems idyllic and I let out an involuntary sigh. "Sounds amazing. Is it lonely?"

He leans on the table so his beard trails the tabletop. How I long to run my fingers through the bristly hair. I wonder if it will be coarse or soft.

"No."

It's a definite answer and I cock my head, waiting for him to give me more.

"People can be assholes; I don't miss them."

I'm reminded of Mark, who left me out here all alone. "You can say that again."

His eyes narrow. "Did someone hurt you, little fish?"

The nickname makes me smile; no one's ever called me little before. Then I notice his clenched fists and I understand in an instant, if I told him about Mark, he'd hunt him down and hurt him. Hurt him bad, maybe even kill him.

My head swims, I feel a rush of warmth, that this big strong man would do that for me. But also, um, reality. However much of an asshole Mark is, I don't want his death on my conscious.

"This omelet is good."

He sits back and I sense his frustration at me changing the subject, but he doesn't push.

"The eggs were laid this morning."

"Really? These are your eggs?" I savor the next mouthful, taking in the rich taste.

"You can meet the girls tomorrow, help me feed them. There's usually a couple of eggs every morning."

Spending my days with chickens instead of people sounds idyllic. I have a vision of life up here. Tending to the orchard, feeding the chickens, and at night watching the stars. Not having to bother with anyone else but ourselves.

Colton takes my plate to the kitchen and I watch him go. A few hours ago, I was terrified of the man, now I'm contemplating a life with him. What the hell is wrong with me?

My body feels weary and maybe my mind is going too, that must be it, exhaustion.

Involuntarily I let out a big unattractive yawn.

"You need some sleep."

He's not wrong. It's been an eventful few hours and after a hot shower and some food, I'm ready to crash.

As if reading my mind, Colton comes round to my side of the table. He leans forward.

"What are you doing?"

Before I know what's happening, he's scooped me up in his arms.

"Relax, I'm taking you to bed.'

My body melts against him and I press my face into his

shirt. It's rough, woolen fabric and smells like wood and fresh rain.

My eyes close as I let him carry me into the bedroom. He pulls the duvet down and deposits me between the sheets.

For a wild moment I think he's going to climb in next to me. There's that tug again, a yearning in my core that I can't explain.

Then he pulls the covers up to my chin and kisses my forehead. A chaste gentle kiss before he backs away.

"Goodnight little fish."

The last thing I see is his figure outlined in the darkness as he switches the light off, then sleep claims me.

6
COLTON

It's early the next morning when Annie shuffles into the living room rubbing sleep out of her eyes. Her hair falls around her shoulders in messy waves and she looks so fresh, so innocent that I think my heart might explode.

I don't know what brought her onto my property, but with every moment we spend together, I don't want her to leave.

"Morning gorgeous." She gives me a confused look as I hand her a coffee mug.

"No one's ever called me that before."

I'm stunned. She is the most beautiful creature I've ever seen, how anyone could not see that is beyond me.

"Then they're blind."

She furrows her brows at me. "Or you are."

It annoys me, this putting down of herself. I can sense it comes from years of teasing, probably about her weight. She doesn't realize how beautiful she is, and her curvy figure is part of that. There's work to do, filling my little fish with confidence. It won't happen immediately, but I'll make her feel good about herself every opportunity I can.

"You wanna help feed the chickens?"

She slips into a pair of my old gumboots, which are so big they look like clown shoes on her, but after the rain last night, the ground is muddy.

I take her on a tour of my property, showing her the raised beds where I grow enough vegetables all year round to never have to visit the shops. She meets Tracey, the goat, who provides fresh milk, and my five fat hens.

She asks intelligent questions and I get the sense she's not just being polite; she's genuinely interested in what I've got going on up here. That fills me with hope.

I want her so much to like it. More than like it, I want her to love it. I want her to be a part of what I'm doing here.

I show her the solar panels that Bear helped me install last year. They provide enough energy so I can live off grid with my own electricity supply.

Her face glows with each new thing and I have a vision of her here with me. Tending the garden, her pregnant belly protruding.

The sound of a car engine pulls me out of my thoughts. I don't get many visitors, but it might be Brandon, needing help with clearing the roads after the storm.

A car comes into view. A white sports car, with a kid behind the wheel. It looks out of place on the mountain.

"Wait in the house sweetheart." I turn to Annie and she's frozen. A look of fear on her face.

"You know this guy?"

She opens her mouth and closes it again. When she speaks it's a whisper. "Mark."

My gut clenches. I don't like the sound of this. "He your boyfriend or something?" It comes out as a growl.

She shakes her head. "No."

The kid gets out of the car and I go to meet him but she grabs hold of my shirt. "Don't let him see me." She darts behind the cabin and I stride forward.

He's a gangly kid, with sharp eyebrows and a mean stare, can't be more than nineteen years old. But if he's done something to hurt Annie, I'll kill him.

"Can I help you?"

He takes a step back as I walk toward him. My fists clench at my sides and I make no effort to hide my distrust.

"Have you seen a girl?"

I'm sure he's talking about Annie, but I'm not handing her over to this mug. "Why, you lost one?"

She snorts as if it's a funny joke. "Yeah, last night."

I fix him with a steely look and he squirms under my gaze. "How do you lose a girl?"

He rubs his nose and glances away. "She jumped out of the car."

This guy's lying through his teeth.

"Now, what you doing to a girl to make her jump out of your car?"

He looks around nervously, and he should be nervous. I'll break his fucking neck.

"Um, I broke down. She ran off. But I can't find her."

So, this fuck knuckle is the guy responsible for leaving Annie out on her own all night. "You left Annie out here, on her own?"

Relief washes over his face. "So, you have seen her, phew. I got home and then felt bad, like she might get eaten by a bear or something, so I tried to come back to…"

He doesn't get a chance to finish. My fingers grab his throat and I push him back against the hood of his car.

"You left a woman out here on her own at night."

His eyes bulge. "I came back for her."

His voice shakes with fear, which is good. I want him to quake, I want him to be so scared he shits himself.

"In the middle of a fucking storm. She could have died out here you useless piece of shit."

His mouth falls open and closed again.

Anything could have happened to Annie out there if I hadn't have found her. A red haze fills my vision, my hand closes around his throat.

"I'll fucking kill you." It will feel good to squeeze his neck till it snaps for leaving my girl like that.

"Colton, stop." Annie's voice cuts through my anger. "Colton, he's not worth it."

She's at my side laying her small hand on my arm. "Don't kill him please." Her calm touch makes me pause. I look at her pleading face. She's right, this asshole isn't worth the jail time.

I loosen my grip.

"You're lucky she's a better person than you'll ever be." I release the guy's neck and he doubles over, gasping for air.

"I won't kill you, out of respect for Annie's wishes. But I will beat the shit out of you."

I pull him up by his collar and my fist connects with his face. There's the satisfying sound of bone breaking which will ruin his pretty boy nose.

"That's for leaving Annie up here." He stumbles back clutching his nose. "And if you ever touch her again, I really will kill you."

He stumbles backwards to the car and fumbles with the door.

"Now get the fuck off my mountain."

The ignition starts and the wheels skid as he takes off reversing all the way down my access road.

Satisfied he's gone I turn to Annie. She's trembling and I fold her in my arms.

"I will kill him if you ask me to Annie."

She shakes her head. "You don't need to do that."

She's looking at the ground and taking her cheeks in my hands I pull her face up so she's looking at me.

"I would kill for you Annie, anything you ask. You're mine, you understand. And I protect what's mine."

Her breathing becomes shallow and her eyes wide. I've just laid out my feelings for her and my body tenses as I wait for her to respond. It feels like an age before her lips part and she says the sweetest words I could ever hear.

"You're mine too."

My lips crash into hers and it's like a storm crashing around us. The air crackles with energy and I put my whole being into the kiss. Showing her with my touch what she means to me.

Her body presses against me, causing an instant rise of blood through my veins and straight to my cock.

My hardness grinds against her and she pushes back, her hips moving against me.

I put a hand either side of her hips and lift her up. She wraps her legs around me, and still joined at the mouth, I carry her into my cabin.

7
ANNIE

My body pulses with energy and heat as Colton carries me inside. He would have killed Mark if I'd given the word, I have no doubt about that. And that thrills me. That this big strong man would do anything for me.

I squeeze my feet together and push my hips into him, making him groan. "Annie, you're driving me wild."

He lays me down on the bed and stares down at me, his eyes hooded and intense. I feel confident under his gaze, confident enough to slide the shirt of his I'm wearing up my thighs so he can see the secret I've been carrying all night and all morning.

My underwear was soaked after the rain last night, when I got dressed in his shirt, I didn't put any panties on.

He gasps as I lift the cotton, revealing my sex to him. My fingers run through the hair and come away slick.

"Oh sweetheart."

His dick is already pushing through his trousers and now he slides them off, revealing a thick cock, which glistens with pre-cum.

My breathing goes up a notch and I think I'm going to pass out. I'm way out my depth here with a dick that big.

He must see my wide-eyed stare because he chuckles. "Don't worry little fish, you'll get used to it."

He slides his knee between my legs and climbs onto the bed.

I prop myself up on my elbows because this is probably the time to tell him I'm new to all this.

"Um." I begin, but his mouth closes around my ear and it sends shivers all the way down to my pussy.

My words turn to moans.

"What's that sweetheart?"

He kisses my neck and I tilt my head to the side, wanting more.

"I, um..." His hand grabs the shirt front and he pulls it open. buttons pings across the room and the heat of his breath glides over my breasts. "Oh god that's good."

His beard tickles my nipples and I know it's soft. Soft with a spring to it that brushes over my nipples making them hard.

I moan again.

His hand slides down my belly and over my mound and then his fingers are tangled in my hair, spreading my lips apart and brushing my entrance.

"You're so wet."

His finger slides along my entrance and then inside. My body bucks at the sensation and he groans.

"You're so tight."

"Because I'm a virgin." I finally mange to blurt out.

He freezes and I'm worried I've done something wrong. His fingers stop moving and a whimper escapes my lips.

"Is that okay?" I whisper.

"Oh sweetheart. That's more than okay. That's fucking amazing."

There's something else I want to say, though I'm not sure how to. As if reading my mind, he raises his eyebrows.

"What is it honey?"

I bite my lip, not sure how to ask for what I need. "You know when you tied me up last night?"

He nods slowly. "Yeah. And I apologize. It was the only way to stop you taking off into the storm."

I shake my head impatiently. "I know, it's fine."

He cocks his head. "Then what is it?"

"I um, I kinda liked it."

Realization dawns on his face and his eyes light up.

"You want me to tie you up?"

I feel silly asking, but the thought of Colton having his way with me while I'm restrained causes a gush of wetness between my legs.

I nod my head.

He chuckles. "Let me get the rope."

A few minutes later I'm completely naked with a hand tied to either side of the bed post. I've never felt so exposed, but also so safe.

Colton strips naked and stands in front of me, his gaze sweeping over my entire body.

"You are gorgeous Annie."

It doesn't feel as stupid as the first time he said it, and I think maybe, just maybe, he might believe it's true.

The thought makes me bold and I move my legs, slowly opening them up and exposing myself to him.

He watches, mesmerized as I let my thighs fall open.

His breathing goes shallow as he kneels before me. "I'm going to make sure you never forget your first time."

His promise is followed by a slow kiss as his hand sweeps up my body. His mouth moves slowly, travelling down my neck, toying with my nipples. I pull at my restraints longing to run my fingers through his hair, but they hold fast.

It's exquisite torture as his kisses travel further south, over my belly and to my sex. When his mouth connects with my pussy, I cry out. It's like volts of electricity are running through my veins, turning my blood hot.

Then his tongue licks my hard nub and I almost come undone. My nerve endings zing to life making my legs spasm.

I pull at my bindings, wanting to run my hands through his hair, to move his head back and forth over me. But I can't move, I must go at his pace and he's going so exquisitely slow.

A finger glides into my opening and then another.

The pressure is building, so slowly, but I want it all now.

"Go faster." He pauses and looks up at me and that's worse. "Go faster."

There's a begging note to my voice. He sits back on his haunches and fixes me with a lazy smile.

My pussy aches for attention and I want to pull him back down. I pull at my hands but they stay fast.

"You didn't say the magic word."

He's teasing me and by the hardness of his cock, enjoying my frustration. I'll say anything he wants right now as long as he puts his mouth back over my pussy.

"Please, Colton. Please, go faster."

I writhe my hips, bucking toward him, longing to feel his mouth on me again.

He captures my hips and holds them in the air. "Anything for you little fish."

His tongue laps at my clit and while one hand holds my hips in the air, the other slides into me, one, two, three fingers.

I'm on the edge of pleasure and I teeter there for a moment before I fall over the top. Stars burst in my vision and I scream out his name as pleasure rips through me. I never knew I could feel like this, feel so good.

But he's not done. His mouth presses against me and I come again, bucking and writhing until I think I can't stand it anymore.

As the second orgasm wains, he climbs on top of me.

"You're ready."

He kisses my mouth and I taste my own saltiness. The rope bites at my wrist as I tug on them, wanting to touch him, but loving the restraint of not being able to.

He throws my leg over his shoulder and pulls my hips upwards, meeting his cock.

I'm at his complete mercy and can only watch as he positions me like a rag doll. His cock lining up with my entrance. The tip running over my glistening lips.

I moan, a guttural sound that I don't recognize as my own voice.

"This might hurt a little."

I don't have time to respond before he pushes inside me. There's a searing pain and then an intense throbbing as my pussy adjusts to his size.

He bends my legs towards my chest and sinks into me further. His hand runs over my nipples and I push my tits out to meet his touch.

"You okay sweetheart?"

I'm so lost in a world of new sensations that I can barely speak."Yah-hah."

"Good cause I'm going to fuck you hard."

The words send a shiver through me. My hips buck and I meet his every thrust. I wrap my legs around him, my heels digging into his back.

"Colton, I'm going to come again."

"Good. Come like a good girl."

Then I'm over the edge, and sliding into my orgasm, even more intense than the last.

I cry out his name and he tenses, groaning into my hair.

"Annie..."

His hot liquid explodes into me, coating my walls and filling me up. We tremble together, sharing this pure moment as one.

Afterwards he unties me and holds me close.

"I never want you to leave." He murmurs, tucking a strand of hair behind my ear. "Come live here, with me."

It seems like the most natural thing in the world and I snuggle into him. "Okay."

He holds me close and I know, I'll always be safe with my mountain man.

EPILOGUE

ANNIE

Six years later…

"You sure that's not going to hurt the baby?"

Colton's concern fights with his desire as he squares my hips over the chair. My belly is even rounder than usual in the third trimester of pregnancy, and I'm horny as fuck. Which is why I sent the girls to their grandma's for the day.

"It won't hurt the baby if you go gentle with me."

His gaze flicks over the cleavage of my swollen breasts. "I can't promise that sweetheart."

"Which is why I'm not taking any chances."

I swing my legs off him and pick up the rope that I left hidden under the table.

Grabbing his hands, I pull them behind the chair.

"Hey, what're you doing?"

His shoulders pop forward and I loosen up a bit. "Making sure you don't accidentally hurt the baby."

Pulling the rope tight I check my knot. It holds.

I walk slowly to the front of him and make a show of taking my top off.

His dick tents in his pants. I unzip him and pull them off him.

"The day you got caught in my net, little fish, was the best day of my life."

I agree. It's six years since I moved in with Colton. Moved into our own little piece of paradise, far away from anyone else.

Molly arrived a year after and Angie eighteen months after that. Now there's a baby boy growing in my belly and I can't wait to meet him.

But my babies are the last thing on my mind as I hover over my husband's thick cock. I lower myself gently, so only the tip slides inside me. Then I pause.

He growls and tugs at his restraints, impatient to be inside me.

"Jesus, Annie, fuck me already."

I slide in another inch and he moans in frustration.

He tugs at the rope and the chair jerks nearly toppling us to the floor. A rope end flicks into the air and then his hands are on me. Pulling at my hips and sliding me down his shaft.

So much for the restraints.

His look is brutish and determined as he lifts me up and down his cock.

I push my hips to him, rubbing against him and feeling the pressure build.

"Fuck, Colton, I'm gonna come."

I explode and a moment later he does too. Impaling me on his cock and holding me in place as his seed shoots into me.

"That's not how that was supposed to go."

He grins. "No? Then I suggest you get thicker rope."

He kisses my lips and wraps his arms around me and I lean

into his chest. After so long together, he's still my rock, my safe place and I know he always will be.

* * *

MOUNTAIN MAN'S VIRGIN

MEN OF MAPLE MOUNTAIN BOOK THREE

MOUNTAIN MAN'S VIRGIN

MEN OF MAPLE MOUNTAIN BOOK THREE

Her ambition got her up the mountain. But when this burly mountain man spies her curves, he won't let her go...

I'm not an outdoors person, I'm scared of the wild.

So how did I end up halfway up a mountain in a flimsy tent? I lied, that's how. A big, massive stonking lie to get my first break.

But I didn't count on Chase. The rugged mountain guide who's making me sweat more than I should.

A night in the wild turns from my biggest fear into my most pleasurable adventure.

But what happens when the trail ends? Can I ever go back to my old life, or has the mountain claimed me for good?

Mountain Man's Virgin is a short and steamy, forced-proximity, city girl/mountain man romance featuring an OTT obsessed hero and the curvy woman he claims as his own. A safe read with no cliffhangers and a happily ever after guaranteed.

1
BROOKLYN

My fingers tap along to the music, connected through my phone and blaring through the car speakers.

Bringing my takeout coffee cup to my lips, I take a sip just as my ringtone blasts through the speakers, making me jump and causing hot coffee to splash over my legs.

"Shoot."

Keeping one eye on the road, I set the coffee down in the cup holder. Patting at the stain spreading across my crotch, I answer on handsfree.

"Hey babe, you there yet?" Lilia's bubbly voice comes at me through the car speakers.

"The last sign of civilization was Maple Springs about twenty minutes ago and there's a big ass mountain in front of me, so yeah, I guess I'm almost there."

"I'm so excited for you," she squeals, making me wince and turn the volume down a notch.

"Thanks babe."

Lilia's my best friend, ever since we met at college and then started interning together at Durant Magazine Group. We both want to be journalists one day and she's as excited as I am to get my first proper assignment.

"Thought I should warn you; Kelvin was asking some tricky questions."

Kelvin's the editor of Mountain Travel magazine, one of the magazines that Durant owns, and the guy I blatantly lied to get this assignment.

"What was he asking?"

"He asked me about our hike to Mt. Hood."

My body tenses. I've never been to Mt. Hood. I've never been to any mountain in my life. But when the journalist who was booked to write the piece on the Maple Mountain trails broke his leg, I pleaded to be given the assignment.

I told Kelvin I was outdoorsy and loved hiking, which might have been a big lie. And I might have accidentally told him that me and Lilia went hiking together.

Finally, he gave in and let me go. After all, it was already paid for and set up. We've got a mountain guide waiting for us in Maple Falls.

"What did you say?" I sip my coffee nervously, wondering if Lilia is about to tell me I have to turn around and come home.

"I told him it was awesome."

My body relaxes. This is why Lilia's my best friend.

"Thank you. I'm sorry I mentioned you, it just accidentally slipped out."

"Don't worry about it, babe. I know you're going to be awesome out there. You got this."

Her words make me smile and set me a little at ease. I wish I could have as much confidence in myself as Lilia does in me.

"Thanks hon. How's thing's back in the office?"

Lilia starts to reply but the phone goes dead. With my eyes on the road, I hit call back but it goes straight to voicemail. I glance at my phone and there's no bars, no signal.

"Great." I'm really in the sticks now.

A tremor of doubt runs through me. I wonder, not for the first time, if I should turn around and head back to Seattle. I've never been hiking in my life; my body isn't built for it. I'm short and round and I prefer binge reading in my sweatpants than galivanting around in nature.

But after three months making coffee and checking print runs, I was desperate to get some real experience. When I saw an opportunity, I took it. I mean how difficult can a two-day hike be.

All I've got to do is walk up a mountain with a trained guide, make some notes, and write a nice piece about the trail.

I've been studying the magazine, and I know the type of thing I need to write. Describe the scenery, mention the wildlife, talk about the peacefulness, recharging from the city, yada yada yada. Easy.

The only thing I'm concerned about is the night that we have to camp on the mountain.

Spending a night in a tent in the middle of nowhere makes me shudder. But I've pushed that out of my mind, trying not to think about it. If it gets me my big journalist break, then one sleepless night will be worth it.

The sat nav tells me to turn left for Maple Falls. It's a gravel road with a wooden signpost that looks like it hasn't changed since the 19th century.

"It's just two days." I prepare myself. Two days in the ass end of nowhere. Do the hike, get the story, and get out. How hard can it be?

The first houses of Maple Falls come in to view. They're more like cabins than houses. Set off the street, up steep driveways, peeping out from between leafy trees. It's quaint, nicer than I expected.

The Main Street, if you can call it that, consists of a line of boutique shops. I slow down, taking in the scattered buildings that line the street. There's a couple of hiking shops, fishing supplies stores, a post office, a convenience store, and a cute looking café.

At the end of the street is a bar, Bear's Brewery. It's got prime position overlooking the mountain.

The tourist office sits across the road, and I pull into a parking space wedging my Mazda hatchback between two enormous pick-up trucks. Both mud splattered, not like the shiny ones on the streets of Seattle.

My coffee is still warm, and I clutch it in one hand, phone in the other, as I enter the tourist office. A kind looking middle-aged lady in thick glasses looks up at the sound of the door.

"Welcome to Maple Falls. How can I help?"

"I'm here to meet someone." I set the coffee down and scroll through my inbox looking for the email with the name of the person I'm supposed to meet. Thankfully there's one bar of signal here.

There's the sound of the door opening and shutting behind me which brings a cool breeze and makes my hairs stand on end.

I find the email. "Chase Amery. I'm doing a walk with him."

"A hike, not a walk." The deep voice comes from behind, making me jump and almost spill my coffee again. I spin around and my heart skitters in my chest.

Standing behind me is without a doubt the hottest man I've ever laid eyes on. He's tall, at least six feet, with shaggy sandy colored hair and pale blue eyes that are staring at me with an intensity that makes me blush.

"Ah-are- you Chase?" I only just mange to get the words out of my mouth because it's gone bone dry.

His pale eyes sweep up my body and land on my breasts. I'm used to men looking at my breasts; they're bigger than average due to my weight being bigger than average. Usually, I hate it, but for once I don't mind him looking.

In fact, I want him to keep that gaze on me, I want him to look at my whole body that way, with a hungry look.

"You don't look like a Scott." His eyes dance and a smile plays at the corner of his lips.

"I'm um..." So distracted by him I can't think straight. Pulling myself together and remembering why I'm here, I step forward with my hand outstretched. "I'm Brooklyn. Scott broke his leg so they sent me."

"Chase." He takes my hand and presses it against his.

His palm is rough with calluses, and a flash of heat races up my arm, wondering what that hand would feel like running over my body.

I drop my hand quickly and drop my head to look at my phone, trying to hide the blush that's climbing up my neck.

This assignment just got a whole lot more interesting.

2
CHASE

The woman in front of me is like a vision from heaven. Wide grabbable hips, long thick blonde hair. Bent over her phone, she's giving me a good view of the v shape of her cleavage, peeping out between the top of her t-shirt.

Perfect round tits and the sweetest pouty lips I ever saw. Damn, she's a fine-looking woman.

She's peering at her phone as if that's going to save her from my lascivious thoughts.

"Um, we're doing a two-day hike…"

"Three days."

She looks up suddenly; her honey-colored eyes show her confusion. "The email I got from Scott says two days."

I'm sure it does. Two days up the mountain with someone called Scott would have been enough. But they've sent the curvy Brooklyn with the amazing tits. I'm making it three days.

"Three days, two nights to see the lakes. They're the jewel of the mountain, I'm sure you want to write about them."

She looks hesitant. "Two nights camping?"

My eyes run over her jeans, light t-shirt, and trainers. She doesn't look like someone who's prepared for the mountain.

"You've got hiking boots, right?"

"Yes." She gives me a huge grin. I don't understand why she's so happy she's got hiking boots, but fuck me, it lights up her eyes making them dance like honey trickling off a spoon.

I have a sudden vision of licking honey off her curvy body.

The blood runs to my dick and I have to turn away or she'll see my hard on and run all the way back down the mountain.

"Good." I head for the door. Not wanting to leave but needing to get away from her before I do something stupid. "You staying at The Crown?"

It's the only hotel in town and she nods.

"I'll pick you up at 5:30 tomorrow."

Her mouth almost hits the floor. "In the morning?"

I give her one of my most charming smiles. "Gotta start early if we want to get to the lakes."

I leave her gapping after me. There is no way that woman has ever been hiking in her life. I'm not sure what her angle is, but I'm determined to find out.

It's still dark the next morning when I pull up at The Crown. It's dead on 5:30 and I expect to be waiting for a while, but Brooklyn surprises me. She comes out of the hotel looking adorable in khakis so new they've still got the crease down the front and a much too big backpack.

"Morning," I say cheerfully.

She shoots me a look that lets me know she may be up but she's not happy about it.

I hold out a hot thermos. "Coffee?"

Her face lights up and the smile goes straight to my heart. I love that it doesn't take much to change her mood. I'm an easy-going guy myself and I hate grumpy people. Apart from my brother, he's the only grumpy person I can stand.

She's struggling under her backpack, and I slip it off her shoulders and undo the zip.

"Hey," she protests.

"I need to check your pack, make sure you've got the right things, and not too much."

"Why wouldn't I have the right things?" She grabs the bag off me defensively and I wonder what she's hiding.

"Relax, I do this with all my clients. The mountain can be an unforgiving place. The weather can change, an accident could happen, we could meet a bear and have to divert our path, I need to make sure we're prepared for all eventualities."

She's gone white. "There are bears on the mountain?"

I'm so used to living with bears that I forget how freaked out some people get, although I would have thought a journalist working for a mountain hiking magazine wouldn't be in that category.

"Only black bears and they mostly stick to the higher ground. We're unlikely to see one."

"Okay." Her voice seems strained, and I change the subject.

I go through her bag, chucking out two sets of sweaters, a pair of jeans, and a roll up pillow.

"Use your jacket as your pillow, it saves on space."

Her gear is a mixture of well-worn and brand-new, and I wonder again what her angle is. In the top of her backpack, she's got a phone, and I take it out and put it in the 'do not need' pile.

"Whoa, that's coming with us." She picks it up. "I don't go anywhere without my phone."

She sticks her chin out defiantly, a real city girl, not wanting to be parted from her tech.

"Suit yourself, but I'm not taking mine."

"But what if something happens to us?"

"What's gonna happen?"

"Like, any of those things you just mentioned. Change in weather, a bear..."

She's working herself up, and she looks adorable. I resist the urge to run my hands over her, to touch her in any way.

"Relax, I always tell the ranger where we're going, so if we don't come back, they'll know exactly where to find us."

She doesn't look impressed. "That sounds slow."

"Yeah, it is. Life moves at a slower pace on the mountain, give it a try, you might like it." She looks down at her phone. "There's no signal once we leave town anyway."

She slips the phone in her back pocket. "I might want to take pictures," she says defiantly.

I shrug. City folk are always tied to their tech. I'm not going to fight her on it.

Once I've done the inventory, her bag's lighter by about half. Finally, we're ready to go and I drive the few miles to the ranger's hut and where the trail begins. I leave a note for Kit letting him know where we're going and when we'll be back. Then, shouldering our packs, we set off up the mountain.

3
BROOKLYN

There's a burning sensation in my thighs, and my back aches from carrying the backpack. Thank goodness Chase got rid of half my stuff out of it before we set off.

My ankles chafe every time I take a step, and I'm sure I'm going to find a fat blister when I eventually peel off my sock. It was lucky I found a pair of hiking boots in my size at the charity shop, but there was no time to wear them in.

It was hours ago that we set off in the faint glow of daybreak. The pale predawn light was just enough to show us a path to the first ridge where we stopped for breakfast.

The sky was streaked with pink as we finished the coffee and ate the bagels that Chase had brought. One good thing about hiking, you must eat a lot of carbs because you need the energy to burn.

We broke for lunch in a forest clearing surrounded by a sea of wildflowers. I've never seen such a vibrant purple in nature before.

But lunch seems like a long time ago as we slog up the winding path. My body aches in places I never knew existed, and this is only day one.

Chase is ahead of me, and I watch his confident figure as he takes long strides, skirting easily around the dips and rock piles of the path. Like a large, good looking mountain goat. If a mountain goat can be good looking.

Every so often he pauses to let me catch up with him. And when he does, I try to get my heaving breath under control and smile like I'm enjoying myself. Although somewhere between the sunrise and lunch, the smile became genuine and I realized I am enjoying myself.

And a lot of that is down to Chase. We've been singing as we walk. Belting out eighties' ballads and nineties hip hop.

He makes me laugh almost as much as Lilia does. Except when I laugh with Chase, I get a funny feeling in my tummy, like I want to throw my arms around him and squeeze him tight. Which is crazy because I only just met him.

The path widens and we come to a clearing in the scrub with a rock ledge behind us. Chase sits on a boulder, and I shrug off my pack to join him.

"We'll stay here for the night."

We're in a dip and the mountain is hidden by the stack of boulders. I imagined breaking camp somewhere a little more scenic. "Why here?"

Chase gives me a mysterious smile. "You'll see."

He gets to work gathering wood for a fire and instructs me to get the tents pitched.

Pulling the yellow canvas out of my pack, I pretend to know what I'm doing. I've never pitched a tent in my life but I can't let Chase know that.

There are some sticks that seem to join to make a long pole. I get that bit figured out but am struggling to find the holes to put them in.

I look up to find Chase watching me.

"Different to the tent I have at home," I mumble.

"Here." He takes the end off me and shoves it through an opening in the canvas, he feeds it through till it pokes out the other end. "Now put it in that metal ring at the bottom."

He doesn't ask me why I don't know how to put up a tent, but it's obvious he's on to me. Not that it matters now. We're halfway up the mountain, there's no going back.

By the time the tents are up, the sun is low in the sky throwing the surroundings into a golden light.

"I want to show you something."

Chase puts his hand out to me, and I take it, feeling it fit snugly into his. He leads me carefully around the rock face to where some boulders stick out making it easy to climb up, like stairs. I follow him up the rock face and we come out onto a flat ledge about ten feet above our camp.

On the other side of the rocks is a ridge that drops away to the valley below.

"This is what I wanted you to see."

The valley is laid out before us, with Maple Falls in the distance and further down the mountain I can make out the winding road that leads down to Maple Springs, the bigger town beyond.

The sun is a burnt orange in the sky as it sets behind the valley. "It's beautiful."

He grins. "Thought you'd like it."

And I do. We sit without speaking for a long time, watching the sky change from orange to gold to pink.

"Have you always lived on the mountain?" I ask.

"All my life. My mother was a cleaner at the Crown Hotel. Me and my brother grew up roaming around the mountain."

"Does your brother still live here?"

His eyes crinkle and he laughs, something he does often. "Oh yeah. Rowan's a grumpy old recluse."

Chase is so good natured I can't imagine how a sibling of his could be anything different.

"My brother's ex-military," he tells me. "Prefers to live alone. Hardly ever comes down the mountain."

I try to imagine what it's like, growing up here. I grew up in Seattle. My parents took me to the beach sometimes, but they weren't into the outdoors. I wonder why not, as I watch the sky turn to pink and breathe in the fresh mountain air.

"Come on," Chase says eventually. "We better eat dinner before the bears come sniffing around."

My body tenses. I can't tell if he's being serious or not. His chuckle reaches me through the half-light.

"I'm joking, there's no bears."

I laugh uneasily. That's all a city girl like me hears about the wild, that there's bears and things that could hurt you. No one tells you about the sunsets and sunrises and purple flowers and the sounds of birds.

I scramble down the boulder feeling my way in the dim light until I reach the campfire. Taking a seat on an upturned log, a feeling of peace washes over me as I watch the flames.

I get it now, this hiking. It's wonderful being out in nature, out in the wilderness. It's only been one day, but I think I'm a convert.

A few hours later I'm woken in the night by a rustling in my tent. My heart thunders in my ears as I strain to hear what woke me.

There it is again, a rustling noise, like something's trying to get into my tent. Like a bear's trying to get in.

I sit up, my heart hammering.

"Chase!" I call out, fumbling in the darkness for the torch. "Chase, there's a something out here."

There's the sounds of a zip undoing and a light flicks on.

"Chase!" I call again, panic rising in my chest.

The rustling intensifies as the zip to my tent comes undone. Chase appears in the door of my tent, his hair ruffled and his eyes blurry from sleep.

"What happened?"

"I heard something." My heart's racing. "I think it was a bear." It feels stupid to say it, but he just nods.

"I'll go take a look."

Before I can protest, he ducks out of the tent and I'm left alone in the dark.

I see his light flicking around outside and hear his footsteps as he circles our camp. My heart's in my throat as I wait for him to come back. Eventually his face appears in the tent entrance again.

"No sign of anything out here."

I'm starting to feel slightly stupid, but no less afraid. "I heard something."

He nods sympathetically. "Might have been the wind, or a twig falling on the tent."

"It wasn't a twig, it was something big, some kind of animal." Although now I'm not so sure. What I am sure about is I'm not getting any more sleep tonight.

He starts to retreat. "I'm going back to bed..."

"Don't leave me."

It comes out as a plea, and I know I'm being ridiculous but we're on the side of a mountain with nothing but a thin bit of canvas between me and the big scary outdoors.

"Sleep in here, with me."

His body stiffens, and I wonder if that's against some kind of trail guide protocol. Don't sleep in the same tents as your clients. But stuff that, I'm scared and I want Chase next to me.

"I feel safe with you," I plead. "Bring your sleeping bag in here, otherwise I won't be able to sleep."

He stares at me for a long time then nods. "Fine. But it's okay. There's nothing to be scared of."

He drags his sleeping bag in and settles down next to me.

It's a small tent, made for one, and with Chase in here, our bodies are pushed up together. Even through the thick layer of sleeping bag, I feel the heat radiating off him. I clench my thighs together. Now that the fear has gone, it's been replaced by a longing in my core. A longing for Chase.

He turns on his side and faces away and a wave of disappointment rushes over me.

I wonder what it would be like to lie next to him, as man and woman, with his arm draped over me.

"I remember my first time sleeping on the mountain," says Chase. "I was with my brother and my dad, when he was still around. We camped out in a big tent, not too far from town. I didn't sleep a wink. Every time the wind blew and the tent rattled, I was sure it was some animal coming to get us."

He rolls over onto his back. "How about you, Brooklyn? When was the first time you slept out in a tent?"

I bite my lower lip, thinking up some lie to tell him, running through plausible scenarios in my head. But there's something about Chase; I don't want to lie to him. I decide on the truth.

"Um, tonight." He doesn't say anything. "Tonight is the first night I've slept in a tent."

"I thought so." Even in the dark I know he's smiling. And I feel relief. He knows my secret and he's not cross.

"Goodnight, Brooklyn."

"Goodnight, Chase."

With him lying next to me, it doesn't take long to drift off to sleep.

4
CHASE

It's the following day as we trudge up the final stretch of the path that leads to the crater lakes. Brooklyn might have slept soundly last night, but I tossed and turned next to her.

Being so close to her was torture. My body was hot all night imagining her touch. I had to restrain myself from reaching out to her in the night.

I settled for watching her sleep instead. Watching the gentle rise and fall of her chest with her lips slightly parted. Laid out like a sweet innocent flower before me. A flower that I want to ravage, tear apart. Satisfy this crazy lust that's been burning through my body ever since I saw her.

But it's more than that. Hanging out with Brooklyn on the mountain has been the most fun I've had in ages. She may be a bad liar, but she's quick to laugh and easy to talk to. I feel like we've known each other a lot longer than just over twenty-four hours.

She's panting hard as we come to the top of the ridge. I take her hand, watching her expression as she looks up at the view

She gasps, which makes me smile. I love showing her all the

secrets of the mountain and the best one yet has got to be the emerald lakes. Left over from an ancient volcanic eruption, the lakes are carved into the crater, with the peak of the mountain behind them.

The volcanoes are long since extinct, but the crater lakes remain, along with a series of small pools, perfect for swimming.

I shrug off my backpack and peel off my t-shirt.

"What are you doing?" She looks alarmed.

"Going for a swim."

Her eyes run over the tattoos on my chest. I can't say it's a bad feeling, having her eyes on me.

"I didn't bring a swimsuit," she protests.

"Neither did I."

I strip off to my briefs and dive into the cool water. The cold hits me like a brick to the head. The water's straight from the mountain and icy cold, but I'm not going to tell her that.

"Come on in."

Hesitantly, she slides off her pack and her shoes. I turn around and swim to the edge of the pool to give her some privacy. I'm dying to see her body, but I'll get there soon enough. I hear a splash behind me, and then she's gasping and spluttering.

"It's freezing!"

I laugh as she flails about with her arms. "Keep swimming, you'll get used to it."

She calms her movements and joins me at the edge of the pool giving me a dirty look. "You could have told me it was this cold."

"And miss the fun? Why would I do that?"

She splashes me with water but she's laughing.

"You want a water fight?" I splash her back and we're both laughing and splashing each other. She squeals, her giggle echoing around the rocks. The sun glints on her laughing face making her eyes sparkle. Not able to restrain myself any longer, I grab her around the waist.

She gasps, her mouth popping open in surprise. Those full lips making my dick ache

"Come here."

Pulling her toward me, her soft skin feels smooth under my touch. Then my lips are on hers, pressing against her. She hesitates for a moment, then she's kissing me back. Her lips soft and pliant, her tongue exploring my mouth.

My hands run down her body and over her ass, pulling her toward me. Wanting to make her mine.

The splashing of a moment ago has gone and we're both still, treading water as we explore each other's mouths.

She shivers in my arms and I pull away. "You're cold."

She nods. "It is, like, zero degrees in here."

"Come on. I'll get a fire going."

Leaning on rock ledge, I pull myself out of the water and then help her out. Through her soaking bra, her nipples are dark, pebbling against the cold.

"Lie down in the sun."

She lies on the rock ledge to dry off. The wet fabric clings to her body showing off her mound and the dark patch of hair underneath.

A zing of energy floods my veins and my cock goes rock hard. I've never wanted a woman as much as I want Brooklyn. And now I'm sure she feels the same. My body aches in anticipation.

But the light's starting to fade and the heat of the day with it. I need to get the fire going and get her warm.

Then I can make her mine.

5
BROOKLYN

It's a few hours later and the heat from the fire sends a warm glow up my legs and through my body.

But it's not just the fire that's making me hot. I run my hands over my lips, feeling the impression of Chase.

When I look up, he's staring at me across the flames. The fire inside me intensifies and my skin prickles with heat.

"Brooklyn." He stands up. His voice is raspy and causes the hairs on my neck to stand on end.

It's a few hours since we had the kiss, and my body hasn't stilled since. We've gone about the business of setting up camp, getting the fire going, and eating a basic meal.

Chase takes his job as a guide seriously, and now he's got the practicalities out the way, his attention turns to me.

And I love it.

He comes around to my side of the fire and takes me by the hand. I tremble at his touch, my whole core burning for him.

"I want to show you something."

He spreads his sleeping bag on the ground next to the campfire.

"Lie down," he says, pulling me onto the sleeping bag.

My lips ready for his kiss, but instead, he lies next to me on his back.

"Look up."

I do as he says and my breath catches in my throat. Above me the sky is ablaze with stars, shimmering like diamonds against the dark sky.

The Milky Way is spread out above us and untold galaxies beyond stretching away to infinity. I've never seen so many stars and never seen them shining so bright.

"It's beautiful," I whisper.

He takes my hand, and we lie for a long time watching the celestial bodies shimmer above us. Eventually he sits up on his elbows and leans toward me. His finger traces the skin of my bare arm making me shiver in anticipation.

"Brooklyn."

Every time he says my name, my pussy clenches, shooting dampness to my panties.

He says it again, this time nuzzling into my neck, his hot breath doing crazy things to my skin.

"I want to make you mine."

His hand slides over my belly and down to the place between my legs. He cups me in his hand. It feels possessive, which should feel wrong, but freakin' heck. It feels good, so good.

"Chase…"

It comes out as a whine, a whimper. This tension that's been building in my body all day, I want him to release it, but I don't know how to ask.

He seems to sense what I need because his hand slips into the top of my pants and slides into my underwear. His eyes are hooded and dark barely visible against the night sky.

"Lie back, Brooklyn, and watch the stars."

As he says it, he palms my pussy entrance causing the heat

inside me to intensify. I gasp as he finds my clit, rubbing his thumb against my most sensitive spot.

My body arches and I sit up on my elbows.

"I've got to tell you something." His hand freezes. "I've not done this before."

"You're a virgin?"

"Yes," I whisper.

His thumb brushes against my clit and I gasp.

"I'll take care of you, baby." He moves so gently, so softly, strumming my hard nub and waking all the nerves endings in my body.

"Lie back and enjoy it."

I do as he says and this time look upwards to the canopy of stars above.

He slides a finger inside me and groans as my pussy tightens around him. With the stars above and him rubbing my core, I feel the whole of the universe pinpointed to my center as he brings me closer and closer to a single point.

My eyes roll back in my head and the stars blur above me. My body writhes and I push against him, getting nearer and nearer to the center of the universe. Then I explode, energy zipping through my body as I climax and the whole cosmos shifts.

I'm floating outside my body, at one with the universe.

Eventually I float back down to earth and come back to myself, gasping in his arms. His face in the darkness is hard to read. He kisses the side of my mouth as he yanks at my pants. I help him shimmy them off. Wanting more from him, wanting all of him.

He pulls his trousers off and his cock sticks out, thick and hard. My core tugs toward him, the fire inside of me still burning.

"Will it hurt?"

He kneels before me and kisses me gently on the sides of my neck.

"Maybe for a little, but then you'll like it."

His cock brushes my entrance, sending me into throws of ecstasy. Then he pushes inside. There's a burning sensation and I think I can't stand it.

He clutches me close to him and we rock together, my pussy adjusting to this new sensation.

Then the burning turns to pleasure. I'm full up, so full of him and it's indescribably good.

He slides gently back and forth, taking it slowly until I can't stand it anymore. "Chase..."

I grab him round the waist, my hands trailing down to his butt. Digging my nails into him, I pull him toward me. The sensation intensifies and I'm focused on that one singular point again

"Chase, I think I'm going to explode."

"Good," he growls. "Come for me."

He hooks one leg over his shoulder and pumps me hard. It takes me over the edge and I scream out his name. The stars explode above us as my body shatters into a million pieces. Chase slams into me grunting as he releases inside me.

We shudder together joined as one as our bodies writhe.

Afterward, he pulls me close and wraps his arms around me, keeping me warm and safe. We sleep under the stars, two people in this tiny universe clinging together on the top of a mountain.

I've never felt so insignificant, yet so content.

6

CHASE

Dawn light wakes me the next morning. We spent the night sleeping under the stars, our bodies pressed together for warmth.

Careful not to wake Brooklyn, I stoke the fire and get a pot of water boiling. By the time the coffee's ready, Brooklyn's sitting up, rubbing sleep out of her eyes.

"Morning." I hand her a mug of coffee and sit next to her, my arm going around her shoulders.

She leans against me as we watch the sky turn from dark to day.

"I don't ever want to leave," she says wistfully.

"Then don't."

She gives me an odd look, but I mean it. I want her to stay here on the mountain with me. I've never felt like this about a woman before, never.

She looks out at the sunrise, her hair shimmering golden in the light. If I could capture this moment and bottle it up forever then I would.

It doesn't take long to pack up our camp, and then we're

ready to head down the mountain. The path back is all downhill and can be done in one day's hike.

She puts her hand in mine, and I clasp it tight, holding onto her as we set off down the path.

Not long after we set off we pass a couple coming the other way with a baby strapped to the man's back. It's Billy and his young wife, I recognise them from Maple Springs. They often come up here to hike.

We stop for a moment to chat. The baby giggles on Billy's back as enthralled by the outdoors as Brooklyn is. An image pops into my mind of the two of us and our own baby hiking the trails. It's a nice thought and I'm smiling as we set off again.

We talk on the way back, getting to know each other. She finally comes clean, telling me about how she lied to get the assignment.

She's nervous telling me, but I laugh at the boldness of it. She obviously wants this so much, to be a journalist. I love that she pushed herself out of her comfort zone to get what she wanted.

"The thing is," she says. "Now that I've spent time in the outdoors, I love it."

She's beaming and I feel a surge of pride, that I showed her the mountain and she fell in love with it, but did she fall in love with me? Because I know in my heart, that I love this woman. That I want her in my life.

Brooklyn talks about the article she's going to write, and I'm caught up in her excitement. But then it hits me.

She did everything she could to get this opportunity because she wants so badly to be a journalist. Brooklyn's got ambitions, and with her bold attitude I'm sure she'll make her dream happen. There's no way she'll want to give it all up to come and live in a tiny town halfway up the mountain.

I couldn't ask her to do that, as much as I want to.

She squeezes my hand. "What's wrong?"

Her look is so innocent, so happy, that I don't want to ruin the moment.

I plaster a smile on my face. "Nothing at all."

It's a few hours later that we reach the start of the track and my pick-up truck. I throw our gear in the back and drive to her hotel.

As we're driving, she turns her phone on to see if there's signal. It immediately rings.

"Hello?"

Her face falls as she talks. I can only hear one side of the conversation but it doesn't sound good. We reach the hotel and I pull over just as she hangs up.

"That was Lilia." She already told me all about her best friend. "Kelvin found out I lied."

It takes me a moment to remember that Kelvin is the editor of the magazine she's writing the article for.

"How did he find out?"

"Did some digging on me. I guess you should never lie to a journalist."

"Are you in trouble."

"Big time. He's furious. He wants me back in the office pronto."

My heart sinks, I know where this is going. I thought we would have more time together, that I could convince her to stay a few more nights with me. But she must go.

"Will you still have your internship?"

She shrugs. "I don't know."

She looks so worried that I don't want to add to her concerns by telling her my feelings. I don't know if she feels the same. And she's too concerned about her situation right now.

"I need to go, Chase." She bites her lower lip and I see the anxiety she's feeling. I put my hands on her shoulders to calm her down.

She looks up at me, her eyes finding mine.

"Go, Brooklyn, write your article and show him how good you are."

A tiny smile breaks through the worry on her face. "Thank you."

I put on a smile I don't feel as I wave her off. As her old car swerves down the road, it feels like a piece of me is driving away with her.

7
BROOKLYN

Two weeks later…

My eyes scan the last lines of the article and then underneath, the byline.

By Brooklyn Jones.

My name in print for the very first time. I should be happy; I should be celebrating. But I'm sitting alone at a cafe opposite the office, feeling nothing but emptiness.

It's been two weeks since I came down from the mountain, as Lilia likes to dramatically call it. She reckons I came back a changed woman, and she's not wrong.

It wasn't just the time in the outdoors that changed me, it was my time with Chase.

My mind goes back to the night we spent under the stars. Just thinking about his hands on me makes my core ache with longing. We shared a connection, something powerful and overwhelming. The kind of connection that you don't realize you've got until it's gone.

When I left him on the mountain, I was so worried about losing my internship, that I never told him how much our time together meant to me. It wasn't until I got back to Seattle that I realized how much I missed him. His touch, his smile, his easy conversation.

I could have emailed the tourist office; it wouldn't have taken much to find his phone number. But did he want to be found? Was I just some city girl that he slept with one night under the stars? Maybe he does that on all his guided trail hikes and I naively thought it was special.

So, I didn't call, and he didn't track me down either.

I sigh. At least I'll always have the memory of that night together, I don't regret a thing.

My gazes drifts back to the article in front of me. I read my name again trying to conjure up the excitement, I know I should feel.

Kelvin was angry that I'd lied to him about my outdoor experience, but he was also impressed by my boldness. He gave me a dressing down and told me that article better be on his desk in the morning. I stayed up all night to write it and emailed it to him, waiting anxiously for his reply.

And he loved it. There were revisions needed, and I worked with him on them. But when I sent the final copy, he even smiled and told me I'd done a good job.

It should be a happy day, seeing my name in print, but here I am, alone in a coffee shop and I feel anything but happy.

I lower the magazine and my heart skips a beat. Standing outside, looking in at me, is Chase.

My mouth drops open as I drink him in. His shaggy hair is pulled back into a man bun, and his beard has been trimmed. His khakis have been replaced with jeans and his walking boots with sneakers.

He pulls at his polo neck shirt, looking out of place on Maddison Street with the skyscrapers behind him instead of a mountain.

"Chase?" He strides into the coffee shop and I stand up to

meet him. My heart beats wildly, hopefully. "What are you doing here?"

"I came to see you."

He catches my hand in his. My pulse jumps under my skin and I can barely breathe.

"Why?"

"Because I can't be without you, Brooklyn."

My heart melts. It's everything I've been needing to hear. I open my mouth to speak, and he holds up a hand to silence me.

"I know the city is your home and you've got a good thing going on here. I can't ask you to give that up." He takes a big breath. "I've been doing a lot of thinking, and I'll move here. I'll move to Seattle so I can be with you."

His look is so sincere, so earnest. He's saying everything I want to hear, but it's not right. Chase's whole life is on that mountain. He works there, he grew up there, he belongs there.

"I can't let you do that."

He shakes his head. "I've thought it all out. I'll get a job in one of the big parks, we can make a life here. I don't care what I do as long as I'm with you."

He clasps both my hands together and his look is so intense so full of meaning. "If you'll have me."

It's everything I want to hear and my heart yearns for him, but I can't let him sacrifice this much for me. He's a man of the mountain, he'd only be unhappy here. He already looks uncomfortable in his city clothes. I can't do that to him.

"You belong on the mountain."

"I belong with you."

His lips meet mine, and the last two weeks of loneliness and hurt come out in that kiss. I need to be with him, but not like this. I pull away.

"Chase, I can't let you do that. There's another way." I bite my lip because while he was planning to move to the city, I made some plans of my own. "You don't have to move here. I'll move to you."

He shakes his head. "No, I can't let you give up your dream here."

"I don't have to. Kelvin's offered me freelance journalist work. I don't have to be based here. I can work from anywhere as long as I go do my assignments every month. It'll mean a few days a month away for work, but other than that, I can base myself wherever I want."

A smile spreads over his face as he begins to understand. "You want to move to Maple Falls?"

"I fell in love with the mountain just as much as I fell in love with you."

He lifts me into his arms and right up off the ground making me squeal.

"Let's go get your things, honey, because I'm taking you home."

EPILOGUE

BROOKLYN

Five years later...

There's a rustling in the tent and I feel a small body climbing over me.

"Mommy, I heard something."

Finn's anxious face appears next to mine in the darkness. I reach an arm out and pull my son down to the floor next to me.

"It was probably the wind, sweetie."

"I think it was a bear."

Tucking him into the sleeping bag, I plant a kiss on his forehead.

"You stay right there between me and Daddy, we'll keep you safe."

He snuggles in between us, and I adjust my pregnant belly so it's away from his squirming body. Chase rolls over and puts a protective arm around his son.

"There's no bears this far down the mountain. I wouldn't let you or mommy camp where a bear could get you."

A gust of wind rustles the tent, and Finn pulls the covers over his head, hiding.

"It's okay, buddy, just the wind." Chase grins in the darkness. "Now give your mommy and the baby some space and come lie this side of me."

Finn clambers over Chase and settles in on the other side of him.

"You okay?" he mouths to me, his face full of concern.

He didn't want to come camping in my third trimester, but I insisted. I wanted to feel the fresh mountain air one more time before I get too close to my due date to risk a mountain hike.

We're up near the lakes where we spent our first night under the stars together. We've taken Finn out hiking since he was a baby, first strapped to my front and then, as he got older, in a toddler backpack on Chase's back.

Chase has shown me every trail and every camping spot. Both Finn and the baby growing in my belly were conceived on the side of Maple Mountain.

My dream of being a journalist has been realized. I write freelance for outdoors and parenting magazines.

Chase and Finn come on most of my assignments. They're like family holidays, where I get paid to hike the trails of the northwest.

Finn's breathing deepens and I know he's gone back to sleep. Now he's asleep again I can relax. My arms wrap around Chase's body, not able to get too close with my big belly in the way.

Soon, he's snoring gently, and I lie quietly, listening to the sounds of them sleeping and the wind in the trees, thinking how blessed I am to have my family and to have the mountain. How glad I am I took a chance and discovered my two great loves.

* * *

Mentioned in this book…

Curious about Billy and his young wife, the couple who love to hike? He's a blue-collar hero and she's a curvy girl with a secret.

Check out Billy here.

MOUNTAIN MAN'S MUSE

MEN OF MAPLE MOUNTAIN BOOK FOUR

MOUNTAIN MAN'S MUSE

MEN OF MAPLE MOUNTAIN BOOK FOUR

He watches her through his lens, his craving for her growing, until he must act...

The moment I see Heather down the lens of my camera, I know she'll be mine.

With my camera, I follow her, my obsession growing.

Her curves, her lips, her smile—they all speak to me down the lens, as I build a private portfolio. An entire room in the basement devoted to her image.

When I finally get Heather in my studio, she ignites a passion that we both crave, giving me everything I ever wanted and making my life full.

She'll never know about the basement, about what's behind the locked door.

Will she?

Mountain Man's Muse is a soft stalker, mountain man romance featuring an OTT hero and the curvy girl who becomes the object of his obsession.

PROLOGUE

KANE

A cold ache spreads through my legs as I crouch in the scrub with my camera poised. There's a scratching noise in the bushes in front of me, and I carefully adjust my lens, getting ready to snap the animal that comes out of it.

Three nights I've camped on the edge of Maple Mountain tracking a male bobcat. Three days I've spent hidden in the brush with my camera ready.

I've photographed the local foxes and squirrels, but the bobcat remains elusive.

The bush moves, and a field mouse scurries out. It pauses, a berry in its paws, and I snap a few pictures. It's not the bobcat I've been tracking, but it'll earn me a few dollars from the right photography sites.

The mouse's ears twitch, and it scampers away in a hurry as if something has startled it. A moment later, I hear human footsteps.

From my position on the ridge, I swivel my camera downwards to the walking path below.

A blue cap comes into my field of vision, dark hair

streaming out from underneath it. It's a woman—two women —but I keep my lens trained only on one.

She stops and turns to her friend, showing off the plumpest lips I've ever seen and deep green eyes sparkling with laughter at some joke I can't hear.

My breath hitches in my throat. She's beautiful.

Click

My finger hits the button before I know what I'm doing. I've got the long zoom lens on, and I'm far enough away that they don't hear the picture being taken.

Below the stunning face is a long neck. A droplet of sweat trickles down her throat, and I follow it with my lens down to the soft skin of her cleavage.

Heat rushes through my body like an electric shock. My blood heats as I watch the rise and fall of her chest. She's panting hard from her climb up the path, her chest heaving up and down to a rhythm that matches the drum of my heart.

Adjusting my zoom, pulling out so I can see more of this beauty.

She's taller than average with wide hips, thick thighs, and luscious curves. But it's her face I bring my lens back to. Those stunning lips. The innocent laughter.

I take another photo. And another. I've never done this before, photographed people without their consent.

But she's not just anybody. I know that already with every fiber in my body. I know immediately that this woman is mine.

Mine.

Leaning against the rocks, she pulls a sandwich out of her backpack. This must be the end of their hike, and I watch as they eat and take pictures of the scenery.

I'm as hard as the rock around me, but I must wait. I'm used to waiting.

Silently, I photograph the woman. Getting to know her.

Every angle, every look. I can't explain this need to capture her image.

Eventually, they pack up their food and head back down the trail. I wait until they're gone before I pack up my things and follow.

Already I know I'm not going back to my life before. As I follow her down the path, I'm already making plans. I'll sell my apartment; I'll find a place here, open a studio, and find a way to be with her.

My life is here now, on the mountain—with this woman who's name I don't yet know.

1

HEATHER

Three weeks later…

The model stares out at me from the pages of the magazine with a nonchalant expression. I tilt my head and pout, wondering if I look as much like I don't give a shit about the world as she does. Although if I had skinny thighs like hers, I reckon I could get away with not giving a shit about anything.

I pinch my too big thighs.

Nope. These chunky flanks aren't going to let me get away with anything.

The bell above the coffee shop door tinkles, and I quickly shove the magazine under the counter.

"Good morning…" My voice falters when I see it's Kane, the wildlife photographer, and my chest flutters like there's a caged bird inside trying to get out.

Kane turned up in town a few weeks ago, and every time he comes in the cafe, my tummy does little flips and my knees go like jelly.

Not to mention what happens to my lady bits. There's a tug,

down there, that makes me squeeze my thick thighs together with longing.

Fumbling to put the magazine away, I meet his penetrating gaze.

"The usual?" I ask, trying to keep my voice calm so he doesn't know what effect he has on me. I mean, the guy is gorgeous—six foot something with shaggy dark hair and a wild beard.

Ursula, my bestie, says I should just ask him out, but what would a guy like that want with a chubby girl who works in a cafe?

He's a photographer, which sounds exotic and awesome, and I make coffee all day, which is dull and boring. Besides, if he was interested, he would have asked me out by now.

He fixes me with a smile that makes my insides melt. "Sure."

I make his coffee slowly, taking my time grinding new beans and frothing the milk.

"How's the studio coming along?"

He's already told me about the cabin he bought on the edge of town and the studio he's building on-site. Why anyone would want to relocate to Maple Falls is beyond me. I've been stuck here my whole life, and I can confirm it's the most boring place on Earth.

Sure, I love the mountain, but even hiking gets boring after a while. I yearn for some excitement, something interesting to happen to take me away from my humdrum existence.

"It's almost finished."

His look is always intense, especially when he's talking about his work.

"So, what are you going to photograph up here?"

"You."

I tilt my head; I mustn't have heard him right. Or he's making a joke. I decide it's a joke and laugh. "Because I'm such model material."

My eyes flutter, and I do a silly pose, like one of the models from the magazine. But he looks dead serious.

"Beauty comes in all forms." His blue eyes bore into mine, and the way he says it sets off tiny prickles of heat over my body.

Is he really suggesting I'm beautiful? This guy's delusional, or he's messing with me. "Not according to fashion magazines."

"I wish you wouldn't read those." He sounds irritable, and I wonder how the hell he knows what magazines I read. He must have seen me stash *Cosmopolitan* under the counter.

I hand him his coffee, and he perches on one of the stools near the counter. He comes in here every day for a coffee and a chat. It's the highlight of my day, but I could never tell him that.

The bell above the door chimes, and a guy in hiking gear comes in with a backpack slung over his shoulder. He must be a tourist visiting town. It's where half of our business comes from.

As he saunters up to the counter, his eyes run over my chest. My body tenses, but I try not to show it. I hate men staring at my boobs, but it comes with the territory of being a big girl. Big girl equals big boobs—which equals lots of unwanted staring.

"Can I help you?" I keep my voice light. It doesn't pay to get annoyed with customers; it's not good for business.

But Kane doesn't seem to have gotten the memo. He's staring at the man with a face like thunder. His fists are clenched, and there's a vein about to pop in his neck.

I'm not sure what's got him so rattled.

"I'm after something sweet."

The man leans on the counter and stares blatantly at my chest as he says it.

"Eyes up, fuck head."

Kane's voice comes out gravelly and cold.

The man turns toward him, and he must see that Kane

means business because he holds his hands up in the air. "Whoa, sorry man. Didn't know she was your woman."

"I'm not…" I start to speak, but Kane cuts me off.

"Get your coffee and get the fuck out."

The guy turns back to me, this time looking me in the eye. "Black coffee. To go."

My fingers fumble with the takeout coffee cup. I've never had a guy stand up for me like that before.

The birds in my chest beat their wings furiously. Not only is Kane hot, but he's also got the coolest job, and he just defended my honor. I think I'm in love.

You could cut the tension with a knife as I make the coffee. Kane keeps his eyes fixed on the man, who drums his fingers awkwardly on the counter. When I hand him his cup, he walks quickly out of the shop, Kane's narrow-eyed gaze following him.

"Um, thanks for that." I say.

Kane's gaze snaps back to me, and it's hard, intense, catching me off guard and making the tug in my core deepen.

"I hate to see assholes disrespecting women."

The flutter in my chest calms. I guess he would have done the same for anyone, not just for me.

Another customer comes in, and by the time I've finished serving them, Kane is gone.

Disappointment rolls over me. I have to wait another whole day to see him again.

2
KANE

My fingers tap the mouse, clicking through the shots from today. There's Heather leaving her house, hair pulled high in a messy bun, her work uniform hugging her curvy figure.

The next shot is a close-up of Heather bending down to pat the neighbor's cat. Her full lips are slightly parted and pulled into a pouty smile.

There's a stirring in my loins as I look at her lips, her chest, her big round eyes. I can imagine those eyes looking up at me, those lips calling out my name as I sink into her.

The pressure in my pants is too much, and I unzip my fly. I give myself a hard stroke as I look at her face, imagining her lips wrapped around me.

One hand flicks through the photos: her skirt riding up her thighs as she walks to work; there's one where she's leaning on the counter, blurred through the glass, but I can make out the line of her cleavage. My other hand grips my shaft, sliding up and down, fantasizing about her legs wrapped around me.

I click back to the close-up, imagining those parted lips screaming my name.

My cock jerks out my release, spraying sticky cum into my palm. Squeezing my eyes shut to keep the image of Heather in my mind, I can almost feel her here with me.

I can feel her breath on my neck, her soft kisses on my mouth. "I love you, baby girl."

Slowly, I open my eyes.

It's just me. Me in a cold, damp basement, sitting at a computer desk with my dick in my hand.

Grabbing a tissue, I clean myself up then hit print on the close-up image.

The printer whirs to life, sucking in a piece of top-grade photographic paper. Slowly, Heather's image appears on the paper, close up and glossy.

Taking it by the corners so I won't leave fingerprints on her face, I scan the wall for a place to pin it.

My computer desk and printer take up one side of the rectangular-shaped basement, where the wall is covered in photos from the first time I saw Heather on the hike.

Turning slowly, I search for a space on the other walls in the room. There are images of her walking in town, at work through the glass, and—my favorite—in her bedroom.

I'm good at hiding, and I'm patient. Once I found out where Heather lived, it was easy to find a place to hide in the trees around the house she shares with her parents. There's a tree with big branches and bushy leaves that has the perfect view of her bedroom.

They're my favorite pictures: Heather sitting on her bed with a magazine spread out before her, hair falling loosely over her shoulders; Heather dressing, her bare shoulders reflected in the round dressing table mirror; then a shot of her reaching up and shutting the curtains. Shutting me out.

My chest tightens. I'm tired of being on the outside looking in. I want to be with her. I want to be by her side. The two of us together, shutting the curtains on the rest of the world.

I think back to today and the man flirting with her at the cafe. After he got his coffee, I followed him and let him know with my fists that she's mine.

He won't bother her again, but others might.

My fists clench just thinking about it. It's not enough any longer to watch Heather. It's time to claim her.

There's a bare spot on the wall in between a photo of Heather in her short pajamas and one of her laughing with her friend. I pin the new picture over her friend's face. It's only Heather I'm interested in. Only Heather that's mine.

The walls are almost full, but I'm not done. I'll never be done photographing Heather.

I make a mental note to pick up some string and small pegs so I can hang photos in rows across the walls.

Switching off the light, I climb the stairs, lock the door, and slip the key in my pocket.

When I moved to Maple Falls, I bought a small property with a simple cabin and space to build a studio.

No one must ever see what's in the basement, especially not Heather.

3

HEATHER

"Hello, kitty."

The neighbor's cat is always hanging around our driveway, and I give it a scratch behind the ears like I do every morning. It meows and rubs against my leg.

When I stand up, my breath hitches in my throat. Kane is walking along the sidewalk coming toward our house. He's as hot as ever with his hair ruffled and his beard unkempt. God, how I long to run my fingers through that beard, to feel it scratch against my thighs.

"Hi," he calls out, looking surprised to see me.

He's got his camera bag slung over his shoulder. I've never seen him without it. What he finds so interesting to photograph in Maple Falls, I have no idea.

He slows down, and I join him on the sidewalk. "I'm on my way to work."

Every time I'm near him, my knees go weak and my heart hammers in my ears. It's so loud I'm sure he must hear it.

"I'll walk with you," he says.

We fall into step together, and he's so close I have an urge to touch him, to clasp his hand in mine.

I reach my pinkie out until it grazes his hand, and I pull away quickly, pretending it was an accident. He'd think I was weird if I tried to hold his hand. The fat, desperate cafe girl trying her luck with every new guy that comes to town.

Except it's only him. Only him who has ever had this effect on me.

"What you photographing today?"

"The sunrise," he says vaguely. "But I'm looking for something more interesting to shoot."

I have no idea what a nature photographer finds interesting. "Like what?"

"Like you."

I give a nervous laugh. It's the same joke he tried yesterday.

"You already said that."

"How about tomorrow?"

I turn to stare at him, wondering what the hell he's talking about. He's looking at me intensely, no sign of a joke on his face.

"Tomorrow what?"

"How about you come to my studio tomorrow and let me photograph you."

My mouth drops open. He's got to be joking with me.

"Are you serious?"

"Of course." His pale eyes bore into mine so intensely that I almost believe him.

"Why do you want to photograph me?"

"Because you're beautiful, Heather."

Now I know he must be completely delusional.

I laugh. "Of all the girls in Maple Falls, you want to photograph the chubby one?"

He runs a hand through his hair and looks frustrated. "I wish you wouldn't say that about yourself. Let me photograph you, and I'll show you how beautiful you are."

His words touch a place deep inside of me, making me

pause. I've never thought of myself as beautiful. I'm shaped differently than any woman I've ever seen in a magazine. But what if he's right? What if he could make me feel like one of those models? Beautiful and desired.

I have a sudden thought and my eyes narrow. Maybe he's one of "those" photographers.

"You don't mean nude, do you?"

His pupils dilate and his eyes widen. A look of pure desire crosses his face. He takes a step closer to me, his gaze dipping to my chest and back to my eyes. "Not unless you want me to."

Holy crap. A zing of heat zaps through my body, and there's a gush of dampness between my legs.

"I'll see you at ten," he says as if it's a done deal. "Bring a few different outfits."

I swallow hard. My body's overheating just thinking about posing nude for him even though that's not what he's asking.

We reach the convenience shop on the edge of the main street, and he pauses. "I need to grab a few groceries."

He ducks into the shop, leaving me to wonder what the hell I just agreed to and why my body's having such a delicious reaction to it.

4
KANE

My lens roves over Heather's body, taking in every inch of her. She's poised on the edge of a stool, one leg touching the floor, the other bent onto the railing. Her hands rest in her lap, playing with the tassel on her over-sized knitted sweater.

"Is it okay sitting like this, or..."

She's self-conscious and nervous in front of the camera.

"You look beautiful. Relax your hands and try a few poses."

She leans back on the stool, which pushes her breasts out. Two perfect mounds straining under her sweater.

"Like this?" She pulls a face and wraps her arms around her body self-consciously. "I've never been photographed before; I don't know what to do."

Oh, but she has been photographed before—many, many times, in many poses. Only she doesn't know it.

Setting my camera down, I walk toward her. "Just be yourself, pretend the camera isn't here."

She pulls a face. "It's hard. I feel frumpy."

This woman is anything but frumpy, and I'm going to show her just how beautiful she is.

"What have you got on under here?" I lift the edge of her sweater, resisting the urge to yank it off.

"Just a top."

"Let's see."

She pulls the sweater over her head to reveal a tight t-shirt. It hugs her body, showing off every curve.

"It kinda shows the fat rolls through."

I fix her with a severe look. "I don't want to hear you talk like that."

It comes out harsher than I mean it to, and she looks startled.

"You have a beautiful body, Heather."

Her eyes are wide as she looks up at me, and I can't resist touching her. My hand rests on her shoulder and runs down her arm.

"Every curve is beautiful." My fingers run over her stomach. "Every dip adds to your character..." I trail them up her rib cage. "Every part of this body is a piece of art."

My fingers stop just under her breasts, twitching to go further. But she hasn't realized she's mine yet, and I don't want to scare her too soon.

Her chest is heaving up and down, and when I raise my eyes, she's staring right back at me. Her back arches, and she drops one shoulder.

Her look is perfect, she's perfect. "Stay there. Right there."

Backing away, I grab the camera and start shooting.

Her penetrating gaze follows me down the lens and makes the blood rush to my dick. "That's it, Heather. You're beautiful."

She pivots on the stool so that she's sitting sideways. Tilting her head, she drops the other shoulder and throws a bold look to the camera.

"You look gorgeous."

My finger clicks image after image. She's got the hang of it now, throwing sexy looks and tossing her hair. "That's it, baby girl."

My words must encourage her because she swivels on the stool so she's front on. Both of her feet come up on the rail, and she slides them open as she leans forward, placing her hands between her thighs on the stool.

Holy shit. The blood pounds in my ears, and my cock pushes hard against my jeans. It's a bold pose, her legs open and her hands between them, shielding her special place, her face tilted upward defiantly.

How I long to push my way between those thighs and fuck her until she's begging for mercy.

"You're so sexy, Heather."

She bites her lower lip, and I almost come undone. My camera drops to my side as I feast my eyes on her.

Her expression changes, and she becomes self-conscious again."Was that, okay?"

My chest is heaving, and my cock aches. "That was more than okay, honey. That was sexy as fuck. You're amazing."

She smiles shyly. "I, um, have another outfit I thought we could try. If you have the time."

I've got all the time in the world for this woman.

"Sure."

While she gets changed, I change lenses. I'm going to want to get some close-ups. With the camera ready, I wait for her to come out from behind the changing screen. When she does, my jaw hits the floor.

She's wearing nothing but a black lacey negligee.

5
HEATHER

My arms hug my body as I step out from behind the screen. I've never done anything like this before. But Kane makes me feel safe, and he makes me feel like maybe, just maybe, I'm not as hideous as I think I am.

His mouth drops open when he sees me, and I wonder if I've gone too far, coming out in a negligee and high heels.

"Is it too much?"

He shakes his head, and when he speaks, his voice is croaky. "Oh, baby, let me look at you."

I drop my arms, and his gaze sweeps over my body. The lace fabric grazes my skin, making me feel sexy, making me feel alive.

I stand up straighter, letting him take in my thick thighs and heavy breasts. His gaze takes in every inch of me, making my skin burn with desire.

"Sit on the stool."

He picks up his camera, a determined look on his face. "I want to capture you like this. You're perfect."

His words make me feel bold, confident. And for the first

time, I feel like there's nothing wrong with my body. If a man like Kane can find beauty in me, then maybe I can too.

The negligee gathers under my breasts and fans out in sheer fabric, covering my stomach rolls and accentuating my wide hips. The panties underneath are matching black lace, and there's not much to them.

As I perch on the stool, I tuck one high-heeled foot onto the rail, leaving the other one on the ground. Kane licks his lips, and I wonder how much he likes what he sees.

He runs a hand through his hair, and I can tell he's flustered. The thought that I'm turning him on makes me feel powerful, confident.

As he picks up the camera, I lean forward, giving my best sexy look down the lens.

He snaps some pictures, and I turn to try a different pose. This time I lean my arms on the stool and tilt my head back so my hair falls down my back and my breasts are pushed into the air.

"Oh, Heather."

Kane groans, and the noise calls to something deep inside off me. My core tightens, and there's a rush of heat between my legs.

The strap of my negligee slides off my shoulders, and I let it slip, throwing a confident look at the camera—at Kane.

He's breathing hard, and there's a lump in his jeans telling me just how turned on he is.

I love that I'm doing that to him.

Feeling sexy and bold, I slide the strap right off my shoulder until the soft flesh of my breast is exposed.

"God, you're sexy." His voice is a low growl, and it makes my pussy gush. There's a pull in my core that I can't ignore.

I fix my stare down the lens as I slide my hand into my negligee.

Kane groans, a guttural voice that makes my nipples hard. "Oh, baby, you're turning me on."

My fingers run over the hard bud of my nipple, sending waves of heat through my body. My head tilts back as I fondle myself to the sound of the camera clicking. I've never felt so sexy before, never felt so bold or so turned on.

"Kane."

"Yes, baby?"

"Are these photos just for you?"

"No one else will see you." He says it with such force that I believe him. "Your body is mine, Heather. No one else will see you but me."

He growls the words, sending a shudder right through me. He's talking possessively, like he owns me. It should scare me, but it turns me on even more.

So much so that I have to pivot on the stool to get my balance.

"You're mine, Heather. Since the moment I saw you."

The words tug at my core and fill me with need. All the while he keeps his camera raised, clicking away at my body. My sexy body.

My hand runs down my breasts and over my stomach. The negligee falls open, and I run my hand over my damp panties.

"Do you want to photograph this?" My palm cups my mound. There's no mistaking my meaning.

I don't know what's making me so bold, but it seems right in the moment. The click of the camera pauses, and he takes a sharp breath. "Oh, baby, you don't know how much."

My hand slides into my panties, my fingers finding my soft glistening folds.

"Holy fuck," Kane growls, and he steps closer, the camera zooming in on my hand. "Take the panties off."

My thumbs hook over the fabric, and I pull them down my legs. My heart beats wildly. I don't know why I'm doing this, but I can't stop. I want him to see me. I want him to watch me down his lens.

My hands slide up my thighs to my wet pussy folds. My palm circles my hard nub, applying just the right amount of pressure.

"You're so fucking sexy, Heather."

The camera clicks, and I part my thighs, letting the lens in, letting Kane in. "I feel sexy. You make me feel sexy."

My fingers, slick with pussy juice, rub against my clit as my other hand teases my left nipple.

The camera moves to my chest, then my face. He moves around me, taking pictures from every angle.

"You're so fucking gorgeous."

My palm rubs my clit, and I let my eyes roll backwards, the soft click of the camera spurring me on toward my climax.

"I'm going to fuck you after this, Heather."

The words are like a shock wave ripping through me. "I'm going to fuck that little pussy so hard. Show you that you're mine."

The dirty words bring me close to the edge.

"Kane!" I cry out as I reach my peak, pressing my palm against myself as waves of orgasm rush over me. The clicking intensifies, and he's photographing my face, my body, my pussy. My whole body trembles under the gaze of his lens.

When I open my eyes, the camera is at his side, and he's looking at me with an intensity that almost makes me come again.

"You're fucking beautiful."

And for the first time, I believe him.

6
KANE

Her chest is heaving, and there's a line of perspiration on her breasts. The scent of her fills my nostrils as she slides her hand down her thighs. "That was fucking amazing."

It's a wonder I didn't come in my pants. The pictures I've taken will keep me wanking for the rest of my days.

She's breathing heavily, and her pussy is glistening and swollen, calling to my cock. Setting the camera down, I take her by the hands and pull her off the stool.

"Heather, I've wanted you since the first day I saw you."

She smiles shyly, which touches my heart. After what she just did, she can still feel shy around me. "So have I. That first day you came into the coffee shop."

I don't tell her that wasn't the first day I saw her. I'd already been following her for a week. There was already a wall of pictures of her in my basement.

Leading her over to the sofa, I pull her down onto the soft rug. She lies beneath me as beautiful in the flesh as she is through the lens.

"It's time you were mine."

My cock's aching in my pants, and I shrug them off. Her eyes widen at the sight of my cock, already hard and dripping.

I run my hand over her thighs, slick with her juice. "Get on your knees."

She does as she's told, and I lean her over the coffee table. There's a full-length mirror on the wall in front of us so I can still see her face.

It's her face that I watch as I flick the sheer fabric of her negligee up and spilt her ass cheeks apart.

She lifts her hips, and my cock runs over her entrance, wet and ready for me. My hand reaches around the front to cup her breast, my thumb grazing her nipple.

With one hand on her tit and the other on her ass, I can control her; and that's what I do now, sliding her down my shaft one inch at a time, watching her eyes widen in the mirror.

"Kane," she says breathlessly, "it's too much."

Her pussy is squeezing me tight, and I stop, letting her adjust. "You want me to stop?"

I slide out, and she whimpers. "No, don't stop."

It's the sweetest sound—a sound I've imagined too many times. I must hear it again. My dick slides right out of her, resting the tip in her entrance.

"No, please, don't stop. I can take it."

Holy fuck, that begging is going to be my undoing. "You think you can take it, baby girl?"

"I can take it. Give it to me, please."

She has no idea what she's doing to me. Her dirty words make my whole body howl.

Pulling her toward me, my dick sinks into her, just an inch, and then slides out.

"Please, Kane. Please fuck me." Her eyes meet mine as she says it. Pleading eyes. "Please, I can take it."

Her pouting mouth saying such dirty things unleashes something animalistic inside of me.

I grab her ass and slam myself inside of her. "Take it, baby girl. Take all of it."

My balls slap against her, and she cries out, her face contorting in pain that turns instantly to pleasure.

"You want it all, you take it all. Take it like a good girl." I thrust into her, clawing at her breasts as I sink myself into her pussy.

I've waited weeks for this moment, and it's as sweet as I imagined, sweeter because now she's moaning in a high-pitched way as I slam my cock into her.

I straighten up and tilt her hips upward, allowing my cock to go deeper. She makes a guttural sound as my balls slap against her.

"Please," she pants. "Fuck me hard."

"This not hard enough for you?"

My cock pumps in and out of her, each time pulling me toward my climax. She's fondling herself between her legs as I slam into her.

The pressure builds in my balls, and I'm not going to last much longer. She meets my eyes in the mirror, and her mouth pops open as pleasure overtakes her.

She screams my name. Her pussy contracts around me, sucking me in and tipping me over the edge.

My cum shoots out, exploding into her and shattering me into a million pieces. My seed coats her walls, claiming her as mine. All mine.

Afterwards, I pull her onto my lap, my arms wrapping around her.

I kiss her shoulders, her hair, her arms. A few hours ago, I could only look at this body through a lens. Now she's mine, and I'm never letting her go.

7
HEATHER

Three weeks later...

My fingers run over the glossy surface of the magazine, and I flip to page seventeen. I'll never get used to seeing myself in print. Yet, here I am. My first modeling job.

Kane introduced me to Adalee, a plus size model who lives in Maple Springs. I was jealous at first wondering about their connection, until she mentioned her devoted husband who's also a photographer and a good friend of Kane's.

Adalee answered all my questions about the industry and being a plus size model.

Kane sent her some of the pictures of me—not the intimate ones—and she shared them with her agency. They found me work right away.

Who knew being too tall and chunky would make me a good candidate for modeling? Plus size seems to be on trend, and I've got another job booked next week in Portland.

Kane came with me to my first job, watching protectively from the sidelines.

He made it clear to the agency that it's fashion clothing only, no underwear and no swimsuits, which is fine by me. I'm happy to keep those shoots for Kane's eyes only.

In the three weeks since I've moved in with him, we've done several private shoots. I love Kane watching me through the lens. I feel so safe with him, and I feel so safe here.

My eyes stray to the basement door that he keeps locked. Kane told me he keeps his old photography kit with expensive vintage cameras down there, which is why he keeps it locked. But he looked away when he said it, and it makes me wonder if he's hiding something.

Laying the magazine on the couch, I pad over to the basement door. The handle is cool to the touch as I fold my hand around it and gently turn.

The door doesn't budge. As always, it's locked.

It could be true that he keeps his expensive camera kit down there, but this is Maple Falls; the last burglary we had was probably in the 90s. It's weird that he's so protective of it. And he's never offered to show me. I've been living here for three weeks and not once have I been in the basement.

I run my hand through my hair, and my finger catches on a hair pin. I pause, remembering the Nancy Drew books I used to love.

Pulling the hair pin out, I straighten it and slide it into the lock. My heart thumps against my ribs as I rattle it in the lock. I'm not quite sure what I'm supposed to do, but I feel the pin catch on something. Carefully, I turn it until I hear the lock click. I pull the pin out, and when I try the door, it swings open.

There's a staircase leading down to a dark basement. My heart's thumping in my chest, and I put my foot on the first step.

I pause. Kane kept this door locked for a reason. He doesn't want anyone in here. But if I'm going to live with this man, there can't be any secrets.

I'm sure whatever it is he's hiding is harmless, but I must know.

The stairs creak as I descend into the darkness.

There's the outline of a desk with a computer and office equipment on it. So far, so harmless.

Fumbling for the switch, I turn on the light. It takes a moment for me to realize what I'm seeing. And when I do, my heart goes still.

Plastered across the walls are pictures, photos blown up large and printed, and they're all of me. All of them.

My hands go to my mouth. There are pictures of me through the cafe window, pictures of me out hiking, pictures of me in the bar with Ursula—but she's been cut out of the photos.

Slowly, I turn around. Every wall in the room is covered in my picture. They're hanging from pegs on strings across the walls. Everywhere I turn is my face staring back at me.

Then I see something that makes me gasp.

Pictures of me at home, in my bedroom, taken through the window. I'm on my bed flicking through a magazine. I'm getting dressed. There's one where I'm sleeping. It must have been the night when it was too hot to shut the window.

My heart's racing, and my mind's in a whirl. Kane was stalking me before we hooked up. He was taking pictures of me without me knowing.

My knees give out, and I sink to the floor. Everything I thought we had, everything I thought he was, is a lie.

There's a creaking noise and footsteps on the stairs. I turn around as Kane comes down the stairs. His face is pale, his expression a picture of devastation.

"Kane," I whisper. "What...?" But I can't get the words out. I don't know what to say.

"I can explain." He crouches next to me, reaches out a hand for me. But I pull away, barely registering the hurt in his face.

"From the moment I saw you, Heather, it was like time stood still."

His pale eyes stare at me, imploring me to understand. "You're beautiful. You're the most beautiful thing I've ever seen. And I wanted to capture that beauty."

His eyes are pleading with me, but I can't comfort him right now. I'm in shock.

I scan the room, and that's when I see them. Hanging in rows hung up by pegs. The shots from our first photo shoot.

Me pulling on my nipple. My hand rubbing myself. My neck stretched out and my face contorted in ecstasy.

I rise onto my knees and stare at the images. They're so raw, so powerful. Is that beautiful, confident woman really me?

"You're so fucking perfect, Heather." He's so earnest, and this time when he reaches for me, I let him.

"I love you so much. I know this is weird, and I can't explain it. But when I first saw you, I had to photograph you, to find out all about you."

I should be running a mile; I should pack my bags and leave. But I don't. Because what he's saying makes some kind of stupid sense.

As I scan the photos from that first shoot, photos of me looking so confident and sexy, I remember that feeling. Kane made me feel that. He made me believe I'm beautiful.

As I look at those pictures—my chest pressed forward, my lips parted, my thighs opened—I feel a pull in my core, a flame igniting between my legs.

I have power over this man. I can bring him to his knees, and that's powerful.

8
KANE

The hurt and confusion on her face pull at my heart and make me hate myself for making her feel this way.

"Heather…" I want to hold her, to comfort her, but she pulls away. "Baby girl. You've got this hold over me."

She's staring straight ahead, and I follow her gaze. It's the images of her on that first photo shoot when she touched herself.

The photos show her in different poses, giving herself pleasure. My dick stirs to life as it always does when I look at those images. They're forever burned into my retinas.

My hand rests on her shoulder, and this time she doesn't pull away. "You're so fucking beautiful. I wanted you to see it too."

My hand travels down her shoulder to her waist. "You're perfect baby, just perfect."

She spins around, and her sadness has been replaced by something else, something raw and wild.

"You made me see that about myself." Her eyes scan mine,

searching for something, and I hope she can see I'm baring my soul, offering it all up to her.

"I love you, baby."

Her gaze darts back to the photos. "They're sexy, aren't they?" Her voice is barely a whisper. She's breathing deeply, almost panting.

"That's because you're sexy."

We're both kneeling on the floor, and I run my hand down her body, sliding it between her legs. She moans, never taking her eyes off the photos. "Kane…"

I let out a breath I didn't know I was holding. Does this mean I'm forgiven?

When she turns to me, her eyes are dark with desire.

"You saw something in me that I didn't see myself." Her hands run up my chest, causing heat to rip through my body. "You made me feel beautiful, sexy."

She whispers the words into my ear as her fingers undo my buttons.

"Because you are beautiful."

Her hands peel my shirt off, and she reaches for my jeans.

"With you I'm sexy. Only you make me feel this way."

She's pulling frantically at my jeans, and I help her pull them off along with my underpants. Flipping her skirt up, I pull at her panties, tearing them off. My hand runs over her pussy, and she's dripping wet.

She pushes my chest, pushing me backwards and onto the floor. "I want to ride you."

The concrete's hard on my back, but I don't care. My cock's stiff and dripping as she straddles me and hoists her skirt up.

Taking my cock in her hand, she guides me into her pussy, and I slide into paradise.

Her eyes stay on the photos, and I love the fact she's getting off on herself. I stare at her images surrounding me, but nothing beats the sight in front of my eyes: Heather riding me, her lips parted as she grinds into my hips.

"Heather," I gasp, "I love you."

She pushes herself against me, riding me hard until her orgasm overtakes her. I explode at the same time, coating her insides with my juice.

She collapses on top of me, and I hold her panting body in my arms.

"I'll take them down if you want. But I can't stop watching you."

She sits up so I can see her face.

"No. I don't want you to stop. You make me feel sexy and confident. I love you."

We cling together. It's a strange love. Others might not understand it, but it's ours.

EPILOGUE

HEATHER

Six years later…

The sheer fabric falls away as I turn, revealing the round bump of my belly.

Click

My hands run over the taut skin where the baby inside me is growing, and I look down at it, a smile playing on my lips.

Click

"That's the shot."

My gaze finds the lens as Kane keeps shooting.

We're in the studio attached to the house where Kane does most of his work. He's made a name for himself as a portrait photographer. Customers come up from nearby towns for baby photos, family photos, and maternity shoots.

Kane doesn't just work in the studio; he also takes his clients outside, into nature. He gets some stunning shots with the mountain landscape.

Occasionally, he disappears into the mountain for a day or two on assignment to photograph the wildlife. But he doesn't like to be away from his family for long.

My modelling career took off, and for a few years, we traveled together doing photo shoots all over the country. It didn't stop once I had kids either. That's the beauty of being a plus size model—it's less restrictive on your body.

"Lean back on the chair," Kane instructs.

I've had maternity photos done for all my babies, and they hang proudly on the wall of the studio.

Kane still loves photographing me, and framed photos of me cover the walls of our house. There's some of the kids too, and I insisted on putting him up on the wall as well.

The X-rated photos we keep for our own private collection. Once the kids are in bed, we unlock the cabinet and pull out the stash of secret dirty photos. Looking through them always leads to quick, urgent sex, the kind where we can't get enough of each other.

Just thinking about those photos makes my core ache. I'm always horny at this stage of pregnancy. As Kane clicks the camera, I slide my hand over my swollen breasts.

They're engorged and aching, the nipples so sensitive. I only have to brush them lightly and they're standing on end.

"Oh, baby girl," Kane groans.

"You got enough nice pictures," I say, my hand sliding down my body. "Now it's time for the dirty ones."

My hand runs over my tummy and down to my panties. They're already dripping wet, and I open my thighs. As my fingers run over my damp panties, the camera clicks.

* * *

Mentioned in this book...

Curious about Adalee the plus-size model and her protective photographer husband? Read Adalee for a sweet and steamy instalove romance.

Check out Adalee.

MOUNTAIN MAN'S REDEMPTION

MEN OF MAPLE MOUNTAIN BOOK FIVE

MOUNTAIN MAN'S REDEMPTION

MEN OF MAPLE MOUNTAIN BOOK FIVE

Does a trained killer deserve love?

When I meet Ewan, the mysterious Scottish recluse who lives in the mansion on the side of the mountain, he seems too good to be true.

He's a chicken farmer living a quiet life, working the land.

I fall into that idyllic life with him, growing vegetables and sipping scotch in front of an open fire.

But why does a chicken farmer have a cupboard full of weapons, always carry a knife, and fight like a ninja?

Who exactly have I given my heart to?

Mountain Man's Redemption is an age gap instalove romance featuring an ex-military mountain man and a younger innocent curvy girl.

No cliffhangers and with a happily ever after guaranteed.

1

EWAN

A gust of wind slams the door to Bear's Brewery shut so hard that it rattles the windowpanes. I glance up from my scotch, and that's when I see her.

My hand freezes with my glass halfway to my mouth. A bolt like lightning travels all the way up my spine, making my head buzz.

Mine.

She's standing in the doorway, her worn jeans tight over thick thighs as she shakes rain off her long dark hair. A purse is strung casually over her torso, the strap resting between the two soft mounds of her breasts. The outline of a bra—and the hint of a nipple—can be seen through her tight t-shirt.

My mouth waters. My dick hardens.

She strides to the bar purposefully.

My gaze follows her. I can't look away.

Bear eyes her warily as she approaches the bar. There's no way this beauty is twenty-one. Despite the lip gloss and confident air, her face is too perfect, too unlined.

She orders a coffee, so he doesn't ID her. Then she takes it to an empty booth.

Sitting down, she pulls a guide book out of her bag. Of course, she's a tourist, just passing through. But what the hell is she doing on her own?

My mouth is dry, and I down my whiskey in one gulp. It burns my throat, the sharp smoky taste reminding me of home.

Home.

The Scottish Highlands where I grew up surrounded by beautiful scenery and biting poverty. I couldn't wait to get out.

I've lived many places since then, but none of them I'd call home.

There's a sharp pain in my skull as the flashback courses through my brain. Gunshots, artillery fire, men calling to each other. Amongst the chaos, I move stealthily through the shadows. The flash of a knife; a blade against flesh.

I press my hand to my forehead, pushing the images out of my mind. My eyes close, and I keep my head down so no one can see.

After a few minutes, the memories fade, and I have myself under control.

When I open my eyes, the girl has company.

My body stiffens. A young laddie closer to her age than me is leaning on the table, though I can tell by her body language that she doesn't want him there.

Standing up, I stride over and stop in front of her. She's sipping her coffee but freezes when she sees me, the cup poised halfway to her plump lips.

Our eyes meet, and I swear a bolt of electricity sparks between us.

"She's wi' me." I keep my eyes on the woman, not bothering to look at the joker who thinks he stands a chance with her, until he's stupid enough to talk back.

"I think she'll decide who she's with."

My head turns to the boy, and when he sees the full force of my gaze, the smart-ass look drops off his face.

He backs away from the table. "Sorry, man."

At least he had the good sense to apologize. I let him stumble back to the bar without hurting him.

When I turn my gaze back to the woman, she's smiling shyly. "Thanks for that. Some guys don't know when they're not wanted."

My eyes narrow as I wonder if she's telling me I'm not wanted. Too bad. I'm going to stick around until I am.

"You want another coffee?"

She nods. "Decaf please, or I'll be up all night."

When I order two coffees from the bar, Bear raises his eyebrows at me.

"You sure you don't want scotch in that?"

He's never seen me order anything else, so I don't wonder at his surprise.

"Jus' the coffee."

The coffee machine is on the end of the bar, and Bear chats as he makes the drinks.

"Did you hear the Ronson place got broken into?"

It's a big, secluded house on the mountain a few miles from my place. "They get much?"

Bear nods. "The Ronson's were fast asleep upstairs. They cleaned out all the downstairs electronics, TV room, office. Even took the kid's tablets."

I wonder at the kind of low-life who steals a kid's stuff. "They catch the guys who did it?"

"Nah," he says and shakes his head. "You got good security at your place?"

Bear's look is all concern.

"Aye," I reassure him. "My defences are good."

"Glad to hear it, buddy."

He puts the coffees down, and I take them with a nod. Bear is one of the good guys on the mountain, always looking out for his fellow locals.

Back at the table, I slide a coffee in front of the woman and take a seat across from her.

"I'm Ewan."

She takes my extended hand, and I clasp her small one in mine, not wanting to let go.

"I'm Bethany."

Bethany. I watch her mouth as she says it, already imaging those pure pink lips wrapped around my cock. Jesus, I don't know what's wrong with me. It's been a long time since I even thought about a woman this way.

"Bethany. That's a pretty name for a lassie."

She cocks her head, her green eyes filled with curiosity. My accent is a dead giveaway here.

"Where you from?" she asks.

"Scotland."

She smiles, her whole face lighting up. "Scotland sounds so exotic. Tell me about it."

Scotland is the last place I'd call exotic.

"It rains most of the time. It's cold. The men are rough and the women rougher."

She laughs, a light tinkling sound that makes my body relax and my heart soften. "Sounds like where I'm from."

"And where's that?"

She waves a hand dismissively and mentions a small town I've never heard of.

"What brings ye tae Maple Mountain?"

She sips her coffee slowly, leaving a pink smear of lip gloss on the rim of the mug. "Probably the same reason you're here."

I highly doubt that. But I'm not going to tell her my real reasons.

"For a quiet life?" At least that's what I've told the few people on Maple Mountain who I talk to.

"Well, that's where we're different. I came looking for adventure." Her eyes sparkle when she says it, and she leans forward. My eyes drift down to the "v" of cleavage poking enticingly out of her t-shirt.

Christ. I'll give this woman an adventure.

"What kind of adventure ye think you'll find in a small toon like this?" Maple Falls is a mountain town of less than one thousand people, with another hundred or so living on the mountain.

She cocks her and waggles a finger at me. "I think I already found it."

2
BETHANY

The man in front of me: Ewan, the Scottish stranger who planted himself across from me without being invited. I should be mad; I should tell him to go away. But instead, I stir my coffee while glancing at him sideways, trying not to be too obvious that I'm checking him out.

The thing is there's a pattern of ink poking out from under his t-shirt, a t-shirt that's pulled tight enough to show he's all hardness underneath.

As he lifts his arm to sip his drink, the muscles in his arms tighten. The guy's buff, like a crush-you-in-his-arms kind of buff.

The thought of this man—this stranger—holding me in his arms sends a shock of heat through my body. My thighs clasp together under the table, and I drag my gaze up to the safer territory of his face.

"What do you do in Maple Falls?" I ask.

His pale blue eyes are fixed on mine, and there's a sparkle of amusement there. Like he knows exactly what I was thinking.

My throat is suddenly dry, and I reach for a water glass.

"I'm a chicken farmer."

My eyebrows shoot up my forehead. Of all the professions, I did not think this mysterious buff man would be a chicken farmer.

"Really?"

He tilts his head. "Aye. Free-range mountain chickens."

His Scottish drawl makes my insides quiver. Under the table, I press my hands between my thighs and squeeze.

"How aboot you, lassie? What dae you do?"

Wow, his accent is killing me. If I spend too much time with Ewan, I'm going to have to change my panties.

I want to ask him all about his chicken farm and how a Scotsman ends up on an American mountainside, but he deftly changes the subject. I get the feeling he doesn't like talking about himself.

"Good question. At the moment, nothing. I'm travelling."

"On yer own?"

His brow creases into a frown, like he's concerned, which is sweet but a little old fashioned, though he's definitely a lot older than I am. There are lines around his eyes and a hard look to his face that tells me he's seen more of the world than I have.

"Yeah. Lots of women travel on their own these days. I can look after myself, you know."

His eyes twinkle again, as if I amuse him. "Aye, I'm sure ye can."

He sips his coffee while regarding me. I could get used to that gaze on me. It makes me feel alive. It makes me feel desirable.

"I jus' wonder why ye chose tae travel alone."

His tone is neutral. He's not judging, just curious.

"I'm not joking when I say I want an adventure. All my friends are getting married to their high school sweethearts. My best friend is already pregnant. And that's fine for her. She's happy. But I don't want to marry a nice boy from town and settle down with 2.5 children—the average American family—in a quiet neighborhood."

I fiddle with my spoon. I'm talking to this man as if we've known each other for years rather than just a few minutes. However, when I look up, he's nodding sagely.

"I want something more than that." I go on because he's looking at me like he understands. "I just don't know what yet."

"Aye, I get it. I used to think the same."

He looks away, and his expression goes dark. His mouth curves into a sneer. "Now, I'd do anything for a quiet life, 2.5 kids, and a quiet neighborhood."

His expression is so grim that I wonder where he's gone. Then, just as quickly, his eyes return to mine, and the dark look disappears.

"You want another coffee, or can I walk ye home?"

This man's hiding some demons, that much is clear. It makes him all the more fascinating. There's no way I'm ready for the night to end. "I'll have a seltzer. If you want to keep talking."

He reaches a hand across the table and tucks a strand of hair behind my ear.

"I'd like very much tae keep talking with ye, Bethany."

Once more a shiver goes through me. My name, in that accent, said by a mysterious stranger. I am in trouble here.

It's only because the bar is closing that we finally leave. It feels like we've only been talking for a few minutes, but in reality, more than three hours have passed. I've told Ewan all about my hometown, my family, and the places I've visited in the three months that I've been travelling.

I realise that I've done most of the talking, and I still know very little about Ewan. Despite that, I feel safe with him, like I've known him my whole life.

I'm staying at the local hostel, and Ewan insists on walking me to the door. It's a small place on the edge of town that provides cheap accommodation to backpackers.

As we approach, there's the sound of muffled house music, the base thumping through the walls.

Ewan takes one look at the place with its faded paint work, the smell of fried onions wafting through the window, and shakes his head. "You're nae staying here."

I wish I wasn't, but it was the only viable option when I decided I wanted to see Maple Mountain.

"It's all I can afford. I'm in a dorm bed."

"Female dorm?"

I wince, knowing what he's going to say. But the shared dorm was cheaper. "No, it's shared."

His nostrils flare, and he clenches his fists. "You're nae sleeping in a shared dorm."

His concern is sweet and makes me feel cared for, but I don't see any other options. "I can't afford the hotel."

The front door opens, and someone lurches past us and throws up in the street. It's the guy from earlier at the bar, the one Ewan chased away.

"Get yer bags."

He's got a determined expression on his face, even though his accent is soft.

"Ewan, I can't go anywhere else. I can't afford it."

"Go pack yer bags, lassie. You're coming wi' me."

For a moment, I can only frown at him. "What do you mean?"

"I've got a spare room at my place. You can stay as long as ye need."

The idea is so strange that I can only stare at him. He misinterprets my look.

"I'll be the perfect gentleman if that's what you're worried aboot."

It is what I'm worried about, but not in the way that he thinks. I'm worried I won't be the perfect lady, that if I spend too much time with this hot man with the panty melting accent, I'll end up jumping him.

But the thought of spending more time with Ewan is too good to turn down.

There's a cackle of laughter from the hostel, and the sweet smell of weed wafts through the window.

"All right." I say. "Give me a minute."

It doesn't take me long to grab my things. As I stuff my belongings into my backpack, I wonder what the hell I'm doing.

I just agreed to go and stay at a strange man's house. Is this the adventure I've been looking for?

3
EWAN

The drive to my place is torture with Bethany next to me in the passenger seat; her thigh is so close to my hand every time I change gear.

But I promised I'd be a gentleman, and a Scotsman never goes back on his word.

I couldn't leave her in that hovel. It's better to have her here, where I know she's safe and no horny backpacker is going to try to get into her bed.

The thought makes my blood run hot with rage, but I suppress my anger, like I was taught to.

We reach my place, and the electric gates swing open.

Bethany leans forward in her seat, her eyes roving over my property. I guess it looks impressive, an architecturally designed house carved into the mountain face.

"This is your place?"

"Aye."

I park the convertible next to the SUV, and as we get out, she looks around with guileless wonder.

"This isn't where I expected a chicken farmer to live."

"Sorry to disappoint ye."

She giggles. "Oh, no, this isn't disappointing."

Slinging her backpack over my shoulder, I lead her into the house.

"Help yerself to anything in the kitchen." I wave in the general direction of the kitchen before heading up stairs.

"You can take the spare room with yer own ensuite. I'll jus' make up the bed."

She follows me slowly upstairs, her curious gaze sweeping over the house.

"Oh, wow," she exclaims when she gets to the landing.

One side of the corridor is glass, a long window looking out to the mountain and the valley below. You can see the lights of Maple Springs, the nearest town to Maple Falls, far in the distance.

"Nice, isn't it?"

I turn to her, and she's got her hands pressed against the glass. Her eyes are wide, an expression of wonder on her face. "It's beautiful."

No, she's beautiful, all wide eyed and innocent. I love that she's so enchanted, not cynical about the world like too many people I've met.

At the end of the corridor is a spare room, and I drop her bag on the floor and fetch a pair of sheets from the cupboard.

"You live here alone?" she asks coming, into the room.

"Aye, jus' me."

She's staring at me in awe with her mouth slightly open and eyes wide. She's fucking adorable. More than adorable. She's sexy as fuck, and my dick knows it too. I'm hard as the mountain rock this place is built from, and it's getting uncomfortable.

Luckily, I keep the lighting in here dim, so she doesn't notice my raging hard on.

I fan out the sheet, and she grabs the other end. As she tucks it in, she leans forward, her breasts pushing against her t-shirt, her cleavage on full display.

Christ, I need to get out of here before I do something entirely ungentlemanly.

"I'll leave ye tae it," I say hastily. "Bathroom's through that door. There's a TV room along the corridor and a lounge downstairs. Help yerself to anything in the kitchen. I'll be oot early tomorrow tae tend the chickens. Just make yerself at home."

She looks surprised, and I know it's an abrupt exit, but I need to get away before my cock explodes in my pants.

As soon as I'm down the hall, I close the door of my bedroom and fall on my bed. Hastily unzipping, I pull my throbbing cock out of my pants.

Bethany's tits are on my mind. Her plump lips and wide eyes. I stroke myself, imagining those lips wrapped around my cock, those innocent eyes looking up at me.

With two quick tugs, I explode, my seed bursting out over my hand and dribbling onto the Egyptian cotton sheets.

Fuck. It's going to take some serious effort to keep my cock away from Bethany. No woman has ever had this effect on me. Never.

It's more than physical attraction. I feel a connection with Bethany, something raw and real. I was taught to trust my instincts, and my instincts are humming right now.

4
BETHANY

Birdsong wakes me in the morning, and it takes me a moment to remember where I am.

Then I remember Ewan, how we talked all night, how he offered me a place to stay. My body tingles just thinking about him, and I stretch lazily, feeling the soft sheets against my body. This has got to be the softest bed I've ever slept in.

Sitting up, I listen for any movement in the house, but it's all quiet. I quickly shower and dress, and about twenty minutes later, I push open the bedroom door.

The door opens to a long corridor. One side of it is glass, showing the view beyond. I stand for a while and look out over the rugged terrain, wondering what brought a Scotsman all the way here to live alone on a mountain.

On the other side of the corridor, there are three doors. My curiosity to find out more about this man is so strong that before I can think too much about it, I'm turning the handle to the first door. After all, he did tell me to make myself at home.

The first door opens to a bedroom similar to mine but smaller. Like mine, it's sparsely furnished, just a bed and a nightstand. I guess Ewan doesn't have much company.

In fact, there's not much furniture in the whole house. There are no side tables or chairs or anything in the long corridor.

The next door leads to the TV room, and it's just that—a flat screen on one wall with a couch facing it and a coffee table.

There are no ornaments, no picture frames, no coffee table books. Just one picture on the wall of a mountain scene with grazing deer, which I guess is Scotland.

My stomach rumbles, and I pad downstairs and find the kitchen. Ewan told me to help myself, but it still feels wrong rummaging through the fridge. So I grab a banana from a bowl and eat it as I inspect the cupboards.

They're as sparse as the rest of the house and strangely tidy. A few cans are lined up in rows arranged alphabetically. I guess the man likes things neat.

Finishing the banana, I wander to the dining room and the living room beyond that.

Again, it's just a flat screen TV, a sofa, and a coffee table, although this room is bigger, and there's a bookcase on one wall. My fingers run along the spines of leather-bound books, some of them so old the leather is coming away from the bindings.

Okay, so this Scottish chicken farmer likes minimalist living and old books. Oh, and he must be some kind of millionaire because he lives in a mansion on the side of a mountain.

I'm wondering who the hell Ewan really is as I wander into another room off the kitchen. This one's full of gym equipment, which explains why he's so buff. He didn't get those muscles from chicken farming.

I'm back at the stairs again, and I climb them, wanting to look out at the view. I'm guessing the bedroom at the end of the hall is his, and I'm not going to snoop around there. But there's another door next to it, wedged between the master bedroom and one of the spare rooms. Only this one's got a push button lock on it.

Curious, I try the handle. It doesn't budge. It's the only locked door I've come across, and I don't know why it would need a heavy-duty combination lock and not just a key.

I'm wondering what's behind the only locked door in the house when Ewan's voice makes me jump.

"Ye had breakfast yet, lassie?"

I turn quickly, my hand on my chest. "I didn't hear you come up the stairs." A guilty flush creeps up my neck, but if he notices it, he doesn't say. "I was just having a look around."

"Aye." His gaze flickers to the door and back to my face. "I've got freshly laid eggs for yer breakfast."

He turns and heads down the stairs. I follow.

No more is mentioned of the locked door, or my snooping around, which I'm grateful for.

In the kitchen, Ewan gets busy whipping up an omelette.

He tells me all about the farm and the chickens and how he's been here for two years selling free-range mountain eggs to the local towns.

"I'll take you for a walk around after we get ye fed."

"I really should get back to town today." It's not what I want to do, but it would be rude to take advantage of his hospitality for too long.

He cocks his head at me. "Why?"

"There's a bus once a day to Maple Springs. I was going to move on today."

He slides the omelette out of the frying pan and onto my plate. "Move on to where?"

I shrug my shoulders. "Don't know. Wherever the road takes me."

He leans on the kitchen counter and fixes his penetrating gaze on me. "It seems tae me the road brought ye here, Bethany."

Damn. Every time he says my name, my insides feel like they're melting.

"What do you mean?" It comes out as a whisper. I couldn't dare to hope this older man could be interested in me.

"Stay here wi' me." He takes my hands and holds them in his. He's so close I can smell his aftershave.

"Stay for a while, or stay forever. But stay."

Then I'm leaning toward him, falling into him. His lips meet mine, and I know that's exactly what I want to do. Stay.

5
EWAN

It's two days later, and my balls are swollen to the size of coconuts—at least that's the way it feels.

Apart from a few kisses, I've kept my word to Bethany and behaved like a perfect gentleman. No matter that it's killing me.

If I don't make her mine soon, my balls are going to explode.

The last two days have been the happiest of my life. She's not shy of helping me with the chickens, donning my old boots and helping feed them and collect eggs, laughing all the while as mud splashes over her clothes.

We've spent the nights having dinner, talking easily, and watching TV. At the end of each night, I've kissed her goodnight at the top of the stairs and then gone to my own room. And it's fucking killing me.

I can see she wants more, but something's holding me back. I'm not the man she thinks I am. I don't deserve a woman like Bethany. I'm torn between my need for her and what she'd think if she knew who I was and what I've done.

Tonight, when we walk up the stairs, I can tell there's something wrong.

She's nervous. Her palm is sweaty when I take it in mine. When I turn to her as we reach the corridor, she's looking at me with big round eyes.

"What is it?"

My heart clenches. This is where she tells me she's leaving.

Instead, she leans forward and stands on tiptoe so she can whisper into my ear.

"I want to sleep in your room tonight." Her breath tickles my ear, the heat of it making my cock stiff.

She's looking at me questioningly, hopefully.

"Bethany, are ye sure it's what ye want?"

She doesn't answer. Instead, her thumbs hook under her t-shirt, and she pulls it over her head.

My breath catches in my throat. Her breasts are perfect mounds encased in a black silk bra. "Bethany…"

She takes my hand and pushes it against her tits. They're soft and pliant, and I move my thumb over her nipple.

She lets out a moan, and the sound is my undoing.

My hand closes over her bra, and I yank it hard. She gasps as the fabric rips. Her breasts tumble out and into my waiting hands.

I push her against the wall, my mouth devouring her, kissing her neck, her throat, her hard nipples. Her hand grasps the back of my head, pulling me into her.

My hand slides up her skirt to her panties. They're already damp, and I yank them off as well.

She gives a little cry as my hand slides over her pussy.

Her little moans are like electric shocks to my dick, turning me into an animal. I should go slow. I should make her cum first. But her little cunt is dripping wet, and I'm going to fuck her like the beast I am.

My finger pushes into her, and she's so tight I can barely get inside her. "You're so fucking tight."

She's panting now, and her cheeks are tinged pink. Sexy as hell.

"Because I've never done this before."

I pull back and look at her in the dim light. "Never fucked a Scotsman?"

She shakes her head. "Never fucked anyone."

Her pussy clenches around my finger as she says it, and I ache to get my dick inside her. The fact I'll be her first makes me swell with a new need I can't explain, a primal instinct to claim her, to make her mine.

"I'm glad I'll be ye first, lassie."

A second finger slides inside her, and I watch her face as she closes her eyes, her head tipped back.

"Keep talking like that," she moans.

I don't know if it's my accent or my words she's getting off on, but I don't care. I slide another finger in, warming her up for my cock, while I watch her face, soft with desire.

"I'm going tae claim ye now, Bethany. Make ye mine."

When I withdraw my fingers, her eyes fly open. "What are you doing?"

There's a pleading note to her voice that makes pre-cum shoot from the tip of my dick. "I'm going tae give ye the real thing."

My dick's already in my hand, and I open her thighs as I line myself up. The angle's off, so I lift her up. She's a big girl, but I'm a strong man, and I like my lassies big.

Leaning her against the wall with her hips tilted out, I find her entrance with my cock.

Her eyes go wide as a slide myself in an inch. Just one delicious inch. But it's not enough. Now that she's balanced on my cock, I hold her hips with both hands and pull her downwards, sinking myself into her pussy.

She cries out, a high-pitched scream that echoes through the house. Her legs wrap around my waist, and she clings on.

I lift her hips and slam in again, and again, and again. Each thrust pulls me closer to climax. Her cries grow higher pitched, and then she's coming, her pussy clenching around me and pulling me over the edge.

I come hard and long, my seed shooting deep inside her womb. My body shatters around her, and I cling to her until every last drop is spent.

Slowly, I slide out of her and set her gently on her feet.

My hand clasps hers, and I kiss her forehead.

"Stay here wi' me, Bethany. Stay on the mountain and be my woman."

She looks up at me in the dark, her eyes wide. She nods. "Okay."

I lead her into the master bedroom, It's her bedroom now too.

She climbs into bed, and I cuddle up next to her, one arm falling protectively over her body.

In a few minutes, she's asleep. But I lie awake. Thinking about a sharp knife slicing through flesh. Thinking about how many lives I took. Do I really deserve to be this happy?

6
BETHANY

Three weeks later…

My back rests against Ewan. His warmth spreads through my satisfied body. We just had another round of mind-blowing sex, and I'm weary and ready to sleep.

He drapes an arm over me, making me feel safe and secure in a way I've never felt before with a man.

The three weeks that I've been at his place have been the happiest of my life.

My days are spent helping with the farm, cooking good meals, and occasionally leaving his mansion for a drink in town or a walk on the mountain.

And the nights. Lordy, the nights. It's like he can't get enough of my body.

He seems to love every part of it, even the squishy bits I always thought were too jiggly. He runs his hands, his fingers, his tongue over my tummy and my thick thighs.

He makes me feel beautiful and sexy. And that makes me bold.

My body has been awakened, and also my heart. Ewan said I could stay as long as I like, and I want to stay forever.

But he's almost twenty years older than me. This might just be a fling for him.

There's so much I still don't know about Ewan. Like why he calls out in his sleep some nights, the headaches that he won't talk about that come upon him suddenly, leaving him holding his head like it's about to explode. Where does he disappear to when one of his dark moods takes him? And why does he keep a locked door in the house?

"What's on yer mind, lassie?"

His ability to practically read my thoughts is incredible. How the hell he knows I'm turning something over in my mind when I'm facing the wall and he's behind me, I have no idea.

This is when I should ask him about his past. I should make him tell me what he's keeping from me. But I'm too scared of what he'll say. I'm too scared it will mean the end of all that we have.

"I'm wondering if I should bake chocolate muffins or chocolate cookies tomorrow."

He leans up on his elbow, and I can feel him looking at me in the dark. He's not buying it, but he doesn't say anything.

"Cookies. Definitely cookies."

His lips graze my shoulder. "Now get some sleep, lassie."

I snuggle against him. Better to live in the moment than worry about his past. Or the future. For now, I'm in bed with Ewan's warm body pressed against me.

I close my eyes and am soon fast asleep.

A sound wakes me. I lie in bed listening, and there it is again, a thump from downstairs.

I sit up quickly to find Ewan already out of bed and dressed.

"What was…?"

He puts a finger to his lips, and I fall silent.

There's a noise again. Someone moving around downstairs. An intruder. My heart leaps into my throat. Bear mentioned there have been burglaries in the area, and a big house like Ewan's would be a prime target.

I suddenly realise how vulnerable we are, living away from town on the side of the mountain, the nearest neighbors a few miles away.

Ewan moves stealthily for someone of his stocky frame, not making a noise as he opens the bedroom door.

I slip out of bed and follow him.

He turns to me and pulls the door almost shut behind him. His face is alert and hard. Not a trace of fear in him.

"I need ye tae hide in the wardrobe."

I shake my head. I don't want to leave him; I'm dreading what's going to happen if he confronts the intruders.

His whisper has a commanding edge. "It's not a request, Bethany. Take yer phone into the wardrobe, and call Kit."

Kit's our nearest neighbor and the ranger on Maple Mountain.

"Don't make a sound, and don't leave the wardrobe until I come tae get ye."

He turns to leave, and I grab his arm. "What will you do?"

A flicker of a smile crosses his face. "Don't worry about me, lassie." Then he slips out the door.

I'm paralyzed by fear. I don't want him to confront the burglars. They might have guns.

I should do what he says and go hide, but my legs are frozen in place.

The door is open a crack, and through it, I see Ewan moving silently down the corridor. He stops in front of the door with the lock and punches a number into the keypad. Then he slips into the room.

My curiosity overcomes my fear, and I pull the door open

and step into the corridor. My heart is hammering in my ears as I pad along the carpet. But I have to know what's in that room.

I come to the open door and have to stifle a gasp.

It's dark, but there's no mistaking what's hanging on the wall: weapons. Long black guns, small pistols, and a rack of knives.

Ewan comes out of the room with a gun tucked into his belt. There's a glint of steel, a knife tucked into his sleeve.

My eyes widen, and they meet his for an instant.

He gives me a hard look as he closes the door and points back to the bedroom. I know what he's saying. He's telling me to go, and this time I don't hesitate.

My feet carry me swiftly to the bedroom. I turn back before I slide through the door, but Ewan is already gone.

Grabbing my phone, I duck into the wardrobe and punch in Kit's number. He answers sleepily but becomes alert as soon as I explain what's happening in an urgent whisper.

"I'll call the cops and come straight over."

"Hurry," I whisper.

"Tell Ewan not to do anything stupid."

He hangs up the phone, and I stare at it in the darkness. It's too late. Ewan's already doing something stupid. But why the hell does he have a room full of weapons?

There's a shout from downstairs; then, the sounds of furniture being knocked over.

I hold my knees to my chest as my heart thumps against my ribcage.

"Please be okay. Please be okay. Please be okay."

I whisper the refrain over and over again into my sweaty knees.

After a few moments, I realise the house has gone still. My

ears strain, listening for any sound, any clue to what has happened.

Suddenly, the light in the bedroom sparks to life.

My hand fumbles on the floor in search of something to defend myself. My hand closes over a shoe, and I hold it up, ready to use if I need to.

The wardrobe door creaks open.

Ewan peers in at me. For a moment, I can only stare at him in too much shock to move.

"For Christ's sake, don't use the slipper on me."

His lips turn into a smile, and I drop the slipper and fall into his arms.

7
EWAN

The last police car disappears down the road, its lights swallowed by the mountain. I lock the gate—not that it's a deterrent for the determined, though. The burglars used a ladder to get over the wall before making their way inside.

Bethany's wrapped in a blanket and sitting on the couch. She's been trying to catch my eye for the last two hours.

She's waiting for an explanation, and I know I can't put this moment off any longer. "You want some hot chocolate?"

She shakes her head. "I've had hot chocolate and coffee and peppermint tea. I don't need another hot drink. I need answers Ewan."

She's right. She does. But she's not going to like hearing them.

Sitting next to Bethany on the couch, I put my arm around her, but she shrugs it off. The slight pierces me straight to the heart, but I can't blame her.

"What do ye want tae know?"

"Who are you?"

It's just before dawn, and the faint glow of sunrise creeps up the valley, throwing a golden light over her face. She's never looked more beautiful.

"I'm Ewan Cavendish, from a small village in the Highlands of Scotland."

She shakes her head. "I know all that. Tell me the stuff I don't know. Tell me why you have a room full of weapons, or how you managed to overcome three burglars with what seemed like ninja skills."

She's referring to the scuffle I had with the would-be burglars. When she came downstairs, I had tied their hands behind their backs, and one was bleeding on the floor where a knife went through his foot. It was the only weapon I had to use.

It's time to come clean. "I'm ex-SAS."

Her eyes narrow. "What does that mean exactly?"

"The SAS are an elite British military force."

I'm not sure how much to tell her. Most of the operations I did were top secret, and I can never talk about them. I'm not even meant to tell anyone I was part of the squad. But if I don't give her some information fast, I'm going to lose her.

"We're trained for covert operations, counter terrorism—that sort of thing."

"What sort of thing?"

Christ, she's so innocent. She's an innocent civilian, with no notion about the nasty aspects of war.

I was trained to kill. Trained to take out threats in a quiet and stealthy way that doesn't fit with the peace-keeping line the modern army likes to spout to the public.

"The jobs no one wants tae know about."

There's a flicker of understating on her face, and she covers her mouth in shock. There's a flash of disgust, and she pulls away from me. "You've killed people?"

And there it is. The moment I lose her.

"Yes," I say quietly. The image of a knife slicing flesh flashes behind my eyes, and I shut them quickly.

"I'm a trained killer, Bethany. I've done terrible things to protect my country."

When I open my eyes, she's staring at me in horror. There's a hard look that's unfamiliar on her innocent face, and it shatters my heart.

Now she knows. Now she knows what I am, and what I've done.

I knew it was too good to last. Men trained for nasty deeds like I was don't deserve to find love.

She stands up. "I need to get some sleep."

But I hear the unsaid words. She needs to get away from me. I disgust her.

"Aye. Goodnight, lassie."

She's already heading up the stairs, and she doesn't look back.

I sit for a long time watching the sun creep up the valley.

When I finally go upstairs, Bethany's not in my bed, and I know she's sleeping in the spare room.

It was a wonderful few weeks, but I knew it couldn't last. Men with blood on their hands like mine don't deserve happiness.

8
BETHANY

Grey clouds hang low in the sky, and rain spatters the window. It's late in the afternoon. I've got my bag packed, but I don't dare come out of the spare room. Once I come out, I have to leave, and it's going to be hard to leave.

I shake my head. I need to leave because how can I stay here with a man who has killed in cold blood?

This is what's been going around and around in my head for the last several hours, ever since Ewan confessed his past to me.

I know he did it for his country, and that makes him a hero, but it frightens me.

The way he took out those burglars. When I came downstairs, one of them had a knife still lodged in his foot. Another had a broken arm.

How can I stay with a man who can commit such violence?

Before I can change my mind again, I sling my backpack over my shoulder and open the door.

I almost trip over Ewan. He's sitting on the floor, his back resting against the wall.

His face tilts up to mine, and he eyes my backpack. "You're leaving."

His expression is neutral and tinged with sadness. My heart breaks as I look at him, and I wonder if I'm doing the right thing.

"Can you give me a lift? I need to catch the five o'clock bus."

"Aye, lassie."

He stands up slowly, the muscles of his arms rippling as he pulls himself up off the floor. My breath hitches as he stands at his full height. We're so close I can smell his unique scent: aftershave and chicken feed and a hint of whiskey. It should be a terrible combination, but it's Ewan's scent, and the pull of that heady combination makes me long to embrace him.

"I understand why you're leaving." His blue eyes find mine. "But there's something I've got tae say first."

My heart thumps so loudly against my ribcage I think he must hear it. But if he does, he says nothing.

"I'm a bad man. I ken that. I've done things I'm no' proud of."

My heart goes out to him. He's struggling with his inner demons, and I get it. Most people would consider him a hero, so why can't I?

"When I left the service, I was haunted by my deeds. I came here, as far away from Scotland as I could get, because I couldn't look anyone I knew in the eye."

He breaks eye contact with me now and looks out the window to the valley beyond, and I wonder how lonely he must have been, up here all alone and far away from his people.

"I thought I'd live a quiet life, disturb no one, and maybe one day the demons that haunt me would go away. They never did."

He sounds resigned, and I wonder how he's not more bitter. He served his country and ended up with PTSD, which is what

I'm sure he's got. It would explain the nightmares, the headaches, and the dark looks.

"Then you came along, Bethany. You reminded me about the good in the world. You reminded me about what it was all for. I love you, Bethany. You make me feel like I could be a good man for somebody."

He turns his gaze back to me, and my heart flutters in my chest at his words.

"I've done some terrible things. But it helped keep my country and my people safe, so I would do them again."

It's a challenge. He's saying I need to be able to accept his past if I'm going to be with him. His gaze is penetrating, but there's also something else. The haunted expression that was always lurking behind his look is gone. He looks free. He looks like a regular guy. A regular guy who sacrificed his own morality for this country. And that is heroic.

I know right then that I'm not going to leave.

My backpack slides off my shoulders, and I let it drop to the floor.

"Ewan." There's a spark of hope in his eyes. "The violence frightened me this morning, but I've never felt safer than when I'm with you."

"Then don't leave." His hand cups my chin. "Stay with me. Always. Marry me, Bethany."

The words are a pleasant shock that I feel all the way to my heart.

"Are you serious?" But I can tell by the intense way he's looking at me that he is.

"Deadly."

"Okay." It comes out as a squeak. I don't even need to think about it. It feels so right to say yes.

The creases on his brow disappear, and he gives the biggest grin I've ever seen on his face.

"You're sure you want an old-timer like me?"

As he says it, he puts his hands on my hips and lifts me up, showing how strong he is. I wrap my legs around his waist. "You bet."

My lips meet his as he carries me to the bedroom.

EPILOGUE

BETHANY

4 years later...

The egg basket drops out of my hand when I see my husband. It lands on the counter, sending eggs rolling every which way. One crashes to the ground and spreads yellow yolk over the kitchen vinyl.

"I've been waiting for ye to get in."

His voice is a deep growl letting me know his intentions, as if I could miss them. "I can see that."

Ewan is butt naked, his erection sticking out thick and long and pointing straight at me. A purple vein throbs as he takes it in his hand.

"Come over here, lassie, and hitch yer skirt up."

I step sideways, trying to peer into the living room. "But the kids?" I whisper.

"Having a nap."

The two-year-old could sleep all day if we let him, but the three-year-old has been skipping her naps lately, and if Ewan has managed to get her down, then we don't have much time.

My eyes travel to his thick cock. There's a tremor in my core and a rush of dampness between my legs.

"We better hurry then."

I pull my panties down, and as soon as they're off, Ewan picks me up and deposits me on the kitchen bench.

He flicks my skirt up and runs a hand up my thighs. "I'd prefer to take my time, but I'm nothing if not adaptable."

The twinkle in his eye is as much of a turn on as the hard cock he's now pressing against my entrance.

In the four years that we've been together, I've seen my husband change from an introspective brooding man to a lighthearted one.

He still has dark moments, but they've been happening less frequently since he's been going to therapy.

The therapist helped him connected with other veterans on the mountain. He started working with Sam and Emily when they set up the veteran recovery center.

He's now more likely to be running the fundraiser BBQ at Bear's Brewery and laughing with the locals than sitting on his own and knocking back whiskey in the corner.

Ewan is an excellent father, tender with the kids, and an exquisite lover.

"Fuck!" I cry out as he slams into me so hard my teeth rattle.

My legs wrap around his waist, and I lift my hips, grinding against him with every thrust. It doesn't take long for my climax to build; then I'm over the edge, calling out his name as my orgasm races through my body.

He comes with me, and we cling to each other as tightly as we did that first night.

And I know I'll always cling to him like this. He's my rock. My safe place. I came looking for an adventure, and I found the biggest adventure of my life. My husband.

* * *

Mentioned in this story...

Curious about ex-military man Sam and what this wounded hero must overcome to claim his curvy woman?

Check out All the Scars We Cannot See.

MOUNTAIN MAN'S FIRST TIME

MEN OF MAPLE MOUNTAIN BOOK SIX

MOUNTAIN MAN'S FIRST TIME

It's only ever been her...

I've been in love with Ursula Riley ever since I was twelve years old. I've watched her grow from a grief-stricken child to a strong and beautiful woman.

When she went away to college, I thought my feelings would cool. But now she's back, with plenty of sass and curves that make my blood run hot.

The problem is her big brother, Bear. He's my best friend and her guardian, and he's fiercely protective.

He'd kill me if he knew what I was up to with his little sister…

Mountain Man's First Time is a forbidden love, dual virgins romance featuring an OTT mountain man who falls for his best friend's curvy little sister.

No cliffhangers and a happily ever after guaranteed.

1

KIT

"She's here."

The whisper travels down the wooden pews of the church to where I'm standing at the altar next to Bear.

He exhales nervously as the distinctive chords of the wedding march fill the old weather-beaten church.

The bridal party starts down the aisle with Colette on the arm of her father. She's beaming, looking radiant on her wedding day, and Bear gives a happy sigh.

But it's not Colette that I'm looking at. Walking ahead of the bride in a simple blue dress that hugs her curvy figure is Ursula. The maid of honor—Bear's little sister and the woman I've been in love with since I was twelve years old.

Her hair is piled high on her head. There are tiny flowers woven through it, and a few wisps hang down, framing her face. She looks so stunning that for a moment I can't breathe.

"She's beautiful, isn't she?"

Bear's talking about Colette, but I only have eyes for the bridesmaid. "Yes. Yes, she is."

The bridal party reaches the front, and Colette takes her

place next to Bear. A look passes between them that's so full of love it makes my heart ache.

I'd do anything to have Ursula look at me like that.

I steal a sideways glance at Ursula, and she must feel my gaze on her because she looks across at me and catches my eye.

She gives me a small smile. Her eyes are glistening, and I can tell she's as happy for Bear as I am.

He's had a tough ticket since their parents died eight years ago. Bear took over the running of the family brewery and became responsible for his younger sister.

Which is why my feelings for her are so impossible. It's why I've kept myself in check all these years.

It was torture when Ursula went away to college, as I wondered if she'd come back with some smart college boy in tow.

But in the months that she's been back, still single and with her figure filled out in voluptuous curves, it's been getting harder and harder to hide my feelings.

I try to concentrate on what the pastor is saying, but my gaze keeps straying back to Ursula.

She's watching Bear and Colette, and my gaze lingers on her profile, admiring her rosy cheeks and bright eyes. Her lips are painted a pale pink, making them look plump and kissable. I've never seen her look so beautiful or seen so much of her cleavage. But that dress seems to float just above her luscious, pillowy…

Bear nudges me, and I pull my attention back to the ceremony. Everyone's looking at me, but I've got no idea what's just been said.

"The rings."

The pastor looks at me pointedly, and I grab the box out of my pocket. Bear shakes his head at me. "You had one job…" he mutters under his breath.

I hand over the rings, and the ceremony continues.

I steal a glance at Ursula. She's got her hand over her mouth, stifling a laugh. Her eyes dance, and I grin back. I know I'm not going to hear the end of it from Bear, but at least I made Ursula smile at me.

"I pronounce you man and wife," says the pastor. "You may kiss the bride."

There are cheers from the audience as Bear lifts Colette off her feet and practically devours her face in a passionate kiss.

Ursula puts her fingers in her mouth and whistles, and I cheer loudly with the rest of them.

When the happy couple breaks apart, they're both smiling widely, and I feel a pang in my heart.

I want this. I want this kind of happiness.

I've never told Ursula how I feel. She was too vulnerable after her parents' deaths. Then she went away to college, and I thought the feelings would fade, but they didn't. I thought Bear would chill with his overprotectiveness, but he didn't. He's made it clear what he'll do to anyone who messes with his sister.

I once saw him lay a guy out at his bar because he touched her ass while they were dancing.

I've sat on the sidelines, and I've waited. But looking at Ursula today, I realize I can't wait any longer. I want this kind of happiness, and I want it with her.

It's time to let her know how I feel.

2

URSULA

The last spoonful of chocolate mousse slips into my mouth and I close my eyes, savoring the taste as it melts on my tongue.

When I open my eyes, Kit's staring at me from his place at the table two seats down.

His eyes are focused on my mouth, and I wipe my finger across my lips, wondering if I left chocolate smeared all over them. That's the only reason I can think of for why he'd be staring at me so intently. Kit—my big brother's best friend and the guy I've had a crush on ever since I can remember.

Too bad any interest he's ever taken in me is like that of a second big brother, as protective of me as Bear is.

I wiggle my spoon at Kit. "Did you try the mousse?"

He cocks his ear at me, straining to hear above the rock music that's blaring from the speakers. If this is the chilled-out dinner music, I hate to think what the band's going to play.

"Did you try the mousse?" I try again, but he shakes his head and pushes his chair back.

Bear and Colette's seats are between us, but they're doing

the rounds of each table, saying hello to their guests before the dancing starts.

Kit sits in the chair next to me, and my body tenses. He looks so hot in his tuxedo with his beard neatly trimmed. As a ranger on Maple Mountain, it's not often I see him out of his casual mountain wear.

"The mousse"—I hold up my empty bowl— "was delicious."

He gives me a sideways look, and I feel my cheeks going pink. I've got the man I've crushed on all my life in front of me, yet I'm talking about mousse.

"I'm more of a crumble man myself."

I cock my head to the side. "I never knew that about you."

"Oh, yeah. Give me a homemade apple crumble, and I'm a happy man."

If only it was that simple. I have a vision of turning up at Kit's cabin with a crumble straight out of the oven. Maybe that's what I need to do to get his attention.

"How's it going at the tourist office?"

I screw my nose up. When I got back from college six months ago with a degree in North American history, I'm not sure what I was expecting to do in the small mountain town of Maple Falls. I must be the most overqualified tourism board rep in the county.

"It's fine, just a little..." I shrug, not sure how to explain what I've been feeling. I'm restless in Maple Falls. I worked my ass off for this degree, but most of my time is spent directing tourists to the local toilets. "...boring."

"You think you'll stick around?"

He asks it casually, but the look he gives me is anything but casual. My breath catches in my throat. Does he really care what I do, or is it an older brother's concern?

"It depends." On you, I want to add.

Just then Bear comes up to the table, his hand firmly

clasped in Colette's. They're so happy together; my big brother looks like he's on cloud nine.

"It's first dance time. You two ready?"

I glance at Kit, feeling shy. As best man and maid of honor, we're supposed to take to the floor after Bear and Colette.

"Sure." Kit clasps my hand as he stands up.

Bear looks at our hands and scowls. "It's a first dance, not a date."

Colette pulls him away before he has time to say anything else, and Kit keeps his hand firmly in mine.

I'm relieved he doesn't back down because of Bear.

"Still far too protective of you, I see."

To say my older brother is protective is an understatement. I've never even tried to bring a guy home to meet him. Not that there's been anyone I'd want to bring home, though. Only Kit.

"I'm hoping now that he's married, he might chill out a bit."

Kit's hand tightens in mine. "Why? You got someone you want to date?"

Do I imagine the jealous look that flickers across his face? I decide it must just be his overprotectiveness again.

"Maybe," I say playfully, which earns me a scowl.

By now we're at the dance floor. The reception is at Bear's Brewery, and a makeshift dance floor has been put down, the place decorated in fairy lights. The rock music from earlier is replaced by Frank Sinatra.

"How did he get so graceful?" Kit whispers as Bear glides across the dance floor, expertly twirling Colette. "Has he been taking lessons?"

Bear will kill me if I let on he's been taking dancing lessons, so I just shrug, but Kit reads the twinkle in my eye.

He raises his eyebrows. "The things people do…"

It's true. Bear has mellowed out since he's been with Colette, and I like my brother mellow. But is he mellow enough not to freak out if I make a move on Kit tonight? Because I don't think I can hold back any longer.

The chorus finishes, which is our cue to lead the other guests onto the floor.

Kit takes my right hand and slides his other hand around my waist. As we step onto the floor, he pulls me toward him.

There's a rush of heat through my body, and I look into his eyes. They're staring right back at me, the pupils wide and intense.

I don't know how to ballroom dance, but with Kit leading the way, we sashay around the dance floor, letting Sinatra guide us.

"You look beautiful tonight, Ursula."

To hear my name on his lips makes my body tingle. Everyone just calls me Urs, but I like my full name. It means bear in Latin, and that makes me feel strong.

"Thank you."

If it were anyone else, I would think they were drunk, but I know Kit never has more than one or two beers. "You clean up okay too."

He grins. "I had my beard trimmed and shaped."

"I can tell." What I don't say is that I'd love to run my hands through his beard, feel it scratch against my skin. "I'm sure the ladies will take note."

I hope Kit doesn't notice the bitter note that comes into my voice. I've seen the way Colette's cousins have been looking at him tonight.

"There's only one woman I want to notice."

My breath hitches in my throat. The way he's staring at me dares me to hope that he's talking about me. "Who's that?" I squeak.

"If you don't know that, then you're not as smart as I thought."

At that moment, he lets go of my waist and twirls me out to

the middle of the dance floor, then reels me back in until my back is pressed against him and his mouth is next to my ear.

"You, Ursula. It's always been you."

His hot breath on my neck makes my hairs stand on end. At his words, my heart lifts, and there's a delicious tremor all the way down my spine and between my legs.

"Kit..." I breathe his name, but he spins me away again. This time when I come back to him, he grabs me by the waist, and I'm looking up into his eyes.

My body is pressed against his, and I feel something hard probing into my belly. Realizing what it is, there's a rush of liquid heat between my legs. My cheeks go red, and my panties dampen.

Kit opens his mouth to say something, but a thick hand suddenly clamps onto his shoulder.

"Getting a bit close there, buddy."

Bear wears a jovial smile, but I can see the tension behind his look. "Come to the bar with me. I want to celebrate my wife with tequila."

Kit gives me an apologetic look before he's whisked off to the bar.

Kit's words whirl around in my head, making my heart race and my body overheat. I need air, and I might need to change my underwear. Being so close to Kit has left pools of wetness between my legs.

My stuff's upstairs in Bear's apartment where I got ready for today with Colette. I head up for a quick breather, hoping to compose myself and change my sticky underwear.

3
KIT

"It's an awesome wedding, man."

We're followed to the bar by the camera crew. I never had Bear down as the sentimental type, but filming the wedding is the one thing he insisted on.

He waves the cameraman away. "Go video my wife, not me."

Bear's grinning as he slips behind the bar and grabs the top-shelf tequila. He snags two shot glasses and pours the liquid into them.

"A toast to my wife."

"To Colette."

We clink glasses, and I swallow the fiery liquid. It burns my throat, and I stifle a cough. I've never been good with shots, but it's my best buddy's wedding day so I've made an exception.

Bear slams his shot glass down on the table.

"When are you going to find yourself a wife, Kit?"

Bear is slightly blurry eyed from the alcohol, but he's in a good mood. Maybe this is the time to tell him about Ursula.

But what is there to tell? We were interrupted before I could find out how she feels.

"I've got my eye on someone."

He raises his eyebrows and looks around the wedding party. The entire mountain was invited and a bunch of people made the trek from Maple Springs too.

Candy's Café did the catering and one of the owners, a woman with her bright blue hair in two bunches, wiggles her butt with abandon in the middle of the dance floor. She clutches her pregnant belly with one hand and her husband with the other. They're both laughing and I feel a pang of envy for what they have.

It seems the entire mountain and beyond has hooked up except me.

"One of Colette's cousins?" Bear says. "That redhead has been eyeing you all night."

I shake my head. "Nah, not my type." I've only got one type, only ever had one type, and her name's Ursula.

Bear narrows his eyes at me. "Is it someone from town? Someone I know?"

"You could say that."

I'm not ready to have this conversation without being sure Ursula wants me too. Luckily, Colette comes looking for Bear before he can ask any more questions.

"Have you seen the guest book?"

Bear shrugs. "We have a guest book?"

She slaps him playfully on the shoulder. "It should be on the gift table, but I think I forgot to bring it down."

She starts to head off, and Bear grabs her by the wrist. "Stay and have a shot with me, wifey."

Colette giggles, and Bear grabs another shot glass.

"One was enough for me." I hold up my hand. "I'll go get the book for you."

Colette gives me a thankful look. "I think it's on the table upstairs."

There's a staircase behind the bar that leads straight up to Bear's apartment, and that's where I head now.

This is where the girls got ready today, and you can tell.

The air is filled with the smell of perfume and hairspray. Clothes trail across the floor. There are empty champagne glasses and strange looking hair styling tools lying on the table.

There's movement in the bedroom, and Ursula appears in the doorway.

"I didn't know you were up here." I don't want her to think that I followed her.

"I came to freshen up."

She sweeps a tendril of hair behind her ear; her finger grazes her throat, and I long to run my lips over the soft skin there. I swallow hard and force myself to look away.

"You see the guest book anywhere?"

"Try the table." She moves to the table in the corner of the room, and I follow.

There's a leather-bound book that's being used as a shelf to display small pots of dark-colored powder that I think might be eyeshadow. My big hands feel clumsy among the delicate makeup pots as I move them out the way.

"Got it."

We've both been rummaging at the table, and when I hold up the book, I realize how close we are.

The tendril of hair has gotten loose again, and I slip it behind Ursula's ear. She looks up at me with clear eyes that seem to see right into my heart.

"Urs…" My fingers run down her throat, feeling her pulse quicken under my touch. "Your skin's as soft as I imagined it would be."

Her hand comes up to stroke my cheek, her fingers running down to graze my beard.

"I've wanted to touch your beard for so long."

My heart melts at her touch, and her words make me bolder. I lay the book on the table, and my other hand slides around her waist. If Bear saw us now, he'd probably kill me. But I don't care.

We're inches apart. I can smell the sweet scent of her perfume mixed with freshly applied lip gloss.

My other hand slides up her cheek, cupping her chin in my hand. "And I've wanted to kiss you for a long time."

Her eyelids flutter shut and her lips part, inviting me in. My mouth presses against hers. She's warm and soft, and I breathe her in. All thoughts of Bear are forgotten. It's just the two of us now as my body shifts against her and my whole universe realigns with a kiss.

4
URSULA

Warmth radiates from my lips and spreads through my body as Kit's mouth slowly explores mine.

I've dreamt about this moment for so long. Ever since I was a little girl kissing my pillow and pretending it was Kit.

Now we're finally kissing—the moment I've longed for—and my body is heating up fast. Kit moves his mouth to trail down my throat, his warm breath tickling my neck and sending shock waves buzzing all the way between my legs.

A moan escapes my lips, and I grind my hips against him. There's a pull in my core that's been building for years and can't be ignored any longer.

His hands tangle in my hair, and he pulls my head back so our eyes meet. "I've waited a long time for this, Ursula."

My hand slides down his front until I find the bulge in his pants. I tug gently and he groans, his eyes rolling closed and the sound sending shocks of heat to my pussy.

"Kit, I want you."

His eyes open. They're hooded and dark with desire. "Not like this Urs. The first time should be special."

He's right. There's something tasteless about making out at my brother's wedding. But now that I'm in his arms, I can't stop.

"Isn't this special?" I run my hand over his cock, stroking him through the fabric. He groans again, and I know I've found his weakness.

A struggle plays out on his face as his hand closes over mine.

"I won't take advantage of you when you've been drinking." He pulls my hand away from his trousers.

"I had a glass of champagne getting ready and another glass with the speeches, but you should know I'm not a big drinker. Anyway"—I slide my hand back to his trousers— "I want you to take advantage of me."

He closes his eyes as I stroke him. "I want you to do all the things that you've been imagining to me."

"Oh God, Ursula," he practically growls. "You have no idea."

"I want this Kit; I want you."

I see the moment his resolve breaks, and it feels like victory.

His mouth meets mine, and this time, it's urgent. A passionate kiss. My pussy's on fire as his hands run down my back and ass, pulling me toward him.

With one arm, Kit clears a space on the table. Then he lifts me up by the waist and sets me down, hitching up the satin fabric of my bridesmaid dress.

"This isn't how I imagined the first time," he says as his fingers trail up my thighs.

Maybe he's right. Doing it at a wedding reception is a cliché, but I'm so overcome with need for him that I don't care. I wrap my legs around his waist and pull him toward me while my hands fumble with his belt.

"I have to tell you something," he says.

My breath catches in my chest, and I wonder what the hell

he's going to say. But at that moment, the door bursts open, and Bear storms into the room.

5
KIT

We spring apart, but it's too late. Bear takes one look at us and the grin slides off his face.

"What the fuck?"

"It's not how it looks." Ursula slides off the table, pulling her dress down.

I'm fumbling to redo my belt, but there's no disguising the hard-on that's sticking out.

"Did you fuck my sister?"

Ursula winces at the words, and I don't blame her. It's not how I would describe what we were about to do.

"That's not a nice way to say it."

There's a dangerous flash in Bear's eye, and before I can defend myself, he crosses the room, his fist connecting with my nose.

There's a stab of pain and a crack that probably means it's broken.

"Fuck, man..."

Blood pours out of my nose and onto my white shirt. But I don't fight back. I'll let Bear have that one.

"We didn't do anything. Not that it would be any of your business."

His eyes flash in anger.

"Of course it's my business. She's under my protection." He turns away in disbelief. "How long has this been going on?"

I'm pissed that it's any business of Bear's. But he was always going to be a problem. I just would have preferred to tell him rather than have him walk in on us.

"It was just tonight. Just one night."

Ursula crosses her arms and fixes me with a look that's as angry as her brother's. "Just one night, was it?"

Shit. Now I've managed to piss off both Riley siblings.

"That's not what I meant."

Bear's look of fury is back. "How dare you mistreat my sister."

He comes at me again. This time, I'm angry. I'm pissed that he thinks I could mistreat Ursula, that he thinks that badly of me.

My aim is low as I swing my fist, landing a hit in his stomach. Bear doubles over, grabbing his waist.

"Kit!" Ursula exclaims, and I hear the shock in her voice.

Bear recovers and lunges at me. I duck, grabbing him around his substantial waist.

I'm a big guy, but I'm not as big as Bear. We wrestle, grasping each other, neither willing to give any ground.

"For God's sake, stop it!" Ursula pushes between us, and we're forced to break apart.

"Stop behaving like children!" She stands between us with her hands up. "This is a wedding. Don't turn it into a brawl."

We eye each other warily.

"I was looking out for you," Bear says. She cuts him off.

"I don't need you to look out for me, Bear. I'm twenty-two years old. I can make my own decisions."

He's breathing hard, still seething.

"I told you you're too protective."

She turns her chastising gaze to me. "And I don't need you to defend me either. You're a mess, Kit. You've got blood all over you."

She turns back to Bear. "What do you think Colette would say if she knew about this?"

Bear drops his head.

"I will not have you ruin my new sister's wedding day. Pull yourself together."

"Kit." Her eyes snap back to me, and I look at her hopefully. "Go home and clean yourself up."

"But..."

She puts a hand up to silence me. "No, Kit. I don't want to hear it. I've had enough of the both of you."

Her eyes flash with anger, and I know there's no point trying to talk to her tonight. Besides, she's right, I can't go downstairs with blood all over myself.

"I'll call you," I say. But she shakes her head, still looking pissed off.

I don't blame her. I practically ravished her and then punched her brother in the guts. What a way to win a woman over.

I head out the back door of Bear's feeling like the biggest ass in the world.

The buzz of my phone pierces through my throbbing temples. Scrambling for it, I come awake quickly and press it to my ear.

"Ursula?"

"Is this Kit?" The male voice sounds uncertain.

"Yeah." I can't hide the scowl from my voice as I swing my legs over the side of my bed and hold my head in my hands.

The punch Bear landed didn't break my nose, but it sure

gave me a headache. I rub my temples, trying to make sense of what the guy on the other end of the phone is telling me.

"Some hikers went up the mountain yesterday, and they haven't come back."

That sobers me up. "How many?"

The guy gives me the details, and I'm already getting dressed as I hang up the phone. As ranger on Maple Mountain, this is what I'm trained to do.

I swallow a couple of painkillers for my head then pull my boots on.

Before I go, I check the messages on my phone. There's nothing from Ursula, only the seven texts I sent her last night apologizing for my part in the scuffle with Bear.

If I'm heading up the mountain, there won't be any signal, and I don't know how long I'll be. She doesn't answer my call, so I leave a quick message and head off to find the lost hikers.

6

URSULA

The suitcase strains under my weight but sitting on it is the only way to get the zips anywhere near each other. After a struggle with the zipper, I finally tug the suitcase closed.

I've been living in the family cabin since I got back from college, and I give it one last look as I wonder when I'll be back.

I'm dragging my suitcase downstairs when there's a knock at the door.

Kit's standing on the porch looking tired and anxious. My heart breaks to see him like that, but I take a deep breath, remembering my resolve.

"Can I come in?"

He never used to have to ask to come into our place. But today he hesitates like he's not sure he's welcome.

I open the door wide, and he brushes past me. His scent of pine needles and woodsmoke is so familiar it makes my heart ache.

He looks rough, like he hasn't slept, and there's a purple bruise above his nose. "You look like shit."

He half grins at me, and the tension falls from the air.

"I've been up the mountain. Some tourists thought it would be fun to stray from the trail and got themselves lost."

"I heard." I don't tell him I listened to his voice message ten times while I tried to make up my mind about what to do.

It's two days after the wedding, and I've been following the search knowing that Kit was leading it—and knowing that I can't stay in Maple Falls.

"You're leaving." He eyes the suitcase wearily.

"There's nothing for me here." Kit winces. I hate hurting him like this.

"I'm suffocating here, Kit. Bear means well, but I'm tired of him being so overprotective. I'm sure Dad would never have been like that."

Kit perches on the side of the couch. "He's scared for you, Ursula. That's why he's so protective. He was made responsible for you, and he takes that very seriously."

"I don't know why you're defending him after what he did."

Kit rubs his nose and winces at the pain.

"Yeah, he wasn't too happy to find us kissing."

I snort out a laugh. "Kissing? Another minute and we would have been…" I can't finish the sentence. Just thinking about it makes my body hot. My gaze meets Kit's, and he stands up and closes the distance between us.

"Stay, Ursula. Stay with me."

His gaze dips to my lips, and I so want to kiss him right now. But I pull back.

"And always have Bear breathing down our necks? No thanks."

He takes my hands in his, and the warmth of his touch makes me tremble. I want to stay with him, but it's impossible.

"Bear overreacted. I won't let him get between us."

"And I won't cause a family feud. Bear's all the family I've got left."

"Not all." His finger slides over my wrist, drawing circles on my skin and leaving a burning sensation that I feel deep in my core.

"You've got me. You've always had me."

"Don't make me choose, Kit. Don't make me choose between you and my brother."

His gaze is so intense I have to look away. I hate that I'm in this position. I hate that it can't just be easy.

"What if you didn't have to choose? Bear was mad, but I'm sure he'll get over it once he knows my intentions."

"And what are your intentions?" My heart's hammering in my chest. This has all happened so fast that it doesn't seem real.

"I'm serious about you, Ursula. This isn't some casual thing. I want to be with you. Forever."

My breath hitches in my throat. It's everything I ever dreamed he'd say.

"I want that too." But it seems so unlikely, living here in harmony with my overprotective brother.

"I don't want to sneak around, Kit."

He rubs his nose. "And I don't want to get punched again. I'll go see Bear and smooth it over."

I hate that I have to get my big brother's blessing, but at the same time, it's nice he cares about me so much.

"Don't get hurt."

Kit growls. "I can hold my own, you know."

He pulls me toward him, and I feel the pure manly strength of him."Tell your nose that."

Kit laughs. It's the best sound in the world. He presses his lips against mine, and this time, it's a gentle kiss. Less urgent. But it still makes my body shiver. I press myself against him, my pussy aching for relief.

"I'm going to get Bear's blessing before this goes any further. I respect my friend enough to do that." He backs away. "And I don't want another bruise."

I watch him go, feeling lighter but anxious.

They don't call my brother Bear for nothing. If he feels his family is in danger, he'll protect them to the death.

I only hope he can see that Kit isn't a threat. He's the one person in this world who could make me truly happy.

7
KIT

It's with trepidation that I climb the steps to Bear's place. The sound of laughter reaches me from inside, and I hesitate.

Bear and Colette are leaving for their honeymoon tomorrow, and they're probably busy packing.

But what I need to say can't wait. I knock on the door.

Colette opens the door. "Kit," she exclaims, eyeing my bruised face, "I had no idea it was that bad."

She gives Bear a dirty look, which means he told her what happened but probably not the whole truth.

Bear comes to the door and eyes me warily.

"What do you want?"

He's got a growl to his voice, but I've been his friend for too long; he doesn't scare me.

"To give you a chance to apologize, numbnuts."

His eyes widen in surprise, but he doesn't laugh at the insult like he usually would. "Me? Apologize? You're the one that took advantage of my sister."

Colette holds up her hands. "Cool it, you two."

She has an immediate effect on Bear, and he looks away, the aggression fading from his expression.

"Kit, come on in." She steps out of the way, and I enter the house with Bear's gaze following my every move.

"Don't know why you're inviting him in. He attacked my sister. Do I have to lock my wife up too?" Bear mumbles, but Colette laughs.

"Oh, honey, I told you. Anyone can see Kit and Urs are crazy about each other. Give the man a chance."

Bear folds his arms, but his look softens. "Is this true?" he asks.

"Yes," I say simply. "I love her."

Bear snorts and looks away. Colette claps her hands together. "Told ya," she says gleefully. "I need to pop out for some milk. I'll leave you two guys to talk."

She pulls her coat on while Bear and I eye each other.

"No fighting, okay?" She kisses Bear lightly on the forehead. Her breezy manner contrasts with the frown carved into his face.

Once the door shuts behind her, he doesn't hold back. "How long has it been going on?"

"I've loved your sister ever since I can remember."

His eyes narrow. "So, you've been sneaking around without telling me?"

"Nah, man. Give me some credit. I only told her how I feel at the wedding." I think back to that kiss, her body pressed against mine. "Lucky for me, she feels the same."

Bear grunts. "Looked like you were taking advantage of her to me."

"You ever know anyone to take advantage of your sister? She's got no problem speaking her mind, and she's as tough as you are."

Bear huffs again, but I can tell I'm getting through to him.

"We love each other. This isn't casual. I want to be with her. I want to marry her."

That gets his attention. He squints at me as if looking at me for the first time, and I don't see my friend. I see the head of the household trying to do the right thing for his family.

"Why do you think you deserve her?"

"Come on, man. You know me. I've been there for the both of you through the hard times. I've got a steady job. I can provide for her." Fuck, this feels weird, selling myself to my best friend. But if that's what it takes to win Ursula, I'll do it.

"There's space in my cabin, and I've got designs approved for an extension. A couple of extra rooms for kids."

He holds his hand up. "Slow down, man. Don't talk to me about kids."

He seems to be softening, but his voice hardens with the next question. "How about other women?"

"What other women?"

"I've seen the tourists that come through here, the women falling over you at the bar. You really gonna give all that up? God knows how many of them you take back to your cabin."

He's got this dead wrong. "None."

"You expect me to believe that?"

"Yeah, because that's the God-honest truth. I've never taken anyone back to my cabin." I take a deep breath. It's time he knew how serious I am.

"I've been saving myself for Ursula."

Bear stares at me. "Come again?"

"I've never been with anyone." His mouth drops open in disbelief.

"When I realized she was the woman I was gonna marry, I never wanted to be with anyone else."

He's shaking his head in disbelief. "You telling me you're a virgin?" I nod. "Urs know about this?"

"Not yet."

He looks away, a slight smile on his face. "That's some fucked up shit."

"You want to talk about fucked up? I see you and Colette with the cameras all the time."

Bear's face reddens, and I know I'm onto something.

"It's cool, man." I hold my hand up, wondering if I've gone too far. "I don't know what you do, and I don't want to know. Just saying. Everyone has their kink, right?"

He stares at me so intensely that I think he's going to hit me again. Then he erupts into a belly laugh that makes his whole body shake.

"You know about the cameras?"

"I know something about cameras, man. Like I said, don't want to know details. That's your private shit."

Bear slaps me on the back, and I laugh along with him. The tension in the air dissipates, and I know I've got my buddy back.

"Do I have your blessing?"

His hand is still on my shoulder, and I wait for him to crush me. "I suppose if she has to be with someone, I'd rather it was you."

I let out a big breath I didn't know I was holding. It's the only blessing I'm ever going to get out of him, and I'll take it.

He squeezes my shoulder tight, his face turning hard. "But you hurt her, you break her heart, I swear to God I will come for you."

Then the grin's back on his face, and he's laughing again.

"I gotta go, man. I've got a question to ask your sister."

He fixes me with a serious look. "You tell anyone about the cameras, and I'll skin you alive."

"You tell anyone I'm a virgin, same goes."

We slap each other on the back, and Bear pulls me in for a

man hug. "You treat her well, okay?" There's a wobble to his voice, and I know that deep down, under his growly demeanor, he's just a man who wants the best for his family.

8
URSULA

As soon as I hear Kit's car pull up, I throw open the door. He steps out of the car, and I'm relieved to see there's no blood. That's got to be a good sign.

"Well?" I'm impatient to know what happened.

Kit saunters onto the porch and slides an arm around my waist. Having him close makes my insides melt and heat travel through my body.

"We have your brother's blessing."

Kit smiles at me, but it's a weird thought. "We have Bear's blessing to…have sex?"

Kit throws his head back and laughs. It's the best sound. "We have his blessing to get married."

His words make me gasp. I may have dreamed of marrying Kit for as long as I can remember, but now that he's asking, I'm stunned into silence.

Kit drops to one knee and takes my hand in his, his fingers running over my knuckles.

"Ursula, I've only ever wanted to be with you. You're beautiful, smart, funny, and courageous. I've known since I was a boy that you'd be my wife. Will you marry me?"

There are tears in my eyes, and I blink quickly. Kit is looking up at me so sincerely, so full of love.

"Yes! Of course I will."

I jump into his arms, almost toppling him over, planting kisses all over his face.

"Whoa, slow down. Let me put this ring on you."

He slides the ring onto my finger, and I hold my hand out, admiring the simple single diamond design. "It's beautiful."

"So are you."

His words melt my heart, and I lean into his chest, a light, happy feeling overtaking my body. Kit slides an arm under my knees, and I squeal as he lifts me up.

He pushes the front door open with his shoulder, causing it to bang against the wall.

"Where are you taking me?"

"Upstairs. We have unfinished business."

There's a hint of a smile on his lips, and I giggle, knowing exactly what he means.

We reach my bedroom, and he throws me gently on the bed. I roll onto my side, leaning on one elbow as I watch him pull off his boots.

Kit peels off his sweater, and he's wearing a tight t-shirt underneath. It stretches across his chest, showing off his muscular frame. I sit up and run my hands over his chest, my legs dropping on either side of him.

Kit kneels on the bed, and I hook my thumbs under his t-shirt and peel it off.

I've seen his body so many times over the years, but this is the first time I've had a reason to touch it.

My fingers rake over his chest, feeling every muscle in his torso. I brush his nipples with my fingertips, and he sucks in a sharp breath. Finding a sensitive spot, I tug on his right nipple, and he groans.

"That feels nice."

A giggle escapes my lips. "I didn't know men have sensitive nipples."

He grins. "Neither did I."

Kit pushes me gently on the bed, and I fall backwards as he climbs on top of me. "Let's see whose are more sensitive."

I like the sound of that. I like the feel of it more as his hand slides up my top. Pulling my bra down, he cups my breast, his thumb brushing my nipple. It's a bundle of nerves that shoots tiny shock waves through my body and makes me shudder all the way down to my core.

A moan escapes my lips, and I open my eyes to see Kit staring intensely at me.

"I like it when you make that noise."

My whole body is on fire as he peels off my top. His gaze roves hungrily over me, taking in my breasts and body. Kit must have seen me a hundred times in my swimsuit at the lake, but suddenly, I feel shy. My hand crosses over my stomach, and he pulls it away.

"You're beautiful, Ursula."

I love it when he says that, and I guess in his eyes, I am.

Kit climbs up next to me on the bed. "I have to tell you something."

My heart stops for a moment. This is where the fairytale ends. This is where he says it's all a joke, that he doesn't really mean it.

"Don't look so worried." He must read my expression because he takes my hand in his and kisses my palm.

"What is it, Kit?"

"I've never done this before."

He seems nervous, and I'm not sure what he's talking about. "Never proposed to anyone?"

He chuckles. "That too. I mean I've never been with a woman before."

He looks down when he says it, like he's embarrassed.

"This is your first time?"

His gaze meets mine. "I was saving myself for you."

My heart melts. For all these years, the feelings I had for Kit, he had them too.

"So was I."

He kisses me then. Slow and deep. Our bodies move together, pressing against each other. My hips grind into his. The friction as my pussy presses against his hardness makes my core ache.

Kit's hand slides up my leggings and runs over the damp heat between my legs. He peels my leggings and panties off, and I help him out of his remaining clothes.

We lie naked, our bodies moving together. My hands run over the smooth skin of his back, exploring every inch of him.

His touch makes me shiver as he explores my body, running his hands over every curve. Until, finally, his hands slide up my thighs and to my aching pussy.

His touch is gentle as his fingers graze my entrance, making me moan.

"You're so wet."

His voice is full of wonder, and I love that this is his first time too, that we're discovering this together.

My hand wraps around his shaft, and I move my palm back and forth, loving the way it makes him groan.

Kit moves on top of me, getting onto his knees. I part my thighs for him, and he slides his cock over my slit.

"We should use a condom," he says.

"Should we, though?" The thought of having Kit's babies is a massive turn-on for me, and when he meets my eye, I know he feels the same.

"Urs, are you sure?"

I nod. "I want to feel you. Kit. Every part of you."

He slides the tip of his cock into me, and already I feel so full. My hips arch, and he freezes.

"Am I hurting you?"

"No," I moan, "keep going."

But he keeps just the tip in as he leans forward, kissing my breasts and nipping my throat.

"I want to take it slow, Ursula. I need to take it slow, or I'll fucking explode just looking at your tight pussy."

The naughty words send a thrill down me. I've never seen this side of Kit before, and I love it.

"Say that again," I whisper.

His breath is hot on my neck as he whispers into my ear.

"I've waited a long time to fuck your tight cunt, Ursula."

As he says it, he slides into me, and I cry out. There's a sharp pain. Then I feel full as my pussy closes around his velvety cock.

"Kit." It's so intense I can barely breathe. "Fuck, it feels good."

"I know, baby." His voice is strained, and I realize he's barely holding it together. I want to make him lose control.

"You can come for me, Kit. Come inside my pussy."

"Fuuuuck."

He thrusts into me, and I grind my hips against him. His eyes squeeze shut, and he's about to lose control. It's the sexiest thing I've ever seen. Suddenly, the pressure that's been building inside me explodes.

"Kit! I think I'm coming."

"Come for me, baby."

My body shatters into a million pieces as I feel Kit explode inside me. He cries out my name as my pussy tugs at his cock, milking him dry.

It's the most amazing feeling in the world, and I dig my fingers into his back, pulling him close to me and clinging to him.

He holds me tight, pinning me down with his arms. We're

joined together, our bodies shuddering as one. Finally, and forever, together.

EPILOGUE

KIT

Six years later…

"How's this for a surprised face?" I widen my eyes and drop my jaw, making Bear chuckle.

"Nah, man, too obvious. You gotta go like this." He puts his hands to his mouth and makes high pitched "oooooh" sound.

I laugh so hard that my eyes water. "I'm not making that noise. I want to get laid tonight."

The laughter drops off Bear's face instantly. "That's my sister you're talking about, bro."

I hold my hands up placatingly. "Calm down. Just messing around."

A grin breaks out over Bear's face. "Me too."

We both laugh, and he hands me the hip flask. I take a swig of bourbon that burns all the way down my throat.

"You think they're ready for us?"

Bear checks his watch. "Urs messaged me ten minutes ago. They're ready."

I take my feet off the dashboard of his pickup truck. "What are we still doing here then?"

"Enjoying some peace and quiet."

Bear looks out at the mountain and raises the flask to his lips.

I know what he means. Family life can be hectic, and it's not often we get time with just the two of us anymore.

When Bear suggested an early morning fishing trip on the day of my birthday, I knew something was up.

It wasn't hard to get him to tell me about the surprise party that my wife has organized. And the fact that she practically fell over herself making sure I went, even though I didn't want to leave her with the kids on her own on my birthday.

"Come on. Let's go."

It's a short walk to Bear's Brewery which, from the outside, looks like it's closed for the day. If it wasn't for the toddler that's pulled the curtain back to peer out at us, I wouldn't know anything was up.

"That one of yours?"

Bear shakes his head. "Looks like an Amery to me."

He makes a show of unlocking the door and indicates for me to go inside first. As soon as I walk in, the lights flick on and everyone yells.

"Surprise!"

My eyes sweep the room until I find my wife. She's grinning at me, and I smile back, hoping I've pulled off the surprised face. "Did you do this?"

I stride up to her and slide my arms around her waist. She's got the baby pinned to her hip, and I give my daughter a kiss on the forehead. Then I give my wife a long kiss on the lips.

There are cheers from the crowd, and someone wolf whistles.

"Happy birthday, Daddy."

Our three-year-old son pushes between us and hands me a piece of paper with colorful squiggles all over it.

"I made a card."

"Thank you, buddy." I scoop him up in my arms, and he squeals with delight.

"And thank you," I whisper into Ursula's ear.

"Happy birthday, man." Ewan slaps me on the back, and I turn to shake his hand. "Ye catch any fish for the barbecue?

"Aye," I say, imitating the Scotsman. "We've got fresh trout."

A child runs between us, chased by an older kid, and Ewan calls out a warning to them.

"Have a birthday drink." Chase hands me a beer, and I take it gratefully.

His older brother Rowan is here too, looking less sullen these days now that he's got a wife and children.

Even Colton and Annie have come down the mountain with their brood of wild kids.

Ursula slips her arm around my waist, and I look around the room, a feeling of contentment in my heart.

It's full of friendly faces. My mountain community. I wouldn't want to be anywhere else.

* * *

Mentioned in this book…

Curious about Bella the bright blue haired woman owning the dance floor at Bear and Colette's wedding?

Sweet as Sin is a steamy instalove romance set in Candy's Café

Check out Sweet As Sin.

MOUNTAIN MAN'S HEALER

MEN OF MAPLE MOUNTAIN BOOK SEVEN

MOUNTAIN MAN'S HEALER

She's trespassing on my land, and that makes her mine...

Rowan

From the moment I see the woman picking wildflowers on my property, I must have her.

I watch, and I wait, and when she falls, I'm right there, ready to be her hero.

But I'm damaged goods; ex-military with too many wounds, the kind you can't see. I let down everyone in my life and this sweet honeybee deserves better than that.

Jenny

There really are bare-chested mountain men in the hills and I know because I saw one. And when I sprain my ankle on his property and get stuck in his cabin; it feels like all my dreams have come true.

But in the morning, he's gone. Did I imagine our connection or is this wounded hero as distant as he is reclusive?

Mountain Man's Healer is a short and steamy instalove romance featuring an OTT obsessed ex-military mountain man and the curvy woman he claims as his own.

1
ROWAN

I never knew a straw hat could be so alluring. But when it's sitting atop the head of a plump golden haired beauty trespassing on my mountain, I'm intrigued.

The hat bobs in the sunlight as it passes between the trees, golden hair spilling out from underneath.

The woman stops when she gets to the next blackberry bush. She plucks a large berry and drops it into the basket she's got slung over her shoulder.

She picks another berry and this one she pops in her mouth. Her teeth bite down sending a spray of purple juice over her plump lips.

A pink tongue flicks out and licks the berry juice off her lips. A bolt of electricity goes straight to my cock and he jumps in my trousers. Christ, those lips.

I lower the binoculars.

Perspiration pours off me, even though it's autumn. My hand reaches for the cold beer on the windowsill and I take a long swig. It does nothing to help cool me off.

Damn this woman who's trespassing on my land.

A fence came down in a storm a few weeks ago. It's near

one of my cattle runs and before I could fix it, she must have mistaken it for a path.

That was three weeks ago. She's been up here every Saturday since, wandering round my land, picking my blackberries and wildflowers, and probably talking to the goddamn butterflies.

It would be easy to mend the fence and put a sign up to say keep the fuck out. But then I wouldn't get to watch her.

I raise the binoculars. She's picking berries with her back to me. It's a sturdy looking back, with broad shoulders and wide hips; a well-made woman. My dick twitches appreciatively.

"Go easy fella."

Yup, I'm talking to my dick. That's what happens when you spend too much time alone.

My dick doesn't usually complain; he's gotten used to it being just him and my hand. But since this honeybee started trespassing on my land, he's been staging a protest. Letting me know how I should be dealing with this particular trespasser.

"We're not in the Middle Ages."

I chide my penis because I know what he's suggesting. And while I'd love to stride over there and rip her bodice open, or brasserie, or whatever women wear these days, that's not how we deal with woman in the twenty-first century.

Casper thumps his tail on the floor, no doubt thinking I'm telling him off. He shuffles over to me and presses his wet nose into my palm.

"I suppose you'd like some company too."

He gives a yelp and that makes the woman look up sharply and toward the house.

"Shit."

I lower the binoculars and hope she can't see in the window from where she is.

Without the binoculars, she's a blurry outline; a splash of

yellow amongst the green trees. She's staring at the house no doubt squinting and wondering who lives there.

She lifts an arm and gives a tentative wave.

"Shit."

Casper yelps again but I remain frozen. I like looking at the woman but the last thing I want is to actually talk to her.

After a while she gives up and lowers her hand. I breathe a sigh of relief as I raise the binoculars.

She walks along the path a bit and stops before a tussock of yellow and white wildflowers. God knows what kind of flowers they are. I don't know shit about flowers but I know they make her smile.

It's a wide, carefree smile and I can imagine she's humming as she picks them.

Her face is pleasingly round with soft dark eyes. Her skin looks fresh and smooth apart from small smile lines at the sides of her lips and eyes. Some people might say she's ordinary looking, but there's a permanent slight grin on her face which makes her beautiful.

She's sweet, I can tell. A gentle soul who's wandered onto my mountain.

My cattle are grazing over the other side of the hill, so she's in no danger of coming across a stray bull. But there's bears in the mountain and while they don't usually come down this far, I can't be sure.

At least that's why I tell myself I'm watching her; to protect her from the bears. My dick twitches again.

"Pipe down you, it's for her own protection."

She puts the flowers in her basket and strolls back the way she came. I lose her in a clump of trees and move through to the kitchen so I can follow her down the path.

She swings the basket looking for all the world like bloody goldilocks skipping through the woods.

So innocent, so sweet and untainted.

"Fuck."

My cock is rock hard against my jeans, rubbing against the fabric. The friction sending waves of electric volts all the way down my legs.

She stops in the path and bends over. Fully bends over with her ass in the air. She must be tying her shoelace or something, but fuck me, those wide hips and grabbable ass...

"Okay, you win."

Keeping one hand on the binoculars, I unzip my trousers. Feeling like a giant perv, I pull my throbbing cock out of my pants and grab it in my waiting hand.

The woman's still bent over and I imagine flicking up her skirt and pulling aside her panties. My cock slams into my fist, fucking my hand like I'd like to fuck her. Ripping that summer dress off and taking her on the side of my mountain, fucking her innocence and sweet cunt.

My seed shoots out of my cock and into my palm. I groan, bent over as I release, shaking all over and momentarily losing the grip on my binoculars.

When I fumble them back to my eyes, it's just in time to see her straighten up. She throws a look over her shoulder to the house and I wonder if she heard me groan.

"Fuck."

She disappears into the trees and I feel her loss like a cold wind to my heart.

A thought strikes me; what if she never comes back? What if she's gathered enough blackberries and this is her last time on the mountain? And I don't even know who she is.

Quickly stuffing my dick back in my pants, I zip myself up and grab my keys.

She must have parked in the carpark a few kilometers down the track where some of the mountain trails start.

If I hurry, I can catch her.

2
JENNY

My skin at the back of my neck prickles and a shiver runs down my spine. It's not an unpleasant sensation.

All morning I've had this sense, like I'm being watched. It's put me on edge, but in a good way, like I've got a hidden admirer somewhere.

When I stumbled across the hidden path a few weeks ago, it wasn't just the plump thickets of blackberries that caught my eye.

There's a cabin, tucked away in the trees and I saw a man there, the first time I came.

A huge guy with a rugged beard and a bare torso. He was chopping wood the first time I wandered down that path.

He didn't see me and I kept myself pressed behind a tree, too much in awe of the muscular display in front of me. His body rippled as he lifted the axe, smashing it down and splintering the wood. With every log, my panties got a little damper until I was dripping wet.

Every Saturday I've come back to the same path, hoping to

run into him, or at least get another show. But I haven't seen him again.

As I walk back to my car, I pop a blackberry in my mouth.

It is the best place for berry picking, and there's wild lilies, which were Mom's favorite mountain flower.

So even though I haven't seen the rugged stranger again, I keep coming back to the same spot for the flowers and berries. Or at least that's what I tell myself.

It's a short walk down the gravel road to my car, where I sling the basket of berries and flowers into the passenger seat.

Before I slide into the driver's side, I look around one more time. My gaze scans the thick trees on either side of the road, but there's no sign of anyone. I swear someone's been watching me all morning. But it could also be a bear, so best not to linger.

It's an hour drive back to Maple Springs, and the whole time, the feeling of being watched doesn't leave me.

There's no phone signal this far up the mountain but as soon as I get into range, the phone rings.

It's Aria, my best friend and business partner.

"Did you see him again?"

She's heard all about my mountain man and she's as anxious as I am for me to see him again. I guess that's what happens when you're newly loved up. I'm happy for my best friend but if I have to watch her canoodling with her husband one more time I'm going to loose it. I love seeing them together but it reminds me of what I don't have.

"No, nothing but berries and flower and trees." I can't hide the disappointment from my voice.

"I was hoping he would be chopping wood again," she says.

"Not as much as I was hoping."

She giggles. And the sound makes me smile. Aria has had acute anxiety ever since I've known her. But since she found love, it's slowly fading away and it's good to hear her laugh so readily.

"So, when are you going to do something about it?"

"Like what? Knock on the door and say, hey, I saw you chopping wood one day and you were kinda hot. Wanna go out some time?"

She laughs again. "Yeah, why not?"

"Um, reasons."

This is such a change, Aria giving me relationship advice.

"Come on Jenny, you're the sweetest, nicest, kindest person I know, probably the sweetest person in Maple Springs. Why wouldn't he go out with you?"

"Aw, you know how to make a girl feel good about herself. But he doesn't know all that about me. I can't go and present him with a CV of my best personality traits."

If only it were that easy. "I'm just happy I saw him once. Maybe he'll be out chopping wood again one day."

She sighs down the other end of the phone. "That's not going to get you a date."

This is rich coming from the woman who was too scared to speak to her sexy neighbor, now husband, only a few months ago.

"Hey, do you ever get the feeling that someone's watching you?"

"Yeah, in the shower some mornings." Her voice goes breathy. "I turn around and Levi is watching me through the mirror. It's so hot, sometimes he comes and joins me, sometimes he just watches."

I roll my eyes, even though she can't see me. I'm happy for my best friend but hearing how everyone else is getting laid except for me isn't helping.

I can tell I'm not going to get any sense out of Aria. "I gotta go, I'm almost in town."

"You going to visit your mom?"

"Yeah, I've got some of those wild wood lilies. She loved those flowers."

"You wanna stop round after? I'm doing lasagna for dinner, there's plenty to go round."

It's kind of her to ask. I'm always a little down after I visit Mom.

"Thanks. I'll make a berry pie for dessert."

I hang up the phone and pull into the Old South Road. It's a quiet part of town. Trees line a wide avenue, throwing dappled light over the street.

There's plenty of free space on the side of the road and I pull in and cut the engine.

My hairs stand on end and I turn quickly, the feeling of being watched strong again. But there's no one there. Just a pick-up truck driving past the end of the street.

I grab the flowers that I picked this morning and get out of the car. It's time to go see Mom.

3

ROWAN

The woman in the yellow dress and straw hat pulls up on the Old South Road. It was easy to follow her into town, staying a few cars back in my pick-up. I'm hoping she'll lead me to her house, so I can find out who she is.

I park around the corner and cut the engine. It's been a long time since I've been to this side of town. Not since Mom's funeral.

The memory comes back unbidden. The small crowd gathered around the grave, some sympathetic looks but mostly accusatory.

I'd come straight off the plane and was looking travel worn and unkempt. My special ops status meant I couldn't tell people what I did for a living. They thought I was away in Europe, living it up while Mom was dying. But the truth was worse.

I shake the memory off. I swore I wouldn't come back here. If that's what people thought of me then I was better off without them.

But I was done with the military also. I headed into the mountains and got myself a small farm holding.

I only come into Maple Springs when I absolutely need to. And never to this part of town.

But the woman in yellow has come here, so I must follow. I slide out of the pick-up and quietly shut the door.

There are big leafy trees and plenty of cars around so it's easy to follow her on foot.

On one side of the street is the cemetery, on the other, a row of houses. She stops in front of a modest house and my breath hitches. Could this be her home? She glances back and I duck behind a tree.

But she's only checking for traffic before she crosses the road.

My heart's hammering in my chest because now I know where she's going.

The ornate gates sit wide open and a line of rose bushes line the entryway. Clasping the bunch of flowers in one hand, she enters the cemetery.

There's a birch tree behind me and I lean against its sturdy trunk as I watch her disappear down the path.

It's the one place I won't follow her, the cemetery.

"Leave all of those." My hand waves at the direction of the blackberry bushes.

My brother sounds unsure. "You want to keep this straggly looking hedge?"

It's two days later and my little brother has come to help clear some land for grazing.

"Keep it."

It's the bush that my yellow honeybee was picking at and I don't want her to be disappointed if she comes back and it's gone.

"I didn't know you liked blackberries that much."

"I don't."

Chase gives me a confused look. But I'm not going to explain anything to him. And he knows better than to push me.

He shrugs and picks up the trimmer, moving over to a patch of wildflowers.

"Leave those too."

His expression is incredulous. "You want me to leave the flowers?"

"Yup."

I fire up my chainsaw and attack a thick sapling. I can feel my brother's eyes boring into me, but that's all the explanation he's going to get.

It doesn't make sense to me either.

This land has been sitting unused since I bought the place and I've been wanting to clear it and increase my livestock for ages. Now that I've got the funds to do it, I don't want to remove this little path she likes walking along.

It'll mean less room for the cattle, but they've got another 200 acres to roam over. They'll still be certified grass fed, organic beef.

The sapling crashes to the ground and I turn the chainsaw off. My brother's still looking at me funny.

"What?" I grunt.

"Nothing. Just you want me to leave half of this and not fix the fence. You're up to something."

He's got me. I didn't realize I had set a honey trap, but now that I've seen what I can catch, I'm not going to destroy it.

But there's no way I'm telling Chase about the lady in yellow, so I maintain silence.

"You mind if I take some flowers home to Brooklyn?" His expression softens at mention of his soon to be wife.

Love's got him even moonier than usual. "Go ahead."

Chase gets to work picking wild flowers while I survey our work.

There's the sound of cattle shucking their teeth as they

chew the cud in the next field. Casper runs around yelping but the livestock mostly ignore him.

Chase has been here most of the day helping me clear a few extra acres of land. We grew up in these mountains, but he never left. He's a trail guide, taking tour groups on day hikes and overnights.

Chase is as bearded as I am, only where my face is set and stony, his has smile lines and sports an easy grin. He's about the only person I can stand and about the only one who comes to visit.

It's a good day's work and I'm in need of refreshment.

"You want a beer?" I ask wiping the sweat from my forehead.

"Sure."

We set down our tools and head to the deck that surrounds the cabin. Grabbing two beers out of the ice chest, I hand one to Chase and pop the tab on the other.

It's cool as a mountain lake and I take a long refreshing swallow.

Chase is nursing his beer, his finger tracing around the rim of the can.

"What's up?"

He keeps his eyes down. "It's almost five years since Mom passed."

Feeling irritated, I take another swallow of beer. I don't like to talk about Mom and he knows it.

"Come to the grave and see her with me." His eyes meet mine, and he's pleading with me.

"No."

"Come on, Rowan, it's been five years. You've got to forgive yourself."

I finish the last of the beer and crush the can in my hand. "Let's get back to work."

I chuck the can in the trash as I stride back to the clearing. His loud sigh follows me down the steps.

He knew what I was going to say. I don't visit Mom. I'm too ashamed about what happened. It's best if I stay out here, on my own.

"She would forgive you, you know." He says it quietly and it makes me pause.

My mother's face comes into my mind, clear as day. She was always smiling like my brother. So proud when I told her I was going on tour. She didn't complain when I couldn't tell her where I was going, or for how long, and that she couldn't tell anyone.

She must have known then about the cancer, but she never mentioned it.

She wouldn't have wanted me to stay with her, or she wouldn't have wanted to see me make the decision to still go.

I shake my head to clear the memory. I let her down. I'm not worthy of her memory.

"I want to get all this broken up before sundown."

My hand closes around the thick handle. If my brother dares to say anything else, it's drowned out by the roar of the chainsaw.

4
JENNY

My tummy churns with anticipation as I make my way up the gravel road from the carpark. It's the next Saturday and I've come on my berry and flower picking mission.

Hell, I should stop fooling myself. I'm here in the hope of seeing the mountain man. It's been four weeks since I saw him wielding an axe like some kind of wilderness hero. And the image of his muscular torso rippling as he swung his tool is imprinted on my brain.

Off to the left is the faint pathway near the broken fence that leads to the track that runs alongside his cabin. I practically skip down the path I'm so excited.

The blackberry bushes near the start of the path are well picked over so I make my way through the trees and further along. On the other side of the trees is where the cabin is closest, about thirty meters away.

It looks different today. Some of the land from the trees to the cabin have been cleared.

Sticks of wood are stacked in piles and there's a heap of

large branches near the chopping block waiting to be cut into logs.

There's no fence between me and the cabin, which is odd, if this land is part of the nature reserve, I would have thought they'd put a fence up.

The line of blackberry bushes is still there and I start gathering. I've got a freezer full of blackberries now and I'll be making pies all winter.

What was supposed to be one foraging trip has turned into a weekly ritual. All in the hopes of seeing the bare chested, axe wielding mountain man.

I work down the line of bushes, keeping one eye on the cabin. As I work, I sing to myself and I'm soon caught up in picking.

My basket is half full when I hear a rustling in the bushes. My heart quickens thinking it might be him, but when I turn, there's no one there.

I've worked my way past the line of bushes and into the next thicket of trees. It's shady in here, and low branches means it's hard to see clearly.

I'm about to turn back to the berries when I hear the rustling again and a noise that sends a shiver down my spine. A snort. An animal snorting, blowing air out through its nose.

My body freezes. There are brown bears in these mountains.

The snort comes again and a rustling, just on the other side of the trees. A shape moves through the foliage.

My foot shuffles backward, my body moving slowly as my mind races, trying to remember what you're supposed to do when you come across a bear. My blood is thumping in my ears and I can't think straight.

The branch in front of me snaps.

My basket drops and I run backwards. This is not what

you're meant to do when you see a bear but try telling my body that.

My foot connects with a tree trunk and I go sprawling on the ground. As I fall, my ankle twists shooting hot pain up my leg.

The bear makes a low braying noise and the branches part. My hands scramble over the tree trunk, trying to pull myself up.

Pain shoots through my ankle and I sink to the ground. The best I can do is cover my head and wait for the attack.

The animal snorts and stamps a foot. I close my eyes preparing for the worst.

Suddenly there's a gun shot behind me.

The animal startles. It gives an angry moo and charges off in the other direction. Somewhere in my brain I wonder at a bear that moos. But my ankle is a hot white ball of pain leaving no room in my brain for anything else.

There are footsteps behind me and I twist around.

Wearing a flannel shirt this time but looking no less hot, and wielding a hunting rifle, is the bearded mountain man.

"You okay?" His voice is as deep as a canyon and raspy as if he doesn't use it much.

His face looms over me and I notice his eyes are the deepest brown, almost black like the center of a blackberry. Which seems very funny. I giggle, but my mouth won't work properly and it comes out like a slurry mumble.

That's when I pass out.

5
ROWAN

Her breasts are pushed against my chest as I carry her into the cabin. She's all curves and softness and she feels so damn good pressed up against me.

My dick is as stiff as a tree trunk, and already oozing sap. I give it a silent warning not to fuck this up.

There's a three-seater couch in front of the fireplace and I lay her on that.

Casper rushes around me, yelping in excitement, and it's probably the noise he's making that brings her round.

She gives me a dreamy smile that quickly turns to confusion when she realizes she's in some stranger's home. "Where am I?"

She sits up on her elbows looking about. She's the first woman I've had in here and I wonder how it looks from her eyes.

Probably bare and devoid of charm. I'm a practical guy and my years in the military taught me to live simply.

Mine's a one room cabin with a bed in the corner and a couch in front of the fireplace. The kitchen is off to the side and there's a small table with two chairs by the wall.

The only other door leads to the bathroom.

"You're in my cabin. You fell over."

"There was a bear…"

She leans her head back on the pillow.

"Not a bear. A bullock."

She gives me a puzzled look. "No, it was a bear, it rushed me."

She's so sincere that I can't help smiling. "No, honey, it was one of my cattle."

"Your cattle?"

Her eyebrows are furrowed and I notice how light they are, the same color as her hair. I wonder if her hair down below is blonde and what it would feel like to touch. My dick spasms and I crouch down hoping she's too confused to notice my hard on.

"What's a cow doing wandering on the reserve? You should keep that fenced in."

"It's not part of the reserve. You were trespassing on my land."

She looks indignant. "I was not, I came down the path."

She swings her legs around and winces as her ankle touches the floor. Pain flickers across her face and I put my hands on her shoulders, gently pushing her back to the couch.

"Take it easy, honey. Let me see that ankle."

Seeming to give in, she puts her legs back on the couch. "My name's Jenny."

"Jenny." I test it out on my lips. "I'm Rowan."

"May I?" I ask and she nods letting me know it's okay to touch her. Resisting the urge to slide my hand up her leg, I slide her shoe and sock off.

She's got delicate feet with bright pink nail polish on the toes, like even her feet are bathed in sunshine.

I press my hands gently, feeling the area around the ankle. She gives a gasp of pain.

"You've twisted it, but I don't think it's broken."

"Do I need to go to the hospital?"

If I thought she really needed it, I'd take her to the hospital straight away, but I've seen enough injuries in my time in the field to know this isn't serious.

"It needs ice, wrapping and rest. That's all."

Standing up, I go to the freezer and root around for something I can use to stop the swelling. There's fishing bait and a lot of frozen meat. I can't expect her to sit there with a frozen steak on her ankle. At the back I find a bag of frozen chicken nuggets and pull that out.

She raises her eyebrows as I wrap them in a cloth and put it on her ankle. "Most people use frozen peas."

"I'm not most people."

She winces as the cold hits her ankle. "We'll need to keep that on for about twenty minutes then I'll wrap it up tight for you."

She doesn't need the hospital. I'll be her doctor right here. Now that I've got her in my cabin, I'll do whatever I can to keep her here.

My dick twitches and I silently clarify to my dick, I'll do whatever I can, within reason, to keep her here. I'm not going to lock the door and hold her prisoner, but if I can engineer it that she can't leave till morning, I will.

6
JENNY

I must be freakin' dreaming. I'm in his cabin. The hot man with the chest carried me, and I'm not a small woman, he actually carried me into his cabin, laid me down and is now tending to my ankle more gently than I'd imagine someone his size can be.

"Did you come here alone?"

"Yes," I blurt out before realizing I'm in the cabin of a stranger and should have some kind of stranger danger control on my mouth. He could be an axe murder for all I know.

"Where's your car?"

"In the carpark down the road." There I go again. Once he disposes of my body he'll know exactly where to find my car to dispose of that as well.

Only I don't think that's what he's going to do. Call it intuition or call it stupid, but I feel safe here. Completely safe with this man.

"You can't drive on that ankle. Not today."

He's right. There's a throbbing emanating from the ankle all the way up my leg and I don't fancy having to put pressure on it. Grabbing my phone out my pocket, I go to call Aria. I'm sure she'll be able to come pick me up and I can get the car another time.

"No reception here."

The lack of bars on my phone confirms what he's saying.

"Internet?" Maybe I can send her an email or a message.

He snorts. "Sorry honey, it's a tech free zone up here."

This is such a strange concept that my mouth drops open, dumbfounded. "How does anyone get hold of you?"

He shrugs. "They don't."

I guess that's the way he likes it. A proper recluse.

I guess there's something nice about that, disconnecting and not being bothered by what's happening online. But that doesn't help my current predicament.

"I don't suppose you could give me a lift to town?"

I've just met the guy but unless he wants me spending the night here, I don't see another way around it.

He cuts me off. "You definitely shouldn't drive, you've been concussed. You can't drive for twenty-four hours and you need to be kept a watch over."

Ohh, maybe he does want me to spend the night. A thrill goes through me and I clamp my thighs tight together containing the delicious shiver between my legs.

"I would take you into town, but my pick-up's got a flat battery."

He turns away when he says it, moving to the kitchen to put some water on the boil. "I was due to go into town on the bike tomorrow to pick one up."

It takes me a moment to realize what he's telling me. "So, there's no way for me to get home?"

"You can take the bed and I'll sleep here on the couch."

I sit up, sending the chicken nuggets rolling to the floor. "Whoa, hold up. You're seriously suggesting I stay here for the night?"

My heart's thumping in my chest. Because while I know it's

completely insane to want to stay with a man I just met, my body has gone all hot and my lady parts squishy and to be stuck here with this man seems like exactly what I want to happen.

Which is insane.

He shrugs his considerably big shoulders. "Sorry honey, I don't see what else we can do."

"You could drive my car?"

He rubs his beard, considering it. "That'll work."

Damn, why did I suggest that? Now there's no good reason to stay.

"You got the keys?"

I fumble in my pocket but my hands come out empty.

"I must have dropped them when I fell." I don't feel at all disappointed that I can't find my keys but I make a show of looking like I am.

"I'll go take a look."

It's getting on to dusk when he heads out to the woods, the yappy dog going with him. I lie back trying to get my breathing under control and silently hoping he doesn't find my damn keys.

It's ten minutes later when he strides back into the cabin.

"Any luck?"

He shakes his head. "The light's getting too dark. I can go back out with a head torch if you..."

He stops mid-sentence as he sees my ankle. My gaze follows his and I give a yelp. My ankle has swollen and the skin's turning blue.

"We need to wrap you up."

Taking a first aid kit from under the sink, he crouches next to me. Removing the frozen nuggets, which are becoming squishy, he takes a compression bandage and begins to wrap my ankle.

His touch is gentle and even through the pain it sends delicious shock waves shooting through my body.

I lie back, wondering what it would feel like if his hand drifted up my calf, up my thigh and to the hot channel between my legs.

"That should do it."

He flicks my skirt down, covering my leg and stands up, moving quickly to the kitchen.

"You hungry?"

All talk of getting the head torch is gone and I don't mention my keys again. Is it wrong to want to stay here for the night? To impose on this stranger?

He cooks some pasta with meatballs and a sauce made from scratch. Then helps me hobble over to the table and we eat facing each other.

"What do you do up here?" It's the question that's been running around my mind ever since I saw him.

"Cattle. I've got a small holding. It's a small herd but I get a premium for the good mountain meat."

"You like living alone?" It's a stupid question. Of course he does, or he wouldn't be here.

"Yeah."

"You don't get lonely?" He takes a moment to answer and I can't see his eyes, hooded in the dark.

Finally, he speaks and his voice is raspy and sexy as hell. "I didn't used to."

There's something about the way he says it and the look he's giving me that sends a shiver down my spine and all the way to my lady parts.

If my ankle wasn't throbbing, I think I'd go over to him and sit right in his lap.

But my ankle is throbbing and I feel very sleepy. I give a great big un-sexy yawn.

"You shouldn't go to sleep; you've had a concussion."

My body feels heavy suddenly. I don't know if it's the shock, or the fall, or because I'm full of pasta and meatballs.

"It wasn't concussion. I fainted," I say shyly.

He frowns at me. "Are you sure?"

"I didn't hit my head. I fainted because of the bear."

"The bullock."

"Whatever." I roll my eyes and a smile tugs at the corners of his mouth. "Whatever it was scared the hell out of me, and I fainted."

Now he is smiling and I know it must sound ridiculous to a tough man like him.

"You take the bed. I'll take the couch."

I stand up but my ankle sends a shooting pain up my leg.

In an instant he's round my side of the table holding out his arm for me to take. I lean into him, breathing in his woody scent.

"Take it easy, Jenny."

He leads me over to the bed and pulls down the covers. I climb between them gratefully. They're soft and warm and it's not long before I drift off to sleep.

7
ROWAN

The bed creaks and my eyes flick open, immediately awake and alert. The fire has burnt low in the grate, giving off a pale-yellow glow. My shoulders ache from being squeezed into this couch, but I don't move.

Through slitted eyes I watch Jenny hobble into the kitchen, just making out the outline of her curvy body in the dim light.

It was worth the lie about the pick-up truck, just to see her in my kitchen in the middle of the night.

She opens a cupboard, closes it, and opens another, closing it with a bang.

"The cupboard to the left."

She startles at the sound of my voice. "I thought you were asleep."

"I was."

"Sorry." She searches in the left-hand cupboard, finds a glass and fills it with water. "Can't sleep."

Considering I watched her for at least an hour, her chest rising and falling, her lips moving softly as air expelled out of them, I know that's not true.

Swinging my legs over the side of the couch, I stretch as I stand up.

"I've got hot chocolate if you want it."

"Yes please." She sounds like an excited child.

"In the pantry bottom shelf."

While she gets the hot chocolate, I stoke the fire, adding a couple of logs and more kindling to get it going again. Flames lick at the kindling and I sit down on the rug, resting my back against the couch.

Jenny comes and joins me holding two steaming mugs. She carefully eases herself to the floor, trying not to bump her ankle.

I pull out a flask of bourbon and dump a generous pour into my mug. "You want some?"

She holds up her mug and I splash a bit into her cup.

We sit in silence watching the flames dance to life.

"There's a lot of military issue gear around here. Are you military?"

"Ex." The bourbon burns my throat as I take a sip of hot chocolate. She's looking at me expectantly, like she wants to know more. I don't like talking about my past.

But there's something about Jenny. She told me she's a florist and she volunteers at the homeless shelter. She's got a nice energy about her, kind and non-judgmental.

I don't know if it's the bourbon, or her openness, but I find myself telling her about my life as it was before.

The never knowing when you'll be called up. Having to dump everything and go, not being able to tell anyone where you were going.

"It must have been hard, leaving your loved ones."

"The only people I loved was my mom and my brother."

She nods quietly, sipping her drink and watching the fire. "Where are they now?"

I stare at the flames for a long time, images of my mother swimming in them. "My mother's dead."

Jenny turns quickly and her hand slips into mine. "I'm so sorry."

There are tears at the corner of her eyes and I wipe them with my thumb. "Are these for me?"

She nods and I'm taken with her empathy, shedding tears for somebody she barely knows.

"I lost my mother too."

She tells me about the accident her mom was in. Taken too soon, leaving Jenny on her own as a young teenager in the care system.

"I decided I wasn't going to let it define me. There's a lot to be thankful for in life and I choose to focus on that."

Her face is glowing in the firelight, making her features soft."You're beautiful."

The words slip out unbidden. I'm not sure if it's her attitude to life or the way the light's falling on her features, but this woman emanates natural beauty.

She turns her gaze on me, studying my face. I set my mug down and capture her chin in my hand. "You're a beautiful soul, Jenny."

Her eyes soften and her lips part. I've been wanting to kiss her mouth since I first saw her on my land four weeks ago, and now I do.

Gently at first and then with more insistence. She responds, slipping her tongue into my mouth and between my teeth.

My hand goes around her head, wrapping my fingers in her hair. She tastes like chocolate and bourbon and blackberries. My whole body comes alive at the feel of her.

My cock springs to attention and this time, I don't hold him back.

I've watched her for so long, wanted her for so long. And now I have her in my arms, I don't waste time.

Gently, so as not to agitate her ankle, I lie her down by the fire. My hands paw at her clothing, sliding off her jacket and fumbling with the buttons on the front of her dress. "Damn things."

My clumsy fingers are too big and she sits up on her elbows. "Let me."

She looks me in the eye as she slowly undoes her buttons. It's pure delicious torture, and it's taking too damn long.

I pull at the remaining buttons and they pop off, pinging across the floor.

"I'll buy you a new dress," I say to her surprised look.

The dress rips as I pull it down her arms, eager to get to her body. The tearing fabric only spurs me on and now I'm like a man possessed.

It's been a long time since I had a woman and I want to take it slow, but my body has other ideas.

With her dress disposed of, she's lying in front of me in cotton panties and a white lacey bra. "Honey, you are gorgeous."

She pulls at my shirt and I rip that off too. Her hands feel cool and soft as they run over my heated body, her nails scraping over my hard torso and driving me insane.

Her panties come off at a single tug. She gasps. She's naked before me, her sex glistening in the firelight. And yes, she does have blonde hair, curly and slick. "You're wet, honey."

"I've been wet since the first day I saw you."

The words send my dick pushing against my trousers and I undo my zipper, letting him out. She gasps and her eyes go wide, looking at my thick member.

"You seen one of these before?"

She nods. "Not that big. Never that big."

Her hands reach out and she wraps me in her palms, sending shock waves ricocheting through my core. Her grip is surprisingly strong and I groan as she strokes me from tip to balls.

Pre-cum shoots out and dribbles over her fingers. I need to get myself in this woman before I explode.

Being careful of her swollen ankle, I grab her leg and swing it over my shoulder. She gasps as her thighs fall open, opening her channel wide up for me. Her pink lips glisten and I run my thumb over her folds, causing her to moan, a deep guttural noise that penetrates right through me.

Her back arches, sticking her titties into the air. It's the most erotic sight I've ever seen.

"Come and give me some of this sweet honey." My cock throbs in anticipation as I look down on those inviting pink lips. My tip runs over her entrance and she shudders.

Pressing forward, my cock slides into her. She cries out.

"You're too big," she moans, even as her hips buck toward me, sinking me into her more.

"Just relax honey, I'm gonna fill you up real good."

Keeping one arm wrapped around her leg so the ankle doesn't get knocked, I ease myself into her a little more. She closes like a clam around me, sucking me into her hot moist pussy.

A whimper escapes her lips. "That feels good."

Damn right it does. She's got a vice-like grip on my cock, squeezing the juice out of me as she wiggles her hips. If she isn't careful, I'm going to lose it any moment.

Her pussy relaxes and I lower myself into her a little more. This time I slide all the way in to the base of my dick, my balls slapping against her back passage.

It's like heaven in here. Better than what I imagined. My cock slides into her sweet nectar, the friction causing volts of electricity to course through my veins.

I run my thumb around her clit and she moans under my touch. Her hand slides to her breasts and she traces circles around her nipples making them hard and dark. I love it that she's getting herself off, adding to the pleasure.

My thumb presses on her clit, increasing the pressure until she cries out. Her pussy convulses as she orgasms, tugging at my penis and almost making me lose control. But I hold on, riding her climax, thrusting into her as she spasms around me.

Knowing she's satisfied, I take her other leg and pull it up over my shoulder, lifting her hips high into the air and letting me thrust deeper.

With both legs wrapped around my neck, I see my cock sliding in and out of her pussy, her creamy juice glistening in the firelight.

She bucks her hips, moving them toward me and letting me sink deeper inside.

Her tits jiggle up and down and it's a visual I know I'll keep with me for the rest of my days.

I pull her further toward me, so she's almost up on her elbows, sinking deeper into her until I feel my balls tighten.

Giving up all attempts at self-control, I destroy this honey pot, fucking her hard. My balls tighten and cum shoots out of me. It's like a fucking freight train rumbling through the cabin.

I snarl as I come, letting out years of pent-up seed, coating her honey pot and bellowing out my pleasure.

Once I'm spent, I lower her legs carefully down and wrap my arms around her. She's exhausted, I can see that, and in a few moments, she's snoring gently in my arms.

As she sleeps in my arms, I wonder what the hell I'm supposed to do now. I've been so long on my own, I know I'm not fit for any woman, and least of all a woman as sweet as Jenny.

I watch her sleep through the night. And just before daybreak, I quietly get up, throw a blanket over her, and slip out into the dawn morning.

8
JENNY

Birdsong wakes me the next morning and I keep my eyes closed, listening to their cheerful calls. My body feels heavy and delicious after last night's antics and I stretch my arms out, expecting to find Rowan next to me. My hand comes down on the empty rug. No Rowan.

My eyes spring open.

I'm on the floor alone, and the fireplace has burnt down to a cold pile of ash. I roll onto my side and wince as my ankle hits the floor.

Pulling myself up onto the couch, I survey the empty cabin.

The sensual memory of last night fades as dull reality sets in. I'm in a dusty cabin, alone with a cold fireplace and a twisted ankle.

Trying not to bump my ankle, I pull myself up and retrieve my clothes. The dress is ripped so I grab a shirt from Rowan's drawer to wear over it.

On the kitchen counter there's a note, written in a hasty scrawl.

. . .

Seeing to the cattle.
Help yourself to food

Brief, to the point, and disappointing. I flip the note over but there's nothing on the back, no mention of how long he'll be, no nice words, no *xxx* not even a *"see you again soon."*

An uneasy feeling grows in my gut. I gave myself to a virtual stranger; what was I expecting, admissions of love?

I shake my head, banishing the negative thoughts.

What you focus on increases, is the motto I live my life by. So, I'm going to focus on the positive, assume that he is coming back and that he wants to see me again and that this wasn't just a one-night sex thing.

Although, the sex was freakin' amazing. I close my eyes remembering the feel of his body pressed against me.

What you focus on increases, and if I could have more of that love making, I'd be a happy woman.

With a smile on my face, I fill the kettle and put on a pot of coffee.

Next to the note is my car keys and my basket, still surprisingly full of berries. Rowan must have found them in the bushes.

Taking a mug of coffee and a handful of berries, I hobble to the table. Easing myself into the chair, I rest my leg on the other chair and inspect my ankle.

It's swollen, and there's a brush of purple bruising under the bandages. But it's not nearly as sore as yesterday and when I test it out, I can put some pressure on it. Enough to get about and I could drive on it, I'm sure.

Picking up the note again I try to decipher any hidden meaning. But it doesn't give anything away and I'm not sure if the car keys are an invitation to leave.

I don't want to be hanging around looking desperate if he

wants me gone. My stomach clenches at the thought. We shared a connection last night. Surely that wasn't just a one-night thing.

I pop another berry in my mouth and as the flavor bursts on my tongue, I have an idea.

Searching in the cupboards I find a bowl, some flour, sugar and eggs. There's no rolling pin, but an empty beer bottle will do.

Humming to myself, I get to work making a blackberry pie.

It's a few hours later and the pie's cooling on the rack. The smell makes my stomach rumble but I don't want to eat it without Rowan. I grab a piece of toast instead and make another pot of coffee.

It's been at least two hours since I found the note. I thought Rowan would have been back by now. He looked after me so well last night, I find it hard to believe he would abandon me without checking if my ankle was any better.

My fingers tap on the table impatiently. They hit something sticky and I peer at the table, suddenly aware of the food stains on it. I didn't notice last night, but the table doesn't look like it's been wiped down for a while.

Under the sink I fine some cleaning gear and get to work giving the place a wipe down. It doesn't look like it's had a good going over for a while. There are cobwebs under the table and grime around the skirting boards.

There's a mop in the corner and I find a bucket on the porch.

I stop at the bathroom because that's a bit weird. But the kitchen and living/bedroom area certainly look better when I'm finished with them.

Feeling satisfied with my work but uneasy about the situation, I lean on the kitchen counter looking out the window.

There's still no sign of Rowan and it's almost midday.

Aria will be wondering where I am. We talk most days, or at least message each other. I decide to make one more coffee and if Rowan isn't back by then, I'll go.

Half an hour later I'm still sitting on my own in the cabin. My uneasiness is turning to anger. How could he abandon me like this? And how could I be so stupid? Not only was I stupid enough to give myself to a stranger, but then I made him a pie and cleaned his house afterwards.

I am such an idiot.

I scrawl a quick, impersonal message on the back of his note:

Ankle is better

Gone home

I hover over the note wondering if I should leave my number, but I've already shown how desperate I am by hanging around all morning waiting for him. If he was interested, he would have come back by now.

Grabbing my car keys, I hobble out of the cabin. It's about a twenty-minute walk to the car and I grab a sturdy looking branch from the wood pile to use as a walking stick.

Feeling angry and stupid, and so disappointed, I hobble to the car.

9
ROWAN

Casper herds the last of the cattle through the gate and I swing it shut behind them. He yelps happily and I rub the top of his head."Good work."

He barks again and grins at me, his tongue lolling.

The light changes as the sun moves behind the mountain, meaning it's getting on to the afternoon.

"Damn."

When I came up the hill this morning to feed the cattle, one of the bulls was caught in the fence, his horns tangled in the wire.

It took all morning to free the damn thing. And doing anything with an angry bull is a tricky business. He tried to gouge me a couple of times and I had to jump back to avoid his horns.

Eventually I had to clip the fence, leaving a gaping hole. Which meant I had to move all the cattle into the back field so they wouldn't get out.

Rounding up cattle isn't easy and when you've got an angry bull it's even harder.

I meant to be back at the cabin hours ago. But I've been out here all morning wrangling with this bull instead. I just hope she's made herself comfortable.

Casper comes at my whistle and we head back to the cabin.

As soon as I pull open the door, I know she's not there.

The place is too quiet. Accusingly quiet.

There's a sweet smell of baking that makes my belly rumble, mixed with the sharp smell of disinfectant.

"Jenny," I call, but I already know she's gone, even before I find the note.

"Damn."

Casper whines and I rub his head. "She's gone, buddy."

The pie's stone cold but looks delicious. I'm touched that Jenny would make a pie for me.

The dishes have been washed; the surfaces wiped. She's cleaned the whole damn place.

My heart swells thinking about this kind sexy woman who cared enough to bake me a pie and clean my cabin. I haven't been looked after like that in years.

Then I think of her waiting for me. I wonder how long she waited, before she gave up on me and left.

Thoughts of Mom crowd my brain; I wonder how long Mom waited before she realized I wasn't coming back.

The thought makes me sit down suddenly.

I'm not ready for this, to have a woman rely on me.

Jenny's too good, she deserves better. I had her for one night, but I already let her down, like I let Mom down. Because that's what I do to people, I let them down. It's why I'm better up here on my own.

My fist crumples her note and I lob it at the bin. It misses and bounces onto the floor, skidding on the slick clean surface. I leave it there as I pull off my boots, mud falling off them and messing up the newly cleaned floor.

10
ROWAN

One week later…

"What's up with you?" Chase fixes me with a concerned look.

"Nothing," I grunt. "Just want to get this finished up."

It's the next Saturday and for the first time since I saw her, Jenny isn't up here picking berries.

Chase lowers his chainsaw. "You're even more surly than usual. What is it bro, girl trouble?"

I'm annoyed my brother knows me so well, but I'm not going to speak to him about Jenny. I'm not going to let him know she's all I've thought about for the past week. Her body is imprinted on my brain; her smile is the first thing I think about in the morning.

Instead, I raise my ax and bring it down hard splintering a log into several pieces.

"You coming to the cemetery next week?"

He's gone from one topic I don't want to talk about to another. This question doesn't even get an answer. I raise my axe and attack another piece of wood.

"It's been five years, man. When are you going to forgive yourself?"

I concentrate on the next log and try to block my brother out.

To my annoyance, he keeps on talking.

"She understood the sacrifice you had to make. She would have forgiven you, but she knew there was nothing to forgive."

"I let her down, Chase." Damn, he's angered me into speaking.

When I chose not to come back when she was dying, when I chose my country over my own mother, I let her down. "I let people down, Chase, it's what I do."

"For god's sake, Rowan, when are you going to get over yourself? You didn't let your battle buddies down; you didn't let your country down."

I throw the axe down and square up to him. My fists twitch and I'm so angry I could pummel him right now.

Chase gives me a weary look and puts his hands up.

The anger goes out of me. He's my brother, I'd never hurt him. I take a step back.

"You're the only one who can speak to me like that and get away with it."

"Maybe it's because I'm telling the truth. Stop being so hard on yourself, bro. You made an impossible choice. Mom understood, and she was so proud of you. Really proud of you."

"I'm not proud of myself."

"That's because you're a sweet guy who cares too much about the ones he loves."

What the fuck is he talking about? This time I almost hit him but he's smiling at me, his eyes dancing with laughter.

I stare at him, the anger dissipating. "No one's ever called me sweet before."

"Come on, bro, you're a big teddy bear."

Now I know he's joking. It's not the image I have of myself.

"A big growly, sometimes scary, teddy bear."

I shake my head. My brother can always make me laugh. But I recognize the truth in what he's saying. There are not many people I've ever cared about in this world, my mom, my brother and now Jenny.

The realization hits me. I care about her. I care about her like she's family. Like she's my own.

"There's a girl involved; I can tell," continues Chase. "Things are different now, bro, you're out of the military. And if you love her, I know you won't let her down."

Chase is right. It's not always an easy life up here. But if Jenny is mine. I'll do all I can to protect her and love her and look after her.

I drop my axe and stride to the shed where I keep the pick-up.

"Hey!" Chase calls after me. "Where you going?"

I don't bother answering as I start up the engine. It's time to claim my woman and I know exactly where she'll be.

11

JENNY

The stone is cool and smooth under my hand as I press it against the gravestone.

"I met a man." I sigh as I say the words and I can imagine my mother giving a sympathetic look and taking my chin in her hands. "What happened, sweet pea?" she'd say.

"He's perfect, Ma, strong and kind, but I don't think he's interested."

"Then he's a fool," I imagine my mother whispering.

Over the next few minutes, I tell her all about Rowan, leaving out the hot sex part. Even the spirit of my mother doesn't want to hear about that.

Then I tell her about my week. What's been happening with the shop and Aria's strange pregnancy craving for cherry flavor; cola, cupcakes, anything except real cherries.

Usually talking to Mom makes me feel better, like therapy, talking out all my troubles. But today, the heaviness on my heart won't lift.

The flowers are from the shop this week, carnations, instead of the wildflowers from the mountain. I arrange them in the vase and then stand up. "See you next week, Ma."

I'm heading down the path that leads out of the cemetery when I see the figure.

There's a large oak tree with a bench underneath it and there's a man on the bench watching me. My heart skips a beat as I recognize Rowan.

My emotions run a gauntlet as I get closer to him. I should be angry, but I've calmed down after a week, and besides, this place is so peaceful, it doesn't seem like the place for anger.

As I get closer and his rugged features come into view, my pulse quickens and my stupid heart hammers in my chest.

"I hoped I'd find you here."

I'm so relieved he came to find me I almost fall into his arms. But I need to play it cool, not fall into bed with him, make him pie and clean his house.

With a massive effort, I calm my run-away heart.

With a nonchalance I don't feel, I put my hands on my hips and wait for him to say what he came to say.

"Sorry, I fucked up."

Blunt and to the point, so much like Rowan. "Go on."

"A bull got tangled in the fence. By the time I fixed it you were gone."

"I waited all morning."

He hangs his head and I almost feel sorry for him. "I know. Thanks for the pie."

"I felt stupid that I cooked and cleaned your cabin."

He raises his eyes and his look is so intense I feel a spasm of sympathy. "Don't feel stupid. That's the nicest thing anyone's ever done for me. I'm the one who's been stupid."

He takes a deep breath and I hold mine, wondering what he's going to say next.

"I let someone down once. I'm scared of doing it again."

Suddenly he looks vulnerable. My big strong mountain man with the soft heart. He's as scared and vulnerable as I am.

All the fight goes out of me and I just want to wrap him in my arms.

I take his hand in mine. "You want to tell me about it?"

We sit on the bench and with the sun coming through the trees, he opens up to me.

He tells me about his mom and the impossible choice he made. That he could have come back when he found out she was dying, but he was about to go on a mission. He thought there would be time.

He tells me about his guilt for not being there when she passed. How he was shunned at the funeral, how he retreated to the mountain.

I hold his hand and let him speak until he's got it all out.

Finally, he turns to me. "Then I met you, Jenny."

My breath catches in my throat. It's what I've been wanting him to say.

"From the moment you trespassed on my land I wanted you."

"I wasn't trespassing if the fence was broken."

That gets a smile out of him and breaks the tension. He takes both of my hands in his.

"I'm glad you did. You've made me want to feel again, want to connect. I was dead inside until I saw you."

The heaviness in my heart dissipates. It's all I've ever wanted, to make a difference in his life, to heal his wounds.

"I love you, Jenny. I may be rough and not for polite society, but I promise I will love you and protect you and take care of you as long as I'm on this earth."

My heart melts at the words. And as I look into his eyes, I know I feel it too. "I love you too, Rowan."

His arms go around me and his lips press to mine. It's a gentle kiss, full of love and hope. He pulls away quickly.

"What is it?"

He points a finger at his trousers and the bulge in them. "Come on, buddy, not appropriate for a place like this."

"Did you just talk to your penis?"

He shrugs. "You live alone too long you develop some strange habits."

I giggle because the thought of him alone up there talking to his dick is too funny.

"You don't have to be alone anymore."

He smiles, the first carefree smile I've ever seen on him and my heart soars knowing I'm responsible.

He stands up and I turn to go, but he stops me with a squeeze of the hand. "There's something I gotta do."

I nod, knowing what he means. "I'll wait here for you."

He kisses me lightly on the forehead. Then sets off down the path that winds between the head stones to visit his mom.

Watching him go, I can't help the stupid smile that spreads across my face. I've been putting good vibes into the universe for a long time and finally someone listened. I went looking for blackberries and I found a mountain man. I found love.

EPILOGUE

JENNY

Five years later…

The leaf is smooth and clear of any signs of disease. Satisfied, I let it go and it falls back into place on the stem of the flower.

Standing up, I survey the row of azaleas. They'll be ready to harvest in a few days' time. I'll take the best bunches to Aria's shop and take the rest to the flower market in Portland.

Once I moved up here, to Rowan's cabin, I sold my half of the shop to Aria.

Rowan gave me a portion of his land to plant up flower fields. A few years later we bought up the neighboring land and I expanded.

Rowan still doesn't like to leave the mountain but he connected to a veteran group online. He chats regularly with an ex-soldier called Kobe who lives on Wild Heart Mountain.

Kobe came back with a damaged leg and a damaged heart. I hope he finds the woman he needs to heal him the same way Rowan did.

I've got sturdy fences to keep the cattle out and rows and rows of brightly colored azaleas and peony bushes.

At the same time, we extended the cabin including new bedrooms for our growing family.

I turn at the sound of footsteps to find Rowan striding toward me. He's got a determined look on his face and I know what that means.

There's a rush of dampness between my legs in anticipation.

"I've got 20 minutes before I have to go pick the kids up." It's not the most romantic of seduction lines, but his lustful look more than makes up for it. "I saw you up here and now I have to have you."

His trousers are already tenting as he takes me by the hand and leads me into the wooded area.

We barely make it inside the shade of the trees when he pushes me up against a sturdy trunk. His lips close around my mouth as his hand runs up my skirt. I'm already dripping when he runs his fingers over my damp panties.

"Take these off."

There's an urgent note to his voice as he tugs on my panties. He doesn't even wait to slide them off, instead tugging hard until the fabric rips.

I shiver as the cool air hits my pussy.

"Turn around."

He flips my body so I'm facing the tree and flicks my skirt up. My bare ass quivers in the cool mountain breeze.

I love it when he takes control like this. My gruff mountain man, taking charge and taking what he wants from me. I'm willing and ready to give him what he needs.

The sound of his zipper causes a rush of wetness, and then his hard cock is pushing at my entrance. I bend over and spread my legs, sticking my ass in the air and opening myself to him.

His cock hovers at my entrance and I wiggle my hips,

willing him to push into me. Then he does. And I'm filled with light and warmth, moaning as he rocks my hips toward him, fitting my pussy around his dick.

My hands wrap around the tree while he pulls me up and down his shaft. My pussy aches with need and I slide a hand between my legs. My fingertips brush his balls while my palm finds my clit, rubbing insistent circles on my hard nub.

The pressure builds and then I'm over the edge, crying out into the mountain. A moment later, he stiffens and comes, shooting his seed into me. Holding me in place while we rock gently.

The urgency gone, he slides out and helps me put my skirt back into place. "I gotta go get the kids."

We leave the two toddlers with a babysitter down the valley for a few hours each day, so I can tend to the flowers and he can tend his cattle.

He kisses me on the forehead. "Love you."

"I love you too."

He squeezes my hand and I watch him go as I lean against the tree. My body still trembling.

My hand goes to my belly and I rub it slowly, thinking about the secret growing inside.

I was going to tell him tonight. I'll bake a blackberry pie and once the kids are in bed. I'll let him know about the baby on the way. The new addition to our expanding mountain family.

* * *

Mentioned in this book...

Curious about Aria and Levi's story? Check out this single dad and neighbour romance.

Check out Levi here.

MOUNTAIN MAN'S STEAMY ANNIVERSARY

BONUS SCENE

MOUNTAIN MAN'S STEAMY ANNIVERSARY

Colette's career is stalled, her oldest son is in trouble at school, and worst of all, Bear has forgotten their ten-year wedding anniversary.

Even a boozy lunch with the girls isn't enough to pull her out of her slump.

But when she discovers the surprise Bear has in store for her, it reminds her of what really matters in life.

Note: Mountain Man's Steamy Anniversary is a bonus short story in the Men of Maple Mountain series. It assumes you have read Mountain Man's Obsession and may contain spoilers.

1

COLETTE

"Anyone for bubbles?"

Brooklyn plunks a glass of Prosecco on the table and deftly extracts the five glasses wedged between her fingers.

"Ooh yeah," I say a little too eagerly. "Fill me up."

After the week I'm having, I could down a whole bottle.

"Anyone hear from the others?"

Heather is flying back from a shoot and Ursula's running late as usual, but both have promised to be here. It's not often we manage to get all seven of us together.

"They'll be here," I say.

"I'll grab more glasses." Jenny heads to the bar and doubles back for her purse. "And another bottle."

It might be the first time that we've all met up when no one is pregnant or breastfeeding, and we don't intend to waste it.

Over the last ten years, these women have been my network, my support system. But it's only been in the last few years that we've been able to get away without the kids. Even today, half the women are on their phones checking messages. I pull mine out of my bag and check mine. But there's nothing from Bear.

The anxious knot that's been sitting in my stomach since this morning grows a little tighter.

"And congratulations on your latest book," says Bethany, holding her glass up in a toast. "I devoured it on my Kindle while waiting for Ali to go to sleep."

I beam at my friends. They're always so supportive of my writing. I don't know what they'd say if I told them about the struggles I'm having with my latest book. After fifteen years of writing historical romances set on the very mountain we live on, for the first time the words aren't flowing. My agent's harassing me for the latest manuscript and trying to make me commit to another four book deal. I should have sent the contract back this week, but it's sitting in the drawer at home and I'm running out of excuses.

We hold up our glasses and tap them together. "Cheers."

Bethany takes a sip of Prosecco and grimaces. "I might start with a coffee."

Jenny comes back to the table with the extra glasses just in time to hear Bethany's comment. She looks down at Bethany's belly with a raised eyebrow. "Does that mean…?"

Bethany holds up her hand. "No way. I'm definitely not having any more children."

Bethany is a stay-at-home mom looking after four children and the chicken farm with her Scotsman up in the mountains.

"Everything alright, hun?" Jenny asks. She's always looking after us and checking in on everyone. "You look worn out. Can I get you a coffee?"

Bethany nods gratefully. "Double espresso, please. Why is it all the other kids could sleep for days and now Ali, almost four-years-old, still doesn't sleep through the night? I'm absolutely exhausted."

We've all been there, so we can commiserate. While the girls offer sympathy and sleeping tips, I check my phone again.

Still nothing from Bear.

But there is an e-mail from the school. It's the third one we've had this trimester from Bear Junior's teacher.

It starts the same as the others, telling me how disruptive he is in class. Then she tells me how a boy got pushed and she thinks it was Junior, but she has no proof. I know it was Junior, because he already told me about the fight he got into.

He was sticking up for his little brother, Wolf. At seven years old, Wolf is a sensitive soul. He loves reading and writing and telling stories, just like his Mama. He's deeply introverted, and that doesn't always sit well with the other mountain boys.

Wolf gets teased a lot, and Junior sticks up for him. I can't really fault that, can I?

No one tells you how hard the school years are going to be. When those chubby little adorable toddlers start getting minds and personalities of their own, that's when parenting really gets tough. I can't help this feeling sometimes that I'm doing it all wrong.

"Everything alright, hun?" Brooklyn's sitting next to me and must have heard me sigh.

The teacher I can deal with. It's Bear's lack of communication that's got me worried. But I'm not going to share that with the girls.

I write about romance. How can I tell them that after ten years of marriage, my own seems to have fizzled out?

It's not that we don't love each other; I love Bear as fiercely as the day we were married. It's just that with him running the brewery and me writing and three kids and worrying about Junior, it sometimes feels like we don't get any time together. And worst of all, today is our anniversary and Bear's forgotten. There was no card, no breakfast in bed, no text message. Nothing.

"Just my little Bear having trouble at school."

I tell the girls what's been going on, and it feels good to talk it out. They're indignant on Junior's behalf, and Annie offers to go in and shank the teacher. I'm not sure if she's joking.

By the time we've talked it through, I'm laughing and feel a lot lighter.

The conversation's interrupted by a loud squeal. Heather stalks across the restaurant dragging her suitcase behind her.

"Hey ladies!"

We jump up, and there are hugs all round. In faux leather pants and a winter coat, Heather always manages to look glamorous even after a six-hour flight.

"What was the job?" Jenny hands her a glass of champagne, and Heather sips it eagerly as she takes a seat.

"Another online catalogue shoot." She screws her nose up, but I've always thought her modelling jobs sounded exciting.

"I'm so sick of doing these mommy roles, you know? I liked it better when I was doing all the cute, high fashion outfits. Now it's all oversize sweaters and leggings. They even posed me with someone else's kids."

Brooklyn pats her leg gently. "There's a reason for that, hon. I hate to break it to you, but you are a mom."

Heather laughs. "I know, I know. I shouldn't complain about the work, but in my mind I'm still in my twenties, you know?"

"Um-humm." There's a lot of head nodding around the table and we all take a quiet sip of champagne, contemplating the last decade.

"I think that's worth celebrating," says Jenny. "We couldn't afford the good wine when we were in our twenties."

Always so freaking positive, Jenny, but you can't argue with that. We clink glasses, and I down the last of my drink.

Bethany gives Heather a nudge. "But do you still do those other shoots?" Bethany waggles her eyebrows and leans forward in her chair. "The ones with Kane?"

We all know what she's talking about. Heather confessed to us one night after a few drinks about the boxes of photos she and her husband keep locked in the basement. Kane's a photographer and his favorite subject is Heather, preferably with no clothes on.

Heather throws her head back and laughs. "Oh yeah. We still do those."

She's never been ashamed of what her and Kane get up to.

"That's what keeps me sane while I'm working. Knowing that when I get home, I can shed the mommy clothes and be my sexy temptress self." The last part is said with a husky voice as she throws us a sexy look over her shoulder, making the whole table giggle.

I'm envious of the way Heather and Kane still have such an active and interesting love life. When was the last time I was a temptress at night?

When Bear and I first married, we couldn't keep our hands off each other. And we used to make videos too. But we haven't had the camera out in a long time. We haven't even looked back at the old videos.

Annie's high-pitched giggle has us all staring over at her. She's laughing at her phone, texting furiously.

"Are you sending Colton dirty texts again?" asks Brooklyn.

Annie blushes, but there's a big grin on her face. She puts her phone on the table and holds up her hands. "Guilty."

"Jeez, you two, aren't five enough kids?" asks Heather teasingly.

Annie shrugs. "Maybe. We don't plan these things; we just see what happens."

"I can tell you exactly what's going to happen if you keep dirty texting," says Heather.

"I wish I had your energy," says Brooklyn. "Two kids are hard enough to wrangle."

"The more you have, the easier it gets," says Annie.

I wish I could be as relaxed as she is with her kids. Parenting just seems to come easy to some people.

"We just let them loose on the mountain. They look after each other." She shrugs.

"Have you ever thought about homeschooling Junior?" she asks me. "I know you work and everything, but it really doesn't take all of your day if you give them some tasks."

She's looking at me pointedly, and I wonder why I never thought of it before. I guess because my work is so consuming, but the idea is intriguing.

"Isn't it like a full-time job?"

"Kinda. But I also use it to help around the place. My kids all know how to trap, how to skin a rabbit. They're learning to cook on an open fire, they know how to navigate by the stars and how to build their own shelter. And then we do a few hours of math and reading and all of that. It's not so hard."

She shrugs again, making it seem so easy. I always envisioned homeschooling as sitting around the kitchen table for hours. It didn't occur to me that you could do all those things. Maybe it's what Junior needs. To be out of the classroom and less regimented with his day.

"Why don't you come around next week? Spend the day with my kids so I can talk you through it a bit more."

"Thanks," I say vaguely. "I might do that." But I'm thinking about how busy next week is going to be with the word count I have to meet if I want to make my deadline.

There's another squeal, and I look up to see Ursula approaching.

"What are you doing here?" she asks, giving me a hug. "I thought you'd have anniversary plans."

The reminder of Bear forgetting our anniversary makes my smile falter and I turn away quickly, but not before Ursula notices.

"Did that useless brother of mine forget?"

"He's got a lot on his mind." I always stand up for my husband, but Ursula can sense I'm not happy.

She grabs her phone, but I stop her. "Please don't say anything. I want to enjoy lunch with the girls."

She gives me a long look but puts her phone away. "Fine. But I will slap him next time I see him."

She slips into a seat as the waitress comes over to take our order.

The rest of the meal is spent in noisy chatter, much laughter, and a few tears from the exhausted and emotional Bethany when Jenny offers to come over and stay for a night with Ali so she can get some sleep.

I check my phone for like the hundredth time after dessert, and there's still nothing from Bear.

I still can't believe that he forgot our anniversary. I thought we were just going through a busy period, a blip that would all sort itself out once I wrote the next book and Junior gelled at school, but what if it's something more? What if he's tired of me? I've been grumpy lately with the stress. Maybe he's not in love with me anymore?

The thought has me slugging back my last drink in a big gulp. I want to be at home. I want to see my kids. I want to look Bear in the eye and make sure there's still love looking back at me.

I stand up quickly, shoving my chair back. "I gotta go, guys. It was lovely to see you." There're hugs all around with promises to make another date soon.

Ursula grasps my arms and gives me a long look.

"Why don't you guys drop the kids over at our place next weekend? They can camp out back if the weather's good."

Gratitude fills me. She's offering us a kid free weekend. Time for Bear and me to be alone, to reconnect. "That sounds great. I'll check with Bear."

But as I leave the restaurant, I can't help wondering if Bear will be so eager to have a weekend alone with me.

2
BEAR

"Here's your drinks, boss." The bar manager slides two bottles of beer across the bar.

"Thanks, man. I'll head off after the pizzas. If you need anything, don't phone."

He gives me a grin. "Okay man. Enjoy your night."

He doesn't know the half of it. If the new young bar manager knew what I had planned, it would make him blush.

It's a relief to have staff you can trust. It's not often that I can sign off completely, but tonight is special.

There's a kids play area in the corner of the family zone, and I wander over and lean on the railing. "Pizza will be ready in five minutes."

There are squeals of delight, and Junior starts up a "pizza" chant that the other kids soon pick up.

I back away from the chaos and slip into a booth opposite Kit.

"Thanks for having the kids tonight, man. Really appreciate it."

I slide him the beer, and he takes a long, slow swig. "No worries. You sure she's got no idea?"

Colette was distracted this morning. She never even mentioned our anniversary, so I didn't either. If she's forgotten, I don't want to make her feel bad, but I reasoned that it will add to the surprise if she thinks I've forgotten completely.

"Nope. I don't think she even realizes it's our anniversary. You sure Urs won't mind having the kids?"

Kit's married to my little sister, who's a notorious blabber mouth. He helped keep my secret, and she doesn't know my three kids are coming to stay.

"She'll be pissed at me for not telling her, but she loves having the kids over."

Colette's been working so hard lately, and she's been worried about Junior and Wolf. She's got a nice day with the girls, and then it's our time to reconnect. I love my wife more than anything, and I hate seeing her stressed. I hope that tonight will relax her.

The door swings open and a blast of cold air billows in, followed by the squeal of children. A Scottish voice booms across the room.

"Dinnae run inside, how many times do I have to tell ye?"

But Ewen's kids aren't listening. They've already jumped into the ball pit and are laughing with the rest of the kids.

Ewan shakes his head as he saunters over and slides into the booth. "Mind if I join ye lads?"

He signals to the barman, who comes over a few moments later with a glass of whiskey, straight. "Might as well stop for a wee dram while we wait for the ladies."

He's not the only one who's hiding in the brewery bar while the girls have lunch.

It's not long before Chase turns up with his two kids.

"The house is too quiet when Brooklyn's not there," he says, sinking into the booth.

"Where's Mommy?" Meghan crawls onto his lap, and he smooths her wild curls back.

"She's having lunch with her friends."

The little girls frowns. "But how will she have any fun without us there?"

"I don't know, honey. I really don't," Chase says with a straight face, while I imagine the girls knocking back tequila shots and cackling with laughter. Which is what they did last time they were here on a girls night. I know, because I watched Colette on the security cameras.

My phone buzzes, and it's Ursula with an angry message about forgetting mine and Colette's wedding anniversary.

"Oh shit."

That means Colette must be upset about it. To be honest, with everything that's been going on, I thought she'd forgotten.

Urs tells me Colette left the lunch early and is heading home, which means I've got to go. I need to get home before my wife.

"I gotta go guys."

I scoot out of the booth and give my kids hasty kisses. "Uncle Kit's in charge. Be good."

Coyote clings on too tight around my neck. "I love you, Daddy."

Then she's gone, racing back into the ball pit, not realizing how those four little words have left my heart feeling full.

My kids are in safe hands, and my bar is in safe hands. Now I can turn my full attention to my wife.

3

COLETTE

It's been ten years since Bear and I were married, and eight years since we moved into our own cabin in the woods. His apartment above the brewery wasn't big enough once we had Junior.

Bear built this place himself with the help from his friends, and I love our home and my family. But when I walk up the path in the early winter twilight feeling lightheaded from Prosecco and trip over one of the kid's scooters for the hundredth time, only to fall in a pile of shoes, I curse every single one of them.

I've told the kids so many times to put their shoes in the rack and their scooters in the garage. Sometimes it feels like I'm the only one who keeps things tidy around here.

Picking up a pair of muddy sneakers that are definitely not in the outdoor shoe rack, I hurl them onto the gravel driveway. They land with a satisfying thud. I chuck another one and then another.

It's satisfying until it's sad. I sink onto the doorstep, feeling like a weight is pushing me down.

Since when did an out-of-place scooter and shoes left on the doormat become such a big deal?

But it's not the scooter or the shoes that's making me upset. It's the looming deadline, and the trouble at school. It's Bear forgetting our anniversary. This isn't how life was meant to be.

Then I think back to lunch with the girls. They've always been my support network. And just talking things through with them has given me some clarity. It's time to take control and make some changes in my life.

I pull out my phone right there on the doorstep and send a quick message to my agent. In fifteen years of writing, I've always done what the publisher wanted. I've churned out books in the same series because my readers love them and they sell. But it's time to try something new. I don't know what that is yet, but I need a break. A long break.

I tell my agent I'm not signing the contract, that I'm taking a sabbatical. It'll ruin her Saturday night, but I don't care. I already feel lighter. I feel like I'm taking back control of my career.

Next, I pull up the email from the school. I'm feeling buoyed by Prosecco and bolder than usual. I reply to the email from the teacher telling her I'm not going to apologize for Bear Junior's behavior. It's not his fault that he finds it hard to concentrate in a classroom environment. If she can't accommodate a child with slightly different needs, then it might be time to take him out of that school.

Next, I message Annie, asking if I can come out on Monday to find out more about homeschooling. It might just be the way forward for Junior, maybe for Wolf too, and if I'm writing to my own schedule now, it's something I can do.

Feeling like a superstar for taking action on two out of three problems, I turn my thoughts to my husband.

It occurs to me that I never mentioned our anniversary to him either. I didn't have time to pick up a card, and maybe he thinks I've forgotten. We barely get time alone together these days, and I miss him.

The realization causes a dull ache in my chest. I've been so busy and self-absorbed lately, but I'd do anything right now to be wrapped up in a warm Bear hug.

He's had a lot going on too with a new manager starting at the bar. If I'm the one who needs to remember our anniversary, then that's what I'll do.

I send Bear a quick text.

Happy anniversary Honey Bear.

Love you.

Miss you xx

Feeling better than I have in weeks, I unlock the door and go inside. The first thing that hits me is the smell of vanilla. Someone's burning one of my scented candles. Me and Bear used to light them all the time when we had the time for romantic nights.

"Hello?" I drop my bag in the entryway, kick off my shoes, and pad into the living room.

Candlelight flickers so softly, I didn't see it from outside. And at the back of the room, a white sheet has been hung over the wooden slats of the cabin wall.

A projector is playing on the white sheet. It's me. A younger, softer, happier version of myself. Smiling and giggling, laughing at Bear behind the camera.

The image changes to our wedding day. Dancing slowly on the dance floor and stopping for a long passionate kiss.

"Bear…?" My voice comes out as a whisper as my husband comes out of the kitchen.

"Happy anniversary, honey."

He didn't forget our anniversary. The knowledge makes my body sag with relief. Of course he didn't forget. He loves me as much as I love him. I can tell by the soft way he's looking at me.

"I thought you'd forgotten."

In his arms are a bunch of white roses, my favorite, and a gift box. He puts them on the coffee table and slides his arms around me.

"Never. Meeting you was the best thing that ever happened in my life. Getting married was the second best thing. I'll never forget, Colette. Ever."

My eyes well up. "But you didn't say anything."

"I wanted to surprise you." He clocks my tears, and concern floods his face. "I'm sorry, sweetie. Was it the wrong thing to do?"

Typical Bear to do something extravagant. I can't believe I ever doubted him. He wipes away my tears with his thumbs.

"Don't quite cry, sweetie. I don't want to upset you."

"They're happy tears." I look around at the flickering candles, the roses. Everything is so thoughtful.

The footage on the protection changes. It's not our wedding anymore. It's one of the many nights where we filmed ourselves.

An image of me in lacy underwear appears on the projection. I'm kneeling on the bed and smiling to the camera, wearing a sexy negligee. My body looks good, sexy, and I ooze confidence.

"Is that the...crotchless panties?"

Bear chuckles. "Oh yeah."

We had a lot of fun with those crotchless panties, and we filmed a lot of it too. We used to watch these old films regularly once the kids were in bed, but I can't remember the last time we brought them out.

On the projection, Bear steps out from behind the camera and he's buck naked.

His butt looks good, full and round, but I suddenly remember where we are: in our living room in the late afternoon. I step in front of the projector, my shadow blocking the image.

Bear gives me a confused look.

"Honey, the kids…"

Bear laughs. "They're at Kit and Urs's for the night."

"All night?"

"All. Night. Long." He says it slowly as he puts his hands on my hips. "It's just you and me, baby. You and me all night long."

He moves behind me and his hands move up to my shoulders, rubbing them gently. The tension I've been carrying around melts out of my body, and I let out a moan.

"I know how stressed you've been, baby, with the latest book, and the kids, and worrying about Junior. I want to give you a stress free night."

"I'm thinking of having a writing break and homeschooling the kids." I blurt it out, not sure what Bear will think.

He pushes his thumbs into my shoulders blades and rubs small circles, not missing a beat.

"If that's what you wanna do, honey, you have my support. Just tell me what you need."

I lean back against him, and he wraps his arms around my front. I sigh contentedly. "I need you, Bear. That's all I need."

"You got me, Colette. Always."

We rock for a moment, enjoying the weight of each other, the connection. As he holds me in his arms, I never want to leave, Bear is my rock, and I'm reminded how I need him. I need this connection. I vow never to let us grow apart, to always take time for each other.

After a moment, he nuzzles into my neck, and I feel the gentle pressure of his hardness against me back.

"After these all these years, being close to you still makes me hard."

Warm breath tickles my neck, making goosebumps stand up on my arms. Bear trails kisses over my neck, and his mouth tugs gently on my earlobe.

My eyes go to the projection on the wall. We're on our old bed that rattled every time we made love. It shook so hard I thought it was going to break.

I'm riding Bear in my crotchless panties. My tits are pulled out of the lacy underwear, and he's sucking eagerly on them while my face is contorted in ecstasy. We're younger, more energetic versions of ourselves, and it's sexy as hell.

"It might be time to make a new video."

Bear spins me around, and his hands snake over my body. His familiar touch has my nipples pebbling and achy. "I like the sound of that."

He kisses me long and hard and I'm overwhelmed by the scent of him: pine trees and hops. So familiar and so sexy.

"I got this for you."

He hands me the package from the coffee table, and I peel it open. Soft pink tissue paper is folded over a black lacy negligee. The fabric is soft and delicate, the thin lace woven into an intricate web. It's beautiful, and the younger version of myself on the video would look great in it. But ten years and three kids have taken their toll, and I'm at least three sizes bigger.

"You want me to wear this?"

"I didn't buy it for me."

He's gotten the sizing right, so I guess my husband understands how my body has changed. But judging by the look in his eyes, he doesn't seem as worried as I am that I might not look sexy anymore. I take a deep breath and decide to go with it. "Give me a minute."

A few minutes later, I edge into the living room wearing nothing by the crotchless negligee, my hands folded shyly over my middle.

Bear goes still when he sees me, and his eyes darken with desire."God, you're sexy, Colette."

His eyes on me are enough to alleviate my doubts. I may be ten years older but my husband still finds me sexy, and that gives me the confidence I need.

I drop my hands and go to my husband. He practically lunges across the room to get his hands on me, pulling me toward him and running his hands over my substantial ass.

His hands grip me around the hips, and he pushes his hard cock into my belly. "Feel what you do to me?"

My thighs clench together as I feel his hardness, his need that matches my own. Pulling his clothes off, I can't get him naked fast enough.

We're joined by our lips as our hands explore each other. Mine run over the familiar contours of his body, the muscles that are kept hard, the butt that fits into my hands, and his glorious cock that stands tall and proud, rubbing against the lace of my negligee.

Bear pushes me down onto the couch and kneels on the rug before me. My legs open for him, and he takes his time sliding his hands up my thighs until I'm impatient for his touch.

He spreads my legs wide and takes his time, his gaze as captivated by my pink flesh as he was the first time we made love.

My pussy gushes heat under his gaze and I push my hips forward, needing his hands on me.

When he finally touches me, it's like electric sparks shooting through my body. Then he leans in and presses his mouth to my sensitive parts, and I almost come undone.

"Oh my God."

It feels so good that my eyes roll back in my head, and I drape my legs wantonly over his broad shoulders.

Bear licks and sucks, knowing exactly where to find my trigger spots. My hips raise of their own accord as I rub against his face, enjoying the feel of his beard grazing my thighs.

I'm facing the projection, and as he works his tongue up my needy channel, I'm watching the two of us. I'm watching Bear then plunge his cock into me as Bear now slides a finger inside. I'm watching the ecstasy on both of our faces.

"Oh my God. Bear…". I grab his hair, trying to hold back the tide of feeling building inside of me. "I'm not gonna last."

He knows exactly the right pressure to lick my clit, and he knows exactly when to plough his fingers into me.

My climax releases in a powerful explosion that has me screaming his name as I cling to his hair. The tension I've been carrying around shudders out of my body, and my legs go rigid and then floppy as I let it go. I should be embarrassed by how quickly I came, but I don't need to be embarrassed around my husband.

Bear sits back on his haunches and wipes the glistening juices from around his mouth. "Wow, you really needed that, huh?"

His cock is standing straight up, and now I want to give him the same experience.

I stand up and walk around the back of the couch. It's a low back and I bend over it, thrusting my ass into the air. "I need you to fuck me now."

Bear's eyes flash dark, and he takes up position behind me. From here, we can both see the projection and the hard fucking our younger selves are having.

Bear's hands grab my hips and he pulls my ass in the air, rubbing his cock along my entrance. His rough hands pull at the delicate lace of the negligee. "You're so fucking sexy, Colette."

Then he plunges inside of me in one deep thrust. I cry out as he fills me up. So good, so familiar, so right.

We both watch the screen, the mirror image of what we're

doing now, and it's sexy as fuck. My hand slides down to my pussy, running slow circles on my sticky core. My fingernails scrape over Bear's balls, and he grunts out a breath. "Fuck, baby. You know what happens when you touch my balls."

I know exactly what happens. Bear goes crazy when I tug at his balls, and that's what I want. To drive my man crazy and make him lose control.

"Come for me, Bear. Take what you need from me and come hard."

"Fuck," he grunts. "Colette..."

He's close to losing it, and that makes me hot as fuck.

I squeeze his balls with my hand as my other palm pushes against my clit.

Bear grabs my tits in his rough hands, pulling me down his shaft, going deeper and deeper with every thrust. It's more than I can take. My eyes scrunch up tight as the orgasm racks me, and I scream his name.

At the same moment, Bear explodes inside of me, his cum hitting the front of my walls in thick strands. He pants my name over and over until every last drop is inside me.

Afterwards, we sit together on the couch, naked apart from a blanket wrapped around us. Bear gets the fire going and makes hot cocoa.

I sip it slowly as I lean into him. I started the day feeling anxious and overwhelmed by life. But I know that whatever the next ten, twenty, or fifty years have in store for us, with Bear by my side, I'm ready for it.

* * *

WHAT TO READ NEXT

THE BIKER'S REVENGE

She's my enemy's daughter and my new obsession.

After three years inside, there's only one thing I want: revenge.

But when a retaliation goes wrong, I find myself with a fire cat captive—Scarlett, my enemy's daughter.

She's half my age and dripping with innocence. Scarlett becomes my revenge, and it's never been sweeter. But when her father comes for her, there's no way I'm giving her up.

The Biker's Revenge is a forbidden love, age-gap romance that starts with a kidnapping and ends with a happily ever after. Featuring an OTT obsessed hero and the curvy girl he claims as his own.

Keep reading for an exclusive excerpt or visit:
mybook.to/UCBikersRevenge

THE BIKER'S REVENGE

CHAPTER ONE

Bruno

The sound of smashing glass breaks the silence. Pans shakes out the rag that he wrapped around his wrist to break the window, sending shards of glass tumbling to the ground.

My eyes dart around the shadowy building, my ears straining for any sign that someone is inside.

But all is quiet at the Chaos Riders HQ. Our intel was correct. The club is on a run out of town, leaving their headquarters unprotected.

I don't expect to find much here, but we'll rough the place up, do as much damage as possible. I want Manny, the Chaos Riders' president, to know that I'm out, and I'm out for revenge.

I give a signal to the boys, and dark shapes emerge from the shadows. Pans is the first one in the window, and he clears the glass with a covered fist so no one gets cut as we climb through.

Flashing lights from the neon sign out front illuminate a bar with dancing poles leading up to the ceiling.

Lyle whistles. "Could get one of those installed at our place, Pres."

I shoot him a dark look. "You keep that in the strip club."

Lyle grins, but he knows I'm serious. My club is a place that's safe for women. There's a time and a place for a strip pole, and it's not front and center of our MC club.

"Where should we start?"

Jesse whistles softly as he twirls a baseball bat in his hand.

It's been a long time since I've been inside the Chaos Riders' clubrooms. It's been years since we were on friendly terms.

The floor's sticky, and empty beer bottles lay scattered on the floor. A thick layer of dust coats the framed pictures of bikes on the walls. The place stinks of vomit and stale beer, making my nose crinkle.

They don't take pride in their clubhouse the way we do. Maybe this little visit isn't going to hurt them too badly. But it's not about hurting them. It's about letting Manny know we're coming for him, letting him know that I'm out and I want my revenge.

"Anywhere you like. Smash it all to hell."

I swing my bat at the wall, feeling a surge of satisfaction as a portrait of Manny crashes to the ground.

The glass frame shatters, and I don't bother trying to muffle the sound.

The boys let out a whoop and let loose with their bats, swinging wildly at anything and everything.

I reckon we've got about five minutes before someone shows up, and I'm not going to waste that time.

Pulling my shoulder back, I swing as hard as I can, connecting with a pinball machine. It gives a strangled beep as the glass smashes. I hit it again and again, thinking about the last three years. Three years in prison, locked up and away from my club and away from my daughter, Lily.

It's lucky I had the foresight to add Gina as one of her

guardians. I did that ten years ago in case something ever happened to me so they couldn't take my daughter away. My bat comes down on the legs of the pinball machine, and it gives a whine as a leg gives out and it sinks to its knees.

Smashing shit up feels good. I spin around, looking for my next target.

The room is in chaos with my guys joyfully destroying the clubhouse.

Lyle has rescued a bottle of bourbon from the bar, and he takes a swig before smashing the fridges in.

Someone's gone through to the kitchen, and there's the sound of pots and pans being thrown to the floor.

There's a staircase, and I head up there. I'm looking for the President's room. I want to destroy something that belongs to the man who put me behind bars, that made me miss out on so much of Lily's life.

"That's for missing her prom."

I swing the bat heavily, getting grim satisfaction as it carves a hole in the plaster of the wall.

"And that's for missing her high school graduation."

The bat makes another hole, and this feels fucking good. Manny put me behind bars. He snitched on me. I was supposed to meet him and his crew for an arms deal. Instead, the cops turned up and caught me with a trunk full of illegal firearms.

I only got a lesser sentence because my sister is the best lawyer in the state.

There's a corridor upstairs with doors leading off to rooms. I try each one, looking for something that Manny would value.

There's a small cupboard at the end, and it's the only door that's locked, which means there must be something worth protecting in there.

I swing my bat hard. It wedges in the door, sending a jolt up my shoulder.

"Motherfucker."

I pull the bat out and swing again. This time, it goes all the way through, making a hole in the door. I reach my hand through, searching for the lock on the other side. My hand finds the doorknob and I turn it, hearing the lock pop open.

There's a rushing sound from the other side of the door, and something comes down on my hand, sending pain shooting up my arm.

"Fuck!" I pull my hand out, and there's blood on my knuckles. Pain sears up my arm, and I see red. Whoever's behind that door is going to pay for this.

My fingers are bent in pain, and I can't grip the baseball bat properly, but I raise it as best I can and open the door.

Someone rushes me. A small ball of fury, hissing at me, all hair and nails, scratching at my arms as they knock me off balance. I step back, pinned against the other side of the corridor. My bat drops to the floor as I wrestle with the wild cat that's tearing at my skin with her nails.

I know it's a woman because she smells good. Her long hair is wild, and every time it whips around my face, I get a whiff of the floral scent of whatever shampoo she uses.

She's got her legs wrapped around me while her fingers claw at my neck. My head tilts back so she can't scratch my face, and I use my arms to try to wrestle her off. But with my injured hand, it's hard to get a grip on her.

She's fighting with everything she's got, like a cornered animal.

"I'm not gonna hurt you."

I try to calm her down, but it only makes her more irate. I don't want to hurt her, but I need to get her off me before she finds an eyeball with one of those nails.

"I need you to calm down."

I try to warn her, but she still gives a surprised oomph when I drop to my knees and roll her onto the floor.

Now I'm pinning her down, holding her still with my one

good arm. Her hair falls off her face, and for the first time, I get a proper look at my attacker.

She's got full, youthful lips, deep red where she's been biting them. Her skin is smooth and tanned, and her wide, dark eyes cast around the room wildly.

My breath catches in my throat. My blood roars in my ears.

Mine.

The word echoes in my head, pounds in my heart, and reverberates through my very soul.

Mine, Mine, Mine.

It's a clear chant in my head that I'm sure she must hear. And maybe she does because her eyes find mine. She stills for a moment, and we stare at each other.

Her look is pure terror, and a flash of anger goes through me, wondering what she's so frightened of.

"I'm not going to hurt you."

I keep my voice steady and calm, like how you'd talk to a frightened animal, and it seems to work.

Her eyes stay on me, and her breathing slows. I can feel the swell of her breasts under me with each ragged breath. And help me, God, but I can't help but glance down to peek at the soft mounds that are billowing up and down as she breathes.

Her top has come unbuttoned, and the white lace of her bra is on show, framing two soft pillowy breasts.

My body responds instantly. And she must feel it because the fight comes back into her. She kicks her knee up, and I duck out the way before she can get me in the goods.

The woman rolls out from under me, and I grab her by the ankle before she can escape. She gives a whimper as I drag her back and pin her under me again.

This time, I pin her legs down with my thighs as I hold her hands over her head.

She looks beautiful splayed out on the ground. More than beautiful. The blood in my veins rushes south, and I have to look away. I have to block the sight of her below me, the scent of her filling my nostrils. Because I'm not an animal and because I recognize this girl. Although she's not a girl anymore, now clearly a woman. She's Scarlett, Manny's daughter.

"I'm not going to hurt you, Scarlett."

Her eyes widen when I say her name, and her nostrils flare. "My father will find you."

She spits the words with such venom that spittle lands on my lips. I flick my tongue out, tasting her on me. Salty and sweet.

"I'm counting on it."

She breathes hard, but when I help her to her feet, she doesn't resist.

Keeping one hand grasped around Scarlett's wrists, I look into what I thought was a closet, the room where Scarlett was hiding. There's a mattress on the floor and a shelf with a few books and a small stack of folded clothes.

"This your room?"

She sticks her chin out defiantly, not giving me an answer. But the way her cheeks flush red tells me everything I need to know.

Manny lets his daughter sleep in a closet. The guy doesn't deserve her.

The sounds of crashing from downstairs have faded, and Jesse appears at the top of the stairs. "Time to go, Pres."

"I guess I'll be the one who has to clean this mess up," Scarlett huffs.

"Not this time, darling."

I lift her off her feet, and she gives a squeal. She's curvy but she's short, and I toss her over my shoulder like a sack of potatoes.

"What are you doing?" Scarlett gives an indignant huff.

I don't answer her because it's obvious what I'm doing. I'm taking her.

"Put me down." Scarlett wriggles on my shoulder, and her small fists pummel my back. I stride down the stairs to where the guys are waiting.

"Who's the girl?" Lyle asks.

I wrap my arms around Scarlett's jean-clad thighs, pinning her in place.

"She's my revenge."

To keep reading visit:
mybook.to/UCBikersRevenge

GET YOUR FREE BOOKS

Sign up to the Sadie King mailing list and you'll get four FREE steamy romance books and access to all the bonus scenes!

You'll be the first to hear about new releases, exclusive offers, bonus content and all my news. You can even email me back. I love chatting with my readers!

To claim your free books visit:
www.authorsadieking.com/bonus-scenes

BOOKS BY SADIE KING

Wild Heart Mountain

Military Heroes

Mountain Heroes

Wild Riders MC

Temptation

Sunset Coast

Underground Crows MC

Sunset Security

Men of the Sea

Love and Obsession (The Cod Cove Trilogy)

His Christmas Obsession (Christmas)

Maple Springs

Men of Maple Mountain

All the Single Dads

Candy's Café

Small Town Sisters

For a full list of titles check out the Sadie King website

www.authorsadieking.com

ABOUT THE AUTHOR

Sadie King is a USA Today Best Selling Author of over 100 short contemporary romance.

She lives in New Zealand with her ex-military husband and raucous young son.

When she's not writing she loves catching waves with her son, running along the beach, and good wine, preferably drunk with a book in hand.

Sign up to her newsletter to receive all the latest news and releases and access to exclusive bonus content.

Sign up at www.authorsadieking.com/bonus-scenes

www.authorsadieking.com

THANK YOU

Thank you for reading my story! If you enjoyed it, please consider leaving a review, they mean so much to authors and it helps other readers find books they might like.

Thank you!
Sadie xx

Printed in Great Britain
by Amazon

59701345R00189